THE
RULES
OF REGRET

ALSO BY MEGAN SQUIRES

Demanding Ransom
Draw Me In

THE RULES OF REGRET

MEGAN SQUIRES

SKYSCAPE

Text copyright © 2014 Megan Squires
All rights reserved.

Published by Skyscape, New York

www.apub.com

Amazon, the Amazon logo, and Skyscape are trademarks of Amazon.com, Inc., or its affiliates.

ISBN-13: 9781477824887
ISBN-10: 147782488X

Cover design by Regina Wamba and Mae I Design and Photography

Library of Congress Control Number: 2014935542

Printed in the United States of America

*I keep thinking that the more I write,
the more space and pages I'll have
for all of my thank-yous.*

*But that just simply isn't the case. With
every book, my list of supporters, friends,
and readers grows, and I just can't find
enough room to adequately articulate how
much you all mean to me.*

*So to all who have been there with me on
this journey, I thank you with all I
have—a heart full of thanks.*

Prologue

"Ma'am, can you recall what she was wearing?"

Mom's thin hands trembled in her lap. The remains of a used-up Kleenex tissue, shredded into snowlike flakes, fluttered near her feet to the hardwood floor. She lifted her head up and sniffed back a tear that almost choked her. "Wearing? Oh, God. I don't even remember."

"She had on my purple Adidas hoodie." I spoke directly to the officer. He looked to be in his midforties, with a short, trimmed mustache that ran the full length of his upper lip.

"Do you have any recent photographs?"

Dad leaned up from the couch with his hands on his knees. He was still wearing his suit from the day before, though the pleats were no longer perfectly creased down the center and haphazard wrinkles crossed back and forth over his legs. "In a box down the hall. Let me go get it."

"We just moved here," I explained, feeling like there should be a reason why our home wasn't decorated with family portraits lining the mantel. We hadn't had much time to settle in, and even if there were extra hours in the day, Mom and Dad were so busy with our family of ten that homemaking wasn't at the top of their mountainous to-do list. They did the best they could, but for some reason, under the scrutiny of the two men in our living room, it felt like that might not be enough.

"Understood." The officer smiled and his partner jotted something down on a pad of notepaper. "How would you describe her features?"

Wiping her nose with the now useless tissue between her fingers, Mom gestured toward me with a wave of her hand. "She looks just like Darby. Irish twins. Only a year apart. Freckles, shoulder-length red hair."

People had asked that all of our lives, if we were twins. For my entire seventh year and her eighth, Anna and I let everyone think that we were. We honestly were alike in so many ways that I often believed we truly were interchangeable, if one person could ever actually be replaced by another. Mom and Dad must have thought it, too, because I got called Anna just as often as, if not more than, my given name.

But one difference was certain. Had the roles been reversed that night, Anna would have done everything in her power to make sure I'd made it safely home.

I hadn't been able to do that, and it was a regret I was certain I'd carry for as long as I lived.

Chapter 1

Six years later

The floor rumbled underfoot, the familiar vibration of an engine echoing on the ground just before takeoff. My heart adopted the same erratic tremble as the 747 outside the stretch of glass windows. I tried to harness its rhythm, but it was no use.

"It will be over before you know it." Lance leaned forward and swept a light kiss across my cheek, just like he did each night before bed. He was kind of a creature of habit, and I'd come to expect certain things from him. Cheek-sweeping kisses were one of those things. "Think about how fast this last quarter went. This is only six weeks—so, like, half that." His hand grasping my hip squeezed, and his blue eyes softened as he hiked the strap of his duffel bag up onto his arm and angled his body in my direction. "We'll be fine, babe. Always have been, always will be."

I probably would have believed that statement had it possessed any ounce of truth. His delivery was convincing enough;

it was the subject matter I had a harder time believing. But even still, the hypnotizing effect Lance had on me since the day of our first phone call hadn't yet worn off. If anything, it had only intensified. I wasn't sure how he was always able to do that, but I figured it had to be some gene passed down to him throughout the generations of charmers that branched out of his family tree. I knew very little about DNA but was pretty positive there was a strand specifically tied to this Casanova gene somewhere in that twisty double helix of his.

I stared straight over his shoulder at the screen listing departures and arrivals, the glowing red numbers and letters obscured by the blur of passengers rushing down the busy corridor with their rolling luggage trailing behind them like obedient dogs. The frenzied bustle disoriented my focus and spread the words on the screen into a fuzzy haze. I'd never taken drugs before—I didn't even know the correct terminology for saying I hadn't—but I was fairly certain the dizzying fog had to be similar to tripping on LSD.

Did you *take* drugs? Or did you *do* drugs? Or was it you took drugs from someone and then did them? All I really remembered was to "Just Say No." And that's what I wanted to do right now—tell Lance that no, he couldn't leave me alone for the next month and a half. I was ready to put my elementary school-learned refusal skills to work.

"We'll be *fine*," he assured once more, stooping down to search my eyes. I nodded quickly, trying to believe him because he sounded so sure. If I looked long enough into those baby blues, it would be all the assurance I'd need. He could convince me with just one heartfelt look, the DNA-certified charmer that he was.

Lance was convincing in all areas of his life. I'm sure that had a little something to do with his selection for the internship in Washington. He was politician material through and through, and even I wasn't immune to his ability to reassure and persuade

4

the most stubborn of individuals. Not only was I not immune, I think I was completely infected.

And I could be quite a stubborn and resistant individual. That might actually explain the nickname of "mule" Lance gave me after our chemistry class together our sophomore year of high school. I had been adamant that we had to note the mass of the volumetric flask prior to filling it with our liquid sample, and he was certain we didn't. We went back and forth the entire duration of the lab and never did turn in our assignment. It seemed like a silly thing to put up a fight over, but I think Lance saw it as an opportunity to challenge me. And when you were someone like Lance—the son of both an affluent lawyer and a representative in Congress—when the opportunity for an argument arose, you jumped on it. It's what you did; it's what you were good at. The challenge was the thrill, and these past six years with Lance by my side had definitely been thrilling, to say the least.

"Darby," he whispered against my forehead, "I'll see you in just a month and a half. It will fly by."

I snickered audibly under my breath. "Maybe for you with your fancy galas and political soirees," I teased, fingering the hem of his red Stanford T-shirt that hugged his toned upper half. "But honestly, the most important thing I'll do this summer is watch paint dry." Lance's shoulders lifted with laughter and he cupped my chin in his hands. I shook my head under his grip. "I'm not joking, Lance. Sonja and I literally have to repaint the town house or Gustov's keeping our cleaning deposit. I'm not being figurative here. We're totally gonna park our folding chairs in front of the wall and watch paint-chip number P7036 dry. You're completely jealous right now—don't even try to hide it."

"He's not making *us* repaint *ours*." Lance popped an eyebrow up that indicated our landlord's favor for his apartment's tenants over mine.

"Because you're a *McIverson*. Seriously, have you ever once had to do anything you didn't want to do?"

Lance twisted his lips and scrunched his nose as though he was really searching his brain for an answer. I'm sure he was. "Yes," he said, thrusting a finger in the air, the lightbulb of recollection illuminating. "My mom once made me eat broccoli for dinner when I was five. I didn't want to do that."

"She made you eat it *once*?"

The last boarding call for his plane echoed over the intercom and I chose to ignore it, hoping Lance was doing the same. If he missed his flight, maybe he'd have second thoughts on leaving altogether. Maybe then we could watch paint dry side by side.

"Yup, just once. Threw it up all over the dinner table and never had to touch it again."

"So you've been a master manipulator from a young age, then," I summarized, the reality of those words hitting me square in the gut. Five more passengers rushed through the hallway, and the attendant pulled on the door to the tunnel leading to the aircraft, about to seal it shut.

"I don't like to call it manipulative, Darby." He brushed my chin with the pad of his thumb and drew me in for a kiss. "I like to call it resourceful." Lance tossed a glance over his shoulder toward the plane and folded me into his arms even tighter. "I'll text as soon as I land, babe. And remember, you have my heart, okay? So I'm always sorta with you."

My mind flitted back to the first time he'd said that, back when we were thirteen, sitting on the front steps to my house. My sister had only been missing three weeks. "I'll never leave you, Darby," he'd murmured after a quick kiss on my nose, his fingers coiled with mine. "You have my heart. It doesn't belong to me anymore." I could see why my sister had a crush on him the moment she'd laid eyes on him. He was completely mesmerizing, and I'd fallen under his spell all too easily, too. "So even when I'm not with you, I still sorta am."

Only the truth of it was that even when he was standing right in front of me, even when his mouth was pressed to mine and our bodies were pushed against one another, it honestly didn't even feel like he was with me. Lance was always somewhere else.

I nodded robotically and my eyes slipped shut, trying to pull all of him into my senses: his expensive cologne that smelled of bergamot and musk; his defined chest that I had curled up against so many nights these past years; the sound of his strong, steady heart that pulsed familiarly against my ear. He bent down to press his mouth to mine and I savored his recognizable minty taste. I was very near the brink of sensory overload.

"See you in six weeks," he said as he strode toward the almost closed doors.

"See you then," I echoed, my voice trailing off as he slid out of sight to get on a plane that would take him three thousand miles away from me.

Once I couldn't see him anymore, I felt like I should go, but I just stood there in the middle of the terminal—unmoving—as the rest of the airport's occupants rushed toward their gates. I contemplated getting on that plane with him—after all, Lance's family purchased a ticket for me just so I could get past the security gates to see him off. But I wasn't meant to follow him. I didn't have a destination. There was no end goal.

So I didn't move, because I didn't have any of those things. I didn't even feel like I really had me anymore.

I might have had Lance's heart, but he was pretty much my life—however messed up our life together had become—and I was fairly positive that ranked higher on the list of things you don't want someone to take off with. Sure, holding his heart meant he couldn't fall in love with anyone because I owned it already and it was supposed to be off the market. But Lance taking my life with him meant I was essentially nonexistent once he slipped out of sight. Since he *was* my life, his leaving drove the final nail into the coffin that was my promise of an unforgettable summer.

This was going to be a painfully long six weeks.

Chapter 2

Want to earn some easy summer cash?
How about $100 a week as a counselor
at Quarry Summit Adventure Camp?
No experience necessary!
Visit www.quarrysummit.org today to learn more!

"What's that?" Sonja pushed a lock of her dark hair back from her eyes with the heel of her hand, simultaneously streaking a strip of beige across her forehead. "Damn," she groaned, tossing the paint roller to the ground. P7036 splattered all over the drop cloth, decorating it in haphazardly placed dime-sized circles.

I shoved the crumpled piece of paper into my pocket and continued coating the wall in a fresh layer, almost acting like I didn't hear her. "Nothing. Just some camp counselor thing I tore off of one of those papers in the student union."

"You getting a summer job?" Sonja flipped her head over to gather her hair in another attempt at a ponytail. Her paint-coated palms left their mark across her black tresses, striping them like a zebra. "I thought we were gonna slum it together this summer. You know, drink all day. Eat Cheetos. Get fat while the boys are away."

Sonja's boyfriend, Rex, would be gone at football training for the next two months, so we swore our allegiance to doing absolutely nothing and enjoying every minute of it. The only thing was, none of that sounded even slightly enjoyable. Not even the Cheetos, and I was a girl with a thing for carb-loaded processed foods in unnatural neon colors.

"I don't know." I swept the brush over the last untouched portion of wall space and chucked it back into the paint can. "This is really the first time in the past six years that I've had any time away from Lance." I plopped down onto the tarp and folded my legs under me like I was sitting on a primary-colored mat in preschool. "If I just mope around, it kinda feels like I'm admitting I don't have a life outside of him, you know?"

"'Cause you don't, Darby." Sonja gave up on her hairdo attempts and let her locks spill over her tanned shoulders. She was stunning in a way that she never seemed to actually acknowledge. Maybe that's what made her even more beautiful. "Lance is your social life. Hell, he's all of our social lives. No one on the peninsula does anything remotely exciting without the McIverson name attached to it," she said in a matter-of-fact tone that I couldn't really disagree with. "So by default, since you're attached to him, nothing you do will be exciting. Face it, Darbs. This is as good as it gets this summer." She waved an encompassing hand across the stark room. We never did invest in any furniture during the past two years we inhabited the space. Guess it would make moving out that much easier.

"Don't you find that more than a little bit depressing?" I rubbed the paint stuck in my cuticles with my thumb, but it stayed put. My nails looked like I had just gotten the world's worst manicure.

Sonja cocked her head sympathetically, but I wasn't looking for sympathy. I was looking for someone to commiserate with. There was a difference—a subtle one—but a difference still. In one instance it was all dumped on you, like you were the sad, sorry case that demanded someone's pity. In the other you were like partners; you literally *co*-miserated together. I wanted that from her because my other partner—the one who had been around for the past six years—was currently residing on the opposite coast from me. I needed her to help lessen the gap that all those states created.

"I doubt he likes being away from you, Darby. You guys are inseparable. The next couple months will be hard on him, too."

I wobbled my head, honestly wanting to believe her. Like maybe if I let her words rattle around in my brain long enough, they might settle in and sound plausible. "I really would like to think that." But a beautiful blonde named Lindsay, among others, sort of made it hard to believe.

"Don't you think part of the reason he accepted this internship is to save up for that ring he's been hinting at?"

My stomach hopped into my throat. Not really hopped. More like vaulted in Olympic gymnast fashion. I was a little worried it was going to fly right out of my mouth and land against our freshly painted wall.

Lance and I had been researching engagement rings for a few months now, and the thought hadn't escaped my mind that this new summer job might be part of that saving process. My tastes weren't extravagant, but the McIverson family's were, and if I was going to be a McIverson someday, I'd need the diamond to match. My finger felt heavy just at the thought of it, like some miniature ball and chain tethered just below my knuckle.

"I'm going to start calling you Deborah so you can get used to it," Sonja teased, twirling a strand of her hair mindlessly between her fingers. She had quite the look going on with her paint-spattered hairdo.

"Please don't," I groaned. "No one has called me that for at least fifteen years."

"Sorry, chica, but you have no choice. Deborah McIverson or Darby McIverson. Which one sounds more worthy?"

"Depends. What do I have to be worthy of?"

"Worthy of the McIverson name and all that goes along with it. I hate to break it to you, but if you think your world is swallowed up in Lance's now, just wait until he's got a ring on that pretty little finger of yours. They'll own you."

And truth be told, Sonja was not too far off in that assumption. Lance's older brother, Heath, had married just three years before to Melissa, a petite debutante with straight blond hair and piercing green eyes, and they'd already contributed to the McIverson succession plan by producing two little clones that were the perfect blend of both their mother and father. By all standards, Lance and I were really dragging our feet—already nineteen and no proposal, no wedding, and no high-powered internships for his family to boast about in their annual family Christmas letter. We were totally on the McIverson slacker track.

"I don't see how it will actually be much different than it is now." I gazed around the room at our paint job. Not too bad. I foresaw a cleaning deposit coming my way in the near future, and if I was also able to secure some kind of summer employment, I just might have enough money for the surprise visit I had planned for Lance in a month.

"You're right," Sonja said. "You're already part of the family. You'll just have the name to make it official."

After six years with Lance, everything about our lives had

become intertwined. Our holidays, our travel, our days and nights—they were all spent together. And at first I wouldn't have had it any other way. Not that I didn't love my own family, but with three older brothers and three younger sisters, it was easy to get lost in the mix. But that's pretty much what we all were—lost.

I knew my mom and dad loved me and they showed it the best way they could. But there was something different about Lance's family. I wasn't just one of the nine Duncans to them. I was Darby, Lance's long-term, loyal girlfriend and an addition to their family. So even if my life did feel swallowed up in theirs sometimes, and even if things between Lance and me hadn't really been all that great recently, I found comfort in the monotony and consistency. Part of me disappeared that night my sister did, and sometimes it seemed like I was never going to reappear. At least that didn't bother the McIversons. They honestly didn't know any different.

"I'm gonna head to the store to stock up on the Cheetos you said you don't want." Sonja snagged my keys off the hook by the back door. My red SUV sat under the parking spot overhang behind our duplex. "I'll only be gone twenty minutes, so you won't be alone long. Need anything while I'm there?"

"Nah," I answered, collecting the paintbrushes to take to the sink to be washed, thankful that Sonja knew me well enough to know I hated being alone. It was nice to have someone who understood and respected my quirks, without my even having to explain those oddities in detail. "I'm good. See you when you get back, Sonja."

"See ya, Deborah."

From: Quarry Summit Info
To: Deborah Duncan
Subject: Camp Counselor Positions

Thank you for your interest in our staffing program at Quarry Summit Adventure Camp. We still have availability for the camp counselor positions, though they are filling up quickly. If you are interested in securing a spot, please complete the attached application and submit it no later than this Friday. You will also need proof of a cleared TB test, as well as fingerprinting documentation.

Our summer camp program runs six weeks long. Counselors reside in the cabins with the campers and have all of their meals provided, with the exception of Saturday, which is considered a "free" day.

Our camp focuses on providing an encouraging, nurturing atmosphere for at-risk youth ages 13–15. We instill the fundamentals for confidence and self-reliance through adventure programs, as well as survival activities that push youth to accept responsibility for themselves and their actions.

Though previous experience is not required for the counselor position, if you have any, please feel free to mention that in your following email and application.

We look forward to hearing from you. Please do not hesitate to contact us with any questions you might have. Counselor orientation takes place June 12th at noon at the rec hall at Quarry Summit Adventure Camp if you are selected to participate in our program. Thank you for your interest in our camp and in the lives of the future generation.

Sincerely,

T. Westbrook

Quarry Summit Associate Director

I skimmed over the email, looking for some hint of personality, but it was completely devoid. Total robot talk. It sounded like a good idea at first, and an easy way to make six hundred dollars, but the more I thought about it, the less the position seemed to be a fit.

I was not outdoorsy. I was never technically at risk. I wasn't even good with teenagers. I was awkward and clumsy during my own early teenage years with my more-red-than-brown hair, the collection of freckles that smattered my nose, and the slight gap between my teeth that wasn't corrected until senior year when Lance's mom gifted the money for braces.

It had taken a long, painful while to grow into my gangly body, and even longer to accept those freckles I had once hated. I'd secretly wished for pimples instead, knowing that they were just a phase and would eventually disappear, whereas freckles were there to stay. It wasn't until one night when Lance traced over every single one with the tip of his finger, telling me how much he loved me and how much he loved them, that I accepted the beauty he saw in them.

So no, I didn't think I'd be much help to anyone currently going through that stage of life. I'd probably make them even *more* at risk by inadvertently screwing them up with my own embarrassing stories of adolescence. Lance was the one who would make a great counselor with his ability to reflect and project his opinions on others. I could only imagine what it would do to a young girl's self-esteem to have someone like Lance tell her she was valuable. If it was even a small fraction of what it did to me back when I was thirteen, she'd think she was the only girl he'd ever laid eyes upon.

I stared back at the formal email and began running my fingers across the keyboard to compose a response.

From: Deborah Duncan
To: T. Westbrook
Subject: Not a good fit, but thank you

Dear T. Westbrook,

Thank you for your prompt response to my email. Upon further thought, I don't think this program is the best fit for me. I just completed my second year at Stanford, where I am studying architectural design. Unfortunately, I do not have a lot of experience with outdoor adventure camps, even less experience with teenagers. I think I'll stick with buildings. ☺

I apologize for taking up your time. Thank you again for the reply.

Sincerely,

Darby

I shoved away from the desk with my palms and snatched my phone out of my purse, eager to call Lance. We hadn't talked since the night before, and I was beginning to go through withdrawals. But since I'd never done drugs, I could only assume the feelings I experienced were withdrawal-like. When someone was a part of your life twenty-four hours a day, seven days a week, even three days apart felt like an unwelcome eternity. We hadn't been getting along much lately (and by lately, I meant the past couple of years), but I'd come to realize that even arguing was better than silence. At least there was interaction. At least there was emotion. As odd of a sensation as it was, and as hard as it was to verbalize, I'd actually been wishing for an argument recently, just to keep the lines of communication open.

When I looked at my phone, I saw a lengthy text already waiting for me.

Lance: You'll never guess who I just had lunch with. . . . Congressman Stanley! You know it's been a dream of mine to rub shoulders with that guy! Invited a few of us from the firm out for dinner this evening. Missing you like crazy, babe. But I think this break in our relationship is what we need. Have fun and enjoy yourself, and don't think twice about me.

I'd already started tapping out a reply about how proud I was of him and how exciting it must be to have a chance encounter with his political idol, when my eyes fell upon those last two sentences. Everything stopped. My key punching, my breathing. And apparently our relationship. I wasn't planning on a hiatus, and wasn't sure I'd be able to get through the next six weeks without "thinking twice" about him. In reality, I'd probably be in a constant state of Lance pondering.

An email alert dinged from across the room and snapped my attention before I had a chance to respond to Lance's text. Probably more spam. I wasn't sure what website I had visited or what list I'd mistakenly gotten myself on, but over half of my inbox was littered with promises of male enhancement and deals on prescription drugs from Canada. I was about to routinely press the delete button when I saw it was from the camp instead.

From: T. Westbrook
To: Deborah Duncan
Subject: See you on the 12th!

Dear Darby,

You are in luck! We have buildings at our camp! And since you already have the perfect camp name (I was a little worried with "Deborah," but "Darby" is right on), you have two advantages over all of our other applicants who made no mention of loving buildings, and who have boring, commonplace names like Ryan, Sarah, and Chris.

We look forward to receiving your completed application and meeting you at orientation on the 12th!

Until then,

Torin

I blinked rapidly at the screen, like the fluttering of my eyelids could somehow magically rearrange the words and letters into a way that made more sense than their current configuration. What in the world was that? If the first email felt contrived and manufactured, this last exchange was a total 180, like an entirely different person penned it.

I was pretty sure the intent of my original message was to decline the position, yet this Torin seemed to have completely overlooked that. I was a little annoyed that this last note demanded another response, because I wanted to just be done with this so I could start looking for a *real* summer job. I wasn't sure why I ever thought summer camp would work for me. McIversons didn't camp, and while I wasn't officially a McIverson, I was sure some of that had rubbed off on me by osmosis or something.

From: Deborah Duncan
To: T. Westbrook
Subject: Again, no thank you

Dear Torin,

I appreciate the encouragement, but I am still declining the camp counselor position at Quarry Summit. After looking at my schedule further, I will need to take time off between the third and fourth weeks of camp to visit my boyfriend in Washington, D.C., and now that I know the campers are at-risk youth, I don't think it would be fair to leave partway through the camp and disrupt any relationships that might be forming while there. Because I cannot be consistent, I don't think this is the best option for my summer employment.

Sincerely,

Darby

Send.

There, that should do it. I scanned over the note again as it sat in my Sent folder and lifted nearly a foot off my seat when the inbox chimed as I was still rereading.

From: T. Westbrook
To: Deborah Duncan
Subject: Luck o' the Irish

Darby,

You are in luck once again! Any chance you're Irish? (I'm guessing so with a name like Darby Duncan.) Our counselors do not need to commit to the full six-week program, and since the gap between the third and fourth weeks brings in a new set of campers, any time taken off then will not affect the relationships you form.

I'm still looking forward to meeting you on the 12th. Be sure to get fingerprinted soon because it can take up to a week before it enters our system.

—Torin

P.S. I will make sure the cafeteria is fully stocked with Lucky Charms prior to your arrival. ☺

Chapter 3

The smell of the pines swept into the Jeep before I was even able to prop open the driver's side door all the way to let it filter in. It was like Pine-Sol cleaner—only more natural, lacking the potent, disinfecting scent that took me back to fourth grade when Lucy Haverson puked all over her desk during our weekly spelling test.

But even now, it was a fitting aroma that summoned an appropriate memory. Because that's how I felt—like I could empty the contents of my stomach onto the crunchy gravel that gripped the tread of my shoes. I wasn't a nature girl. Give me buildings and concrete and I was in my element. Tall, ominous trees and looming mountain peaks that framed them like a Bob Ross painting made me feel anything but comfortable. I started to regret my hasty decision already. Maybe I should have sent out just a few more résumés.

"Welcome!" a slight woman with a chin-length blond bob shouted as she scurried toward me across the small parking lot, startling me like she'd just fired a gun into the crisp, thin air. "You must be Darby." She extended a calloused, tanned hand in my direction. Her blue-and-red flannel shirt was tucked into jeans that rose well above her navel, and her boots looked more like practical military garb than actual footwear. While the term *mountain woman* wasn't one readily at hand in my vocabulary, she fit the description to a T in a sort of adorable, sort of scary way.

"I'm Marla Westbrook. You'll meet my husband, Curtis, during orientation. Here, let me help you with your bags." She didn't wait for my reply and popped the back of the Jeep open, tucking her clipboard up into her armpit. With two strong grasps and a slightly audible huff, she yanked my luggage out of the trunk and swung around toward the stretch of cabins that sloped down the hillside. "Let's get these dropped off and then we'll meet in the rec hall with the rest of the counselors. You'll be in the Spruce Cabin with the thirteens," she called over her shoulder, her voice gruff and authoritative. I trailed her obediently, because even though she was a tiny bit of a woman, she had the overwhelming presence of a drill sergeant. And she sort of frightened me. "You'll have six campers bunking with you at a time."

"You said 'meet the rest of the counselors—'" I tripped over an ill-placed log that outlined the dirt path on the way to the sleeping quarters. After stumbling two feet, I reclaimed my balance before Marla had the chance to notice my falter. Good thing, because I was fairly certain there was nothing that would stop her from commanding me to drop down and give her twenty—and I had small, weak arms that trembled just thinking about it. "Does that mean I'm the last one?"

"Yup," she grumbled. Her whole no-nonsense demeanor made me cower, like I was five years old again and just got in trouble for sticking my hand in the cookie jar. "Last one to commit to the position. Last one to be fingerprinted. Last one to show up for orientation." She didn't look back at me as she spoke and instead continued down the trail.

Though it was midmorning, the farther we hiked into the canopy of trees, the darker the surroundings grew. *Flashlight.* That was the one thing I had forgotten to pack. I highly doubted these pathways were equipped with solar-powered ground lighting like our backyard at the rental. Stumbling my way through this summer was something I'd need to get used to. I could really use something to guide my path.

"This is it," Marla said, kicking open the door to the second cabin on the left with the steel toe of her shoe. The walls were flanked with four sets of metal bunk beds, their plastic mattresses bare, and two low dressers rested under the windows on either side. There was an open door at the back of the boxlike structure that I assumed housed a toilet and a shower based on the chipped tile floor that peeked out, its grout dark and stained. From the looks of things, this camp had been in operation for quite some time.

Marla dropped my bags onto the ground, a small cloud of dust billowing out from underneath them, and she wiped her hands across one another briskly. "You can unpack after orientation, but this is your space. Feel free to decorate it as you wish, but these kids likely won't notice—nor appreciate it—so don't put yourself out too much."

My eyes traveled down to my pink duffel bag—the one containing nothing but cartons of craft materials and teenybopper posters. I groaned. I so wasn't cut out for this. I wondered if Marla needed any bonfire kindling, because she was welcome to the entire bag if so.

"Let's head back up the hill. You have a lot to learn, Darby." Marla propped the rickety door open for me and I walked through, met with the unfamiliar sounds and smells of the forest that made my stomach roll with hesitation.

"Yes. Yes, I do."

. . . .

"So that's the procedure in case of an emergency," Curtis concluded, his large hands folded across his chest as he casually balanced his weight on the edge of the metal stool. His gray handlebar mustache obscured his mouth when he spoke, though the permanent smile was evident underneath, despite the whiskers that curled over his upper lip.

Curtis and his wife were quite the odd pairing. While Marla probably didn't weigh more than one hundred pounds soaking wet, Curtis was a big bear of a man, but more like a teddy bear rather than a grizzly. The warmth in his green eyes and the upward pull of his mouth indicated nothing but compassion and kindness. But I guessed you needed that balance, especially when working in the field they did. I imagined Marla knew how to get unruly youth in line, and I also supposed Curtis did a great job easing any of their fears and troubles that might unexpectedly arise during a week at camp.

"We will have a different medical staffer on hand each week, so get to know each of them and get to know them well. We've yet to have a week that doesn't involve injury in one form or another."

A girl with two sleeves of colorful ink coating her arms and a headful of black, spiky hair slipped her hand up. "What types of injuries should we be prepared for?"

Curtis wobbled his head as though he was recalling past incidents. "Mostly cuts and bruises, an occasional broken limb, lots of stomach issues and vomiting," he said, stroking his mustache the way they do in movies. I really liked his mustache and how deceiving it was. How it made him appear tough and intimidating, yet that seemed to be so far from the actual truth about his character.

I always felt like an open book. I wore my heart on my sleeve. My emotions were written all over my face. Insert any other cliché descriptor for vulnerably expressing oneself, and I could be its poster child. What you saw was what you got when it came to me and I sort of hated that. Maybe that's why I'd tried so hard all these years to be someone else. Then at least what you saw wasn't the entire story.

Curtis twisted the curled edge of his mustache, rolling it between his fingers. "Like I said, usually just routine illnesses, but at least once a summer we have an attempt, so be prepared and on the lookout for any signs or indicators."

"An attempt?" a boy in the row behind me said, cocking his head. His hair was fiery red and his skin was so pale he could have been an albino. I'd never seen anyone who looked the way he did, but I could say the same for the girl with the intricate arm drawings, too. Pretty much everyone I grew up with had been preparatory school material with their crisp polos and pressed, pleated skirts. No one at the orientation was wearing anything that required any kind of ironing at all. Though it should have been a relief—an excuse to relax and for once just be comfortable—it felt more constricting than the blue-and-khaki uniforms we'd been required to wear back at our private high school.

"An attempt. A suicide attempt," Curtis clarified, his body bowing toward us slightly. "These aren't your typical happy-go-lucky campers. They're not here because Mom and Dad wanted a week of quiet away from the kids. They're here because this is the last straw—the last resort." He paced the length of the stage, his gaze deliberately meeting each counselor in attendance as he swept across the floor. "They won't like being here, they won't like the food, they won't like you. Be prepared for that. If you are, it will make your job that much easier."

I pinched the bridge of my nose and clenched my eyes shut, attempting to draw in a cleansing breath, but the headache that pulsed just behind my eyes disallowed my focus to fall anywhere but on the rhythmic beating that vibrated my skull. What had I gotten myself into? The open position at Burger Bill's sounded like a dream job right about now.

"Hey. You okay?" I snapped my head up and folded my hands quickly into my lap. The dirty-blond-haired boy sitting immediately to my left tilted his upper half closer, so close that he was almost touching me. "You all right, Darby?" His shoulder pressed against mine.

It concerned me that everyone knew my name when the rest of the counselors still maintained their anonymity. I guessed that's what I got for being late and for being so transparent and all. And I was sure it wouldn't be the last time I forced myself to stand out. Nothing about this experience felt natural to me. I'd already achieved sore-thumb status by sticking out so blatantly and I was only one hour in.

I didn't look directly at him but centered my vision on Curtis's shoes as they scraped across the wooden stage. He continued the pacing and I studied his strides like there would be some test on it in the very near future. "I'm fine, but thank you." It was a nice gesture, I supposed, and I didn't want him to think it went unnoticed.

Blond boy hugged his arms tighter to his chest and slunk down into his seat, clearly comfortable not only in his chair, but with everything Curtis was saying about the counselor experience as well. This couldn't be his first time at camp. Maybe we could be friends. I could definitely use someone to show me the ropes.

"Like I mentioned earlier," Curtis continued, "Saturdays are your days. Your Sabbath, your day of rest. Spend it wisely because the remaining six belong to us. Are there any more questions?" He steepled his index fingers in front of his mouth and surveyed the room with a sweeping gaze. "Oh, and one more thing. You'll be paired off. This will be your buddy, your right-hand man. As you've probably already figured out, cell reception is not one of the luxuries we have here. Instead, you'll be using these." Curtis yanked on the clip of a walkie-talkie and released it from his belt. He waved it in the air like he was ringing a bell. "This is your line of communication, your lifeline. Don't lose it—especially during your survival overnighter. Now, do you have any questions?"

"Do we get to pick partners?" a girl with tight, corkscrew-like ringlets that could rival Shirley Temple's asked hopefully. I couldn't help but notice her eyes fall on the boy to my left. Maybe she had a thing for ratty-looking guys with horrendous posture and weird close-sitting tendencies. To each his own.

"You'll be partnered with the person sitting next to you," Curtis explained as he refastened the walkie-talkie to his Levi's belt loop. "Maggie and Ran," he continued, looking down at a couple in the front row, "since you are only with us for the first three weeks of camp, you'll partner together." They both nodded, though I was pretty sure they had some type of partnership already. I couldn't help but notice the smiles and quiet laughter they'd exchanged throughout the orientation. Watching them interact made me homesick, or withdrawal-y, or whatever it actually was, and I longed for Lance, or maybe just the familiarity of our daily routine. I was grateful this new couple would only be at camp a portion of the time, because I didn't think I could survive six weeks without insane amounts of envy turning me green and distracting my focus and my attention.

Curtis stepped down from the low platform and began weaving through the three rows of rickety aluminum chairs, pairing off counselors as he went. He stopped in front of me and then looked to the boy at my side. "Tor and Darby, you'll be a team."

Tor. Why did that sound familiar?

The boy dipped his right shoulder and angled his head back. "Howdy, partner," he said, extending a hand toward me. The gloves he wore were made of shabby gray yarn, and the tops of all the fingers had been haphazardly cut off, so they unraveled at the edges. I took hold of his hand, squinting to recollect where I'd heard that name before.

"Tor?" I asked, lifting my brow. "Torin Westbrook?"

"In the flesh." He smiled, two dimples piercing his unusually pink cheeks, which looked as though he'd been out skiing on a sunny day without sunscreen. His lips matched their rosy color, like if he were a girl, he would have intentionally done his makeup in a way to make them like this. Aside from that, nothing about him was feminine at all. No, he was quite literally a rugged bundle of tattered clothing, broad shoulders, and long, shaggy hair.

"Nice to put a face to the emails, Darby." He smiled and revealed a sliver of a gap between his upper teeth. If mine had been as small and moderately charming as his, I probably would have opted out of that embarrassing year of braces as a seventeen-year-old. It was funny how what might be considered an imperfection to some people could look absolutely perfect when it was on the right person. "You'll be happy to know we have an abundance of Lucky Charms on hand in the dining hall with your name on them."

"Oh." I smiled, chuckling slightly. I tugged my hand from his grip, but Torin's still hovered in the space between us. I thought about swatting it away because having it suspended there made me nervous, but just laced my own fingers together instead. "Just because I'm Irish doesn't mean I like Lucky Charms."

His green eyes grew into silver dollars like I had just admitted to committing some egregious crime. "But they're magically delicious!" He laughed again and tugged on the drawstring of his worn sweatshirt, pulling it back and forth through the hood. His jeans had holes at the knees, and he wore shoes identical to his mom's, which would be endearing if he were four, but he wasn't four, so it just seemed a little silly. "Do you have any questions about anything my dad covered?" Torin lifted his chin toward the stage as if to recall the past hour's worth of instructions in one swift motion.

"I have a lot of questions. The first one being: What on earth am I doing here?"

"Well," Torin said, looking down at his nails rather than at me. He had the aloof, indifferent act down pat. "My first guess is you needed the money. Judging from your email, I bet you have plans to spend that money on the flight to visit your boyfriend." He ran the pad of his thumb over his nail bed. "My second guess is that you sub-consciously want a challenge. And you'll definitely find that here."

"One out of two isn't so bad," I said, shrugging. "Unless you count it percentage-wise, and then in that case you get fifty percent. Which is an F. Which is honestly as bad as it gets. So it's actually pretty bad." The rest of the paired-up counselors started to filter out the door, but Torin didn't look like he had plans to go anywhere the way he was slouched down into his seat. He looked quite at home.

"I've never been too good in school." He laughed, suddenly bolting upright with his palms pressed to his thighs. "So. Want a tour?"

"You know this place pretty well, I gather?" I shadowed Torin as he stood and walked out through the rec hall doors, his gloved hand catching the handle to hold it open for me. The sun beat down overhead, but there was still an unexpected chill in the mountain air, which seemed odd for June.

"You could say that, considering I was born here." He kicked a rock across the parking lot and it hopped like it was skimming the surface of a pond before it wedged against the base of a truck's tire tread. Boys like Torin didn't exist back at home, and I didn't quite know what to make of him or how to even act around him.

I tried to envision him decked out in the Ralph Lauren–style threads of the guys I usually hung around with, and the thought made me giggle silently to myself.

"You were born here?" I said, hoping my words would mask the fact that I was laughing at him. "As in, this is your home?"

Torin swiveled to face me but continued walking, just backward, with long, intentional strides. I figured he really knew this place like the back of his hand if he was able to blindly guide his way around. "Yessiree. Mom and Dad started this camp back before I was born. Used to just be an adventure camp, but we changed the focus seven years ago after my older brother committed suicide."

I blanched. Any other comments that were waiting to fall out of my mouth hung back in my throat. I swallowed them down quickly, tasting the bitterness of each syllable. That was a lot of disclosure from someone I'd known only five minutes. All he knew about me was that I might like Lucky Charms, which I actually didn't, so he really didn't know anything at all. But I suddenly knew he had a dead brother. I thought about opening up to him a bit but decided against it, still too stunned to really speak.

Torin picked up on my hesitation and smiled cautiously.

"Don't feel bad," he said, continuing his backward movement. "Reinventing the camp was a huge part in their healing process. I can't even begin to tell you how many lives it's probably helped." He ran his gloved fingers through the length of his blond hair. It was at that awkward stage where it looked like he was due for a haircut by the way it curled around his ears and hung on his neck, but judging from the rest of his overly casual look, I guessed this was the way he liked it. I actually kind of liked it, too. "We get dozens of letters every year from campers and parents who say Quarry Summit saved them. Feels like we're using Randy's death for good, you know?"

"Yeah," I said, my breathing still unsteady. Maybe it was the altitude. Or the withdrawals. "I'm so sorry, Torin. I honestly had no idea."

He winked, which caught me completely off guard. Not necessarily the winking part, but the part where it made my stomach flip-flop. I hadn't been ready for that type of visceral reaction. "You should have done your research, fancy pants Ivy Leaguer. It's in our mission statement."

"The term Ivy League refers to an athletic conference, not academics. Stanford's a Pac-12 school."

"Gotcha. I thought it meant something else," he said, thumbing his chin in the slight little divot that made it a little like a butt chin, but much cuter than the ones I'd seen before. "I do not think it means what you think it means," Torin recited in a strange, foreign accent. I gave him a puzzled look and he lifted his hands in the air as he shook his head dubiously. "*The Princess Bride*?" He tilted toward me, awaiting my reply. I offered him a blank stare as my only response because that was all I had. "Inigo Montoya? 'You killed my father'? 'Prepare to die'?" I shook my head, totally clueless, and you would have thought I'd just admitted to not knowing the Pledge of Allegiance. Apparently this Inigo fella ranked pretty high in the necessary repertoire of common knowledge.

Torin smirked wryly. "So I'm the one who grew up on a secluded mountaintop, but you're the one who sounds like you were completely robbed of your childhood."

"In more ways than you know." *Wow. That was totally cryptic.* I added, "I was only robbed because we had eight childhoods going on at once. Mine just got thrown into the mix. Kinda like trying to watch eight TV shows on eight different TVs at once—each story blends with the other and it all just becomes a cacophony of chaos."

Torin held back to wait for me to walk the few feet to catch up with him and then he resumed his pace at my side, facing forward this time. I wasn't sure where we were going, but I followed. "You're one of eight? That's crazy." His eyes were wide. "And you seem a little crazy, too, you know that? Attending such a prestigious school but not knowing the entire script of *The Princess Bride*? Total crazy status."

We rounded a turn and headed down the incline past the cabins that dotted the hillside. A thick line of trees skirted the structures, and I could see wires that hooked between each of them like tightropes in the sky. "It's only seven now." I kept my eyes held to the ground. "Only seven kids in my family, I mean."

He halted for a moment, then continued once he realized I was still moving forward. "That something you want to talk about?" The sensitivity in his tone was alarmingly comforting, and though he'd just admitted to losing a sibling, I didn't want to talk, so I just said, "Nope," and then he said, "Okay," without even missing a beat, like he could completely read my social cues. "But it does sound like fun," he added, "having all those siblings around."

I shrugged. "Trust me, it's more fun in theory than in reality."

"Okay," Torin said, nodding. His endearingly disheveled hair bounced along his ears. "I can do that."

"Do what?" I followed at his side, and when the trees opened up into a small clearing, I lifted my gaze to meet his.

"Trust you." He pointed a finger above us toward the rope ladders, zip lines, and netting strung in the canopy of trees. "Because that's the theme of our first exercise." Torin bent down to snatch two helmets off the forest floor. He passed one to me and then gathered the black harnesses that rested on a nearby tree stump, their straps and buckles tangled together. "You ready to put all your trust in me, those ropes, and this carabiner, Darby?"

My face went white, not that I could see it, but I could feel it. I could feel all the blood literally rush away from my head, leaving behind a ghostly pallor of pale flesh, like Albino Boy's back in the rec hall. What had I signed up for? I choked down the bile that crept up my throat.

"I'll take your lack of an appropriate response as a yes," Torin said as he fitted the helmet onto my head.

Chapter 4

"Please don't do that again." Torin scrunched up his face, entirely disgusted. He shuddered like he had just witnessed something truly revolting and a shiver ran through him head to toe.

I stared down the length of the tree at my vomit that puddled at its base.

"I'll try not to," I groaned, wiping my mouth with the back of my hand. "But no promises. I think I have an unusually responsive gag reflex."

The trees swayed at my periphery and I clutched on tighter to the bark, splinters wedging under my nails. I'd always considered myself environmentally conscious, but the term *tree hugger* was much more fitting in this moment. I didn't think the Jaws of Life would be able to pry my grip from this thousand-year-old redwood. I was pretty sure the tree might have just gotten to second base with me.

"You're not going to fall," Torin assured from his perch on a two-by-two-foot platform nailed to the tree opposite me. Two thick wires connected us, one about six feet above the other. "See?"

He leaped off the wooden base and a scream burst out of me, burning my already raw throat. My bloodcurdling wail bounced off the surrounding trees like a game of pinball. Torin chuckled as he dangled by his harness, swinging back and forth as though he was on a child's playground rather than suspended one hundred feet in the air.

"See?" he said again. "This will catch you. You can trust that."

Though he was by no means a bodybuilder—I was certain Lance could bench-press double what Torin could—he surprised me with his upper-body strength as he pulled himself back up to the platform with just the use of his arms as he glided up the wire hand over hand.

"Plus," he continued, ignoring the fact that I wasn't looking at him and had now pinched my eyes completely shut, "you need to be able to do this if you expect our campers to do it."

"I don't think I actually expect them to do it. This is pretty terrifying, you know," I called out to him.

"Well, that's just great, Darby." I could hear the sarcastic quality in his voice and assumed he was rolling his eyes, because that's what you did when you took that tone with someone. "If that's the case, then you'll be just like everyone else in their lives. Way to be the change."

"What's that mean?" I questioned, peering out of just my right eye like a pirate, which was fitting since he was sort of asking me to walk the plank. I almost wanted to tack on an "arggh" at the end of my question, but that would make me a dork. Torin already thought I was crazy. I wasn't sure I wanted dork status to make the cut as well.

"I mean, if you don't expect anything from your campers, then that's what you'll get—nothing. And that's what they're used to giving, so you'll make their job very easy."

"I told you I wasn't cut out for this," I retaliated, frustrated with both myself and Torin, but mostly with Lance, who had left me to fend for myself for six weeks. Being tethered to a tree in the Trinity Alps Wilderness was not my idea of the perfect start to summer. I could almost taste the Cheetos on the tip of my tongue and longed for the boring, uneventful routine Sonja and I had originally planned for our break. I even missed the beige P7036 hue that coated our walls.

"It's about overcoming," Torin said, his gloved hand still outstretched in my direction. If he thought I was going to grab ahold of it, he was crazy, and I'd already claimed that title. Though it did seem like it took a fair amount of crazy to work at this camp. Why couldn't I have signed up for a program that involved logic and reason? I was good at those things. I would even settle for science camp over this. Nerd goggles and test tubes were much more my speed.

"Tell me ten things about you."

My eyelids popped open and the bird's-eye view of the forest instantly surged a dizzying rush to my brain. I dug my nails deeper into the bark to center myself. "What? Why?"

"Because you're my partner." Torin dropped down onto his platform and swung his legs over the side. He kicked them back and forth like he was on the dock of a pier. "We should get to know one another since we'll be spending the next six weeks together."

"Oh . . . yeah . . . I guess so."

He kept up with the leg swinging and I tried not to look at it because it made my knees unhinge and my stomach feel weightless, two things I didn't really enjoy when my feet weren't fully planted on the earth's surface. "What do you want to know?"

"Whatever you want to tell me." Torin shrugged. "But here's the deal: with each thing you tell me, you need to take one step forward on the rope."

I tried to vehemently shake my head, but it probably looked more like an uncontrolled tick because I was clinging so tightly to the tree that any movement I made was hindered by my death grip. "I don't like that idea. Self-disclosure and tightrope walking for me, while you just sit there? Hardly seems fair."

"Oh." Torin grinned knowingly. "So you're one of those."

"One of those what?"

"One of those who think everything needs to be fair." He brought his knees up to his chest and hugged them. It made him look young, like a little boy just climbing a backyard tree. It also made him kind of adorable. "Fine. Then I'll tell you ten things about me, but you have to take a step with each one."

"Not in any way to be mean, but I don't have this over-whelming urge to get to know you right now." I really didn't like that I was coming across as rude, but being up this high in this tree made my whole censor start to disintegrate. "I'm a little more focused on not falling to my death."

"Darby, I'm pretty sure I can guarantee your survival, if that's what you're worried about. Remember, this forest is my home." Torin lifted up and rose to his feet, popping his knuckles together. Crack, crack, crack. "Let's try something different. What is something you're looking forward to? Some goal you have?"

I didn't know where he was going with this, but I had no choice but to either play along or make myself comfortable in this formidable evergreen. I resigned to the first option because, although the tree and I were becoming quite intimate, I would rather get out of its branches sooner than later. "A goal? I don't know. To visit Lance this summer, I guess."

"Okay, that's a good one. Let's go with that." He held out his hand toward me once again. "So to reach that goal, you have to do several things first, right?"

"Um, yeah."

Torin waved me forward, but I didn't budge. "Pretend I'm Lance—"

"Ha!" I belted out. "I'm sorry, but that made me laugh."

"I can see that. No worries." Torin just smiled, apparently unaffected by my slipup of laughter. I wasn't usually rude. I didn't know what it was about this guy that brought that out in me. "Pretend I'm Lance and I'm at the airport awaiting your plane's arrival." His light eyes opened widely and met mine. He had the same friendly eyes as his dad and I wanted to stare at them longer, but that felt a little creepy, so I shifted my focus back to the tightrope. "In order to get on the plane, what's the first thing you have to do?"

"Buy a ticket."

"Very good." Torin congratulated me like I was a kindergartner who had just spelled my first word correctly. "This is where you take one step forward."

"No, Torin. I don't think I can." I shook my head so he could see and bit my bottom lip between my teeth.

"Visiting your boyfriend isn't incentive enough?" Torin pursed his lips and I was surprised that he came off a little bit like a jerk. But maybe that was just me casting my views on him already because, in all fairness, I really wanted him to be a jerk. I didn't want him to be endearingly disheveled and sincere the way he sort of made himself out to be. So I kept telling myself he was acting like a jerk, hoping that maybe he'd rise up to meet that projection. So far, so good. By late this afternoon, I was pretty sure he would reach full-on jerk ranking.

"Okay then," he continued. "Let's modify. Pretend I'm Lance and I'm in a burning building."

"Why are you in a burning building?"

"I don't know. I was cooking you a candlelit dinner and the place went up in flames." Torin fiddled with his harness and it made me nervous that he was being so casual so high up. One false move and he could tumble to his tragic death. Though I didn't really know the guy, it would be sad to see him go so early on in our obligatory friendship, even if he did end up being the complete jerk I hoped he was. Regardless, I really wished he would leave his harness alone. "You need to come rescue me and get me outta here."

"There is no way I could rescue Lance from a burning building. He's easily twice my size. I'd call the fire department."

"You're making this harder than it needs to be with your sensible logic and reason, Darby." Torin tugged at the hair that curled out from under his helmet, fidgeting with frustration. "This is an exercise, one in which you need to take some initiative in order for it to work." He threaded his fingers together at the nape of his neck and angled his face toward the sky, like maybe the inspiration would somehow rain down on him and he'd suddenly have the perfect words to convince me to budge from my post. Unfortunately, I didn't see the sky opening up at all to grant him that wish. "Okay. Let's try this again. I'm Lance and you've just caught me cheating on you."

"That wouldn't happen," I replied quickly, adamantly. "If we're doing this, it has to be believable. Lance wouldn't cheat." That is, he wouldn't cheat again, that much I knew. Or at least that much I'd hoped. We'd traveled down that road a few too many times and I was hoping we were finally on an alternate route.

"Let's go with the cheating example."

"I don't like it." In fact, I hated it.

"That's why we're using it. I need something to get you to step off that platform. Protecting your relationship is the perfect motivation." Torin reached up to grasp the wire overhead and shimmied his body and weight onto the rope underneath. It bowed under his boot-clad foot, pulling the suspension with his weight. "Though I find it a little odd that saving the guy you're *in* a relationship with from a burning building wasn't important enough, but whatever."

"Please don't judge me, Torin. And please just get to the point," I murmured, trying to marshal any ounce of bravery I had. I slipped one hand off of the trunk and reached toward the wire, but my fears wrapped around every muscle in my body, controlling them more than my resolve, and I yanked my hand back and secured it on the bark again.

"I've got an even better one," Torin said as he bounced up and down on the ropes. I felt the small vibration of his movement echoed in the tree and I just about lost what was left of my lunch again. "Pretend I'm the girl he cheated with."

That got my attention.

I tried to recover my surprised expression, but he took notice.

"He wasn't that good anyway," Torin teased in a catty voice, several octaves higher than his natural one. "I just did it to make his girlfriend jealous."

Seriously, what was he trying to accomplish with this?

"She's all petite and quirky in a sort of sexy way and goes to some Ivy League—"

"It's a Pac-12," I interjected. Wait, did he just say sexily quirky?

"And I bet he's only with her because they've been together since they were like, what, twelve?"

"Thirteen," I corrected. I knew he was doing this to get me mad, and I hated that it slightly worked. Maybe they used brainwashing at this camp as one of their techniques. I wouldn't put it past them. I really should have done more research.

"But if she's really as important to him as she thinks, then why is he here with *me* now?"

"Because it's his internship."

"It's his job to go out every night and hook up with random girls?" Torin's voice resumed its low, natural tenor, like he wasn't joking at all anymore.

"What makes you think he's doing that?" I bit down hard on my lip, feeling like Torin knew something I didn't, though I knew that couldn't be the case. I hated the insecurity that took hold of me and made me question the current status of my relationship with Lance.

"Does it make you angry to think that it might be true?"

"Of course it does," I said, relaxing my grip. "But at you and not him. Because he's not cheating. I have his heart."

"Well, that sounds sweet and very young-love-ish and all, but he's a college guy in a city all the way across the country with no one holding him accountable. In my book, that's the perfect recipe for cheating, and for getting away with it. And he doesn't need to be in possession of his heart to get into another girl's pants. Pretty sure that body part is not necessary."

I gritted my teeth until they hurt. "Lance wouldn't do that, because he's committed to me. We're committed to each other." And he was all I had. I'd proven before that even if he wasn't 100 percent committed, I wasn't about to let go of him. That wasn't in my plan.

Torin cupped his hand around his ear and leaned forward. "What? I'm sorry, I couldn't hear that. You're going to need to come closer."

I totally got what he was doing and I wasn't about to be manipulated by his attempts at trickery. I instead chose to just raise my voice. "He's committed to me," I repeated.

"You have to come closer. I'm having trouble hearing you."

"You're a colossal ass!" I said, megaphoning my mouth, knowing full well he had no trouble hearing *that*. The other counselors back at camp probably heard it ringing clearly through the trees like a siren whistling in the distance. It was the first time I'd ever called a guy that, and it actually felt kind of good in a way that doing something wrong oddly makes you feel good.

"Maybe I am a colossal ass, but you're the stubborn one." Torin moved two feet forward with such confidence that you'd think he was some species of monkey that grew up swinging between the branches. "So tell me again how you know he's not cheating on you?"

"Because I trust him," I admitted. And I did, or at least I needed to.

Torin nodded. "Meet me halfway."

"What?" I whipped my head in his direction and the end of my ponytail hit my cheek.

"Meet me halfway, Darby." With one hand holding on to the rope above him, he slid forward on the wire and kept another hand extended my way. "You just told me you are able to trust a person a continent away that you can't even see. That takes a huge amount of trust. If you can do that, then you should easily be able to trust this wire since you're actually *watching* it as it holds me securely." He smiled widely and his tiny gap and dimples all showed at the same time. I kind of liked it when they did that because it was some irresistible cuteness trifecta. "It's easier to put your trust in objects than in people, and since you just proved you can do the harder of the two, this should be a cakewalk. C'mon, meet me halfway."

"But I don't trust *you* yet." I loosened my arms slightly and contemplated putting one foot in front of the other, but I just couldn't will my body to follow through. This was really hard.

"You don't actually need to trust me, though it would be nice if you did," Torin said, pulling up the corner of his mouth the same way his dad did. "All you have to do is trust what you see. Tell me what you see."

I breathed in deeply and that Pine-Sol scent infiltrated my lungs. Nausea swept through me like a fog curling onto the coast. "I see a goofy mountain man suspended a hundred feet in the air like some crazy trapeze artist." What was it about him that made me so snarky?

"Okay, if that's your interpretation of this, that works." He bent his knees and pushed up, bouncing on the taut wire just like earlier. "And now?"

"I see that you have a serious death wish."

"Less about me, more about the rope."

I pursed my lips and gave in. "I see that the rope is holding your weight."

"Do I weigh more or less than you?"

"More, I hope." I laughed, because Torin had at least fifty pounds on me.

"So if the rope can hold a hundred-seventy-pound guy, do you think it will hold you?"

"Yeah, obviously. But I'm not confident it will hold both of us at the same time."

"Would you rather me wait over here on my platform, then?" He gestured behind him with a glance flicked over his shoulder.

"No, stay where you are." With a movement that wasn't my own, I slipped one foot onto the rope, still gripping the tree with my hands. I had no idea what possessed me to do it, and for a transitory moment I thought maybe there was some type of wizardry going on at this camp, along with the brainwashing I was fairly certain they utilized. Nothing in me wanted to take that step, but I just did it like I was under some spell.

"Would it help to know that we've had three guys all my size on this rope at once before?"

"Since I haven't gotten to the 'trusting you' part yet, no, not really. I'd need to see that for myself."

"Close your eyes. Sometimes it's easier to see with your eyes closed." Torin's voice was unusually soothing given the circumstance. It surprised me that anything could calm the nerves that crawled through my body. I felt them scurrying across every surface of my skin, their antlike tickle making me shiver. "Lift your right arm—just like that, you got it—and now place your right foot onto the wire."

I begrudgingly did as I was told and felt the bend of the suspension rope under the tread of my shoe. I decided to make up my own spell—"hocus-pocus, keep my focus"—just in case the whole wizard speculation might actually be true.

"Now do the same with your other hand and foot." I kept my eyes shut and slid both hands and feet onto the wire. I wobbled back and forth, but managed to correct myself by tightening my grip on the overhead rope. "Now you can either shimmy toward my voice or you can place one foot in front of the other and walk toward me, but I suggest you open your eyes if you choose to do that."

Since opening my eyes was out of the question, I crept my way across the tightrope, inch by unsteady inch, until the sound of Torin's voice got louder, like we were within normal talking range. I didn't dare to open my eyes until I felt his breath on my skin and smelled him right under my nose. Just like his voice and his eyes, he had a comforting scent—some kind of spice that reminded me not of cologne, but of something in my mom's potpourri dish back home. Whatever it was, it eased my anxieties and encouraged me to take one more step forward until I bumped straight into him. The ropes swayed against the impact and Torin hooked an arm around my waist to steady me.

When I opened my eyes, he was staring straight down at me with his wide, green gaze. All at once, the reality that I was suspended in the trees like a bird on a power line flooded my senses and I sunk under his grasp, my legs giving out from under me like they were mush. "Steady, Darby. You've got this." With an arm still secured around me, he slid forward to the platform and I clung to his back, not letting go even when I had two feet firmly planted on the wooden surface. "You did it!" Torin spun around and threw me a high five. "See? Not so bad."

"It kinda was so bad."

Torin reached up to unhook my carabiner from the wire and reattached it onto another rope at the other side of the tree that sloped down at such a steep angle it could only mean it was a zip line. He tugged on it twice to ensure its safety. "I don't think he's cheating on you, by the way. A relationship that's endured six years—most of them teenage—can easily survive a six-week sabbatical." He clipped his own hooks onto the rope right behind mine. "Plus, you seem like a nice girl, Darby. Aside from that ass comment and possibly being a touch crazy. But I'm chalking that up to nerves."

"Thank you, I guess."

"You're welcome." Torin nodded and propped his hands on his hips. His jeans were low enough that the waistband of his boxers peeked out above them. "So do you want to do this on your own or tandem?"

"Tandem." I said quickly, my knees unlocking again. This lack of control over my own muscles was getting really aggravating. "I find it difficult to do things by myself." And that was true, though I was surprised I had so readily admitted it.

"I don't think that's the case, Darby. You came here on your own." Torin shoved his hands in his pockets coolly, like he was just waiting for the bus. A bus that apparently picked up its passengers in the sky. Was there anything that made him uncomfortable?

"I came *here* so I could go *there*." I pointed a finger at the ground below and then in the air, indicating Washington, D.C. "This is a means to an end for me." I tightened the base of my ponytail and prepared my body for the weightless sensation I knew was inevitable.

"I hope this turns out to be more than just that." Torin's face fell slightly and I thought I saw a shadow of hurt sweep through his eyes. They were cloudier than before and it kind of made me feel guilty, knowing that my statement was responsible for them looking that way. "I know you come from a big family, but I don't. And even though I tell myself each time I won't let it happen, all of the counselors and campers end up being that to me— my family."

Suddenly, unexpectedly, he wrapped both arms around my waist. My breath hitched, and when he pressed his chest against my back, it was such a weird feeling—to be this close to a boy who wasn't Lance. I wanted to pull away, but realized I had just asked him to do this by saying I wanted to ride the zip line together rather than separately. That was all this was. "Always recognize that human individuals are ends, and do not use them as your means to your end." Like before, with his weird *Princess Bride* imitation, Torin searched me for some sort of recognition. "Immanuel Kant? The German philosopher?"

"I know who he is," I said, gripping Torin's arms as he scooted us to the edge of the platform. My toes hung precariously over the wooden plank.

"I think if you look at this experience in that light, you'll leave with more than just six hundred dollars in your pocket after you've put in your six weeks." Torin tugged me closer to him and hiked one leg around my waist, readying to push off with his other. All the blood rushed away from my brain and left me light-headed and disoriented, and I wasn't sure if it was from the fact that I'd soon be sailing to my possible death, or the reality that this guy's warm body was pressed so closely to mine.

"I don't know if I want more than these six weeks," I whispered, pulling a long breath through my nostrils. I was sure he had heard me, but if he did, he ignored it as we slid off the platform and sped down the length of the wire, the fringe of the forest whirling past at dizzying speed until our feet met the ground below after just a few seconds of free fall.

I pressed up on trembling legs, and when Torin's arms stayed wrapped across my body, even after he unclipped the hooks from the rope overhead, I knew without a doubt that all I wanted was for this experience to be that means to an end. I didn't need more family members—between my own and Lance's, I had an abundance already. I had enough blaring TV stations to have my own cable company.

And I honestly didn't even need any more friends. All I truly needed was the money. Even if it wasn't one for Torin, the whole experience really was just a way for me to get from point A to point B.

Unfortunately, it might have been a bit easier to make the journey had I been assigned a different partner.

Chapter 5

The blare of the bugle jolted me out of slumber and my body reacted instantly, popping up vertically at the startling sound of the wake-up-call horn. As things would have it, the reality that I'd tucked myself into a bunk bed last night took a moment to make itself known, and when it did, it was in the form of warm blood spilling down my forehead. I reached up toward my hairline and felt the thick gash resulting from the contact with the metal bed frame hovering overhead. *Crap.* That was going to leave a mark.

I found some Kleenex tissues in the adjoining bathroom and held them to my head as I dressed and got ready, but the blood quickly seeped through the folded-over sheets, staining my hands. Though I hated to admit it, this was going to need some medical attention.

There was a map on the inside of the door and I located the medical office on it. From the looks of it, I figured it was just next to the rec hall. I knew where that was, probably the only place I actually could find my way to.

It was another cool June day and I wondered if this temperature wasn't actually unseasonable, but just how it was in the woods. It sort of felt like home, how the peninsula always stayed chilled despite the rest of California's tepid temperatures. But it was about the only part of this whole camp thing that reminded me of home, and even that was a significant stretch.

When I got to the medical room, the door was already propped open with a brick and I could hear hushed voices on the other side. They were talking about test results and counting out months until the holidays, and I didn't want to interrupt them because it felt a little like intruding. But the blood that tinged the tissue pressed to my forehead didn't leave me much of an option. I rapped on the door with my knuckles, hating that I had to break into their conversation all because I was a clumsy mess.

"Come on in," a friendly voice answered as loud footsteps echoed across the ground. The door stretched open more and Ran stood on the other side. Maggie sat on some type of medical bed, her legs swinging over the edge. When she saw me, she rushed over to stand behind Ran's shoulder.

"Darby?" Ran asked, pulling the tissues from my forehead. His piercing-blue eyes examined the slice at my hairline, but I was totally distracted by his mouth. His lips were perfect, almost unreal. I thought for a moment how unfair it was that they hired such an attractive medic, because I had already begun to feel dizzy at the sight of the blood trickling down my face. Having someone who looked like Ran as the medical staffer just exacerbated that spinning sensation. It was unfair on all kinds of levels, like I was a glutton for punishment.

"What did you do?" He lowered his eyes to mine.

"Sat up too quickly. Hit my head on the bunk." My pulse began to throb under the injury, and the headache that formed accompanied its rhythm.

"You had a tetanus shot recently?" Ran asked as Maggie took my hand to walk me to the cot that she had been sitting on earlier. I lifted myself up onto it, and Ran grabbed a bottle and some gauze from a shelf lined with medicine at the far wall.

"Yeah," I grumbled. "I think last year."

Ran tilted the bottle upside down as he paced back toward me, hiking a leg up onto the bed. "Good," he said, then hesitated as he drew the gauze up to my face. That hesitation could only mean one thing. "This might sting a little."

I gritted my teeth rather than bite my lip, and was glad I chose that option because it stung much more than just a little, and I probably would have gnawed completely through my lip had my teeth been pressed into it. It felt like a branding iron pushed against my scalp, the burning sensation affecting at least three layers of skin, I was sure. I sucked in a searing breath and counted to ten as I closed my eyes to endure the sudden pain.

"Sorry," Ran said as he tore open a butterfly bandage. Maggie's face held an empathetic grimace as he pressed the sticky side to my forehead, rubbing his thumb against it. It reminded me of Sonja's ability to naturally show sympathy and instantly filled me with the slight nausea of homesickness. "You lucked out—don't need stitches. But this will probably scar. Since it's so close to your hairline, it really won't be noticeable."

"What's going on?"

My stomach and body jumped at the unexpected sound of Torin's voice. He stood in the doorway at the back of the room and had close to a dozen backpacks looped across both of his arms, a slight sheen of sweat coating his brow, his cheeks reddened with exertion. When he saw me, he dropped everything to the ground and hurried over to my bedside, like maybe he was actually a little worried about whatever it was that brought me to the medical office. At least, that's what it felt like. At least, that's what I hoped it was. "What did you do, Darby?"

I jumped again. Why was I so jumpy?

"I hit my head," I groaned, which was quite appropriate to do because it really did hurt like hell. "On the bunk bed."

"Ahh." Torin nodded like it wasn't the first time he'd heard this. "Well," he said, thumbing his chin in a small circular motion. He cocked his head just slightly to the right. "This makes you look kinda hard-core. I was gonna suggest some ink like Tara's, but you can hold your own with a gash like that."

"How do you know I'm not covered in tats already?"

"I don't see any," he said, squinting an eye and scanning me up and down. His eyes hung a little too long below my collarbone where I, of course, wouldn't have any tattoos, so it was glaringly obvious he was using it as an excuse to check out my nearly nonexistent rack.

"Maybe they're all covered up," I suggested, for whatever reason I wasn't sure. "Maybe I have more ink than the Bic pen factory coating this freckly skin of mine."

Torin laughed unrestrictedly. "Well if that's the case, I'd love to see it. Go for it—strip down and show us this masterpiece you boast of."

I ignored Torin. Ran chuckled quietly, slipping my hair behind my ear to pull it away from my forehead. "Come back in tonight, and I'll get a clean bandage on this for you."

"No can do. Tonight's the overnighter. If she needs a bandage, she'll have to take it with her."

Ran flipped around to face Torin. They were eye level, and even though they looked nothing alike—Ran with his dark hair and Torin with his dirty blond—they both were equally attractive and I couldn't decide who was better looking. There was something classic, yet equally bad boy, about Ran, and despite Torin's overly casual demeanor and mildly unkempt appearance, they were both intriguing in their own right.

I sat there for a few minutes rating them. Ran had a perfect mouth, but Torin had those irresistible dimples. They were both built—Ran probably more so, with Torin just a bit on the leaner side. Ran had a strong jaw, but Torin's permanently rosy cheeks won out over that. I shook my head and scolded the irrational thoughts away. I shouldn't be concerned about the looks of other guys, much less about judging who was hotter like they were competing in some pageant they didn't even know about. How hard had I hit my head?

"Overnighter?" was all I managed to squeak out through the mess of hormone-laced thoughts running laps around my brain.

"Yeah." Torin motioned toward the ground littered with backpacks. "Tonight is our survival run-through."

"That's what the backpacks are for?"

"Yep. I came in here to stock them." Torin stood at the wall with the rows of bottles and bandages and gathered an armful of supplies. "But Maggie and Ran will stay back. We need to have a medic on the grounds at all times, and everyone who goes out for the overnighter needs a partner."

"I'm fine hanging back," Maggie said, exchanging a look with Ran. I wondered if they wanted company. If being the third wheel got me out of a night alone in the forest with Torin, I'd happily volunteer for that tricycle position.

"I can stay back if we need more people at camp," I said, pressing my palm to my forehead. The bandage was doing a good job of keeping the gash from opening, and the sting from earlier was now completely gone.

"Nah, Darby, you're with me." Torin unzipped the backpacks and slipped medical supplies into them. From what I could see, he placed a few Band-Aids, an Ace wrap, and some packets of gauze into each.

I nodded, figuring I wouldn't have gotten out of it that easily, but it was worth a shot.

"Would you mind helping me carry these to the rec hall?" Torin looked up at me under a lock of hair. He flicked his head to sweep it back instead of using his hands, which would have been more effective. I never quite understood the use of the neck to do things the fingers were meant for. Like calling a waiter over or requesting the check or waving at a friend. A head nod seemed like a weird stand-in for jobs that were created for fingers. "We need to pass them out to the other counselors."

"Yeah, sure." I hopped off the cot and draped several packs across my arms just like Torin had them arranged when he walked into the room.

I found it hard to believe that whatever I needed to survive a night in the woods was contained inside these bags. I was pretty sure I would need a U-Haul full of equipment. In reality, that might not even be enough. I think I was total semitruck status.

In fact, I found it hard to believe there was anything that might help me survive that summer at all.

. . . .

"Watch out!" Torin yanked me by the wrist, pulling me back onto the path before my leg brushed against the feathering plants lining it. I jerked to the side with his sudden movement and narrowly missed the patch of greenery he pointed to. "Poison oak."

"Seriously?" I said, shaking my head. "I'm not cut out for this."

This phrase had become my mantra over the past two days, and I was sure it wouldn't be the last time it fell from my lips. Torin had suggested tattoos earlier and this would be a great one for me: "I'm Not Cut Out for This" in thick, black Old English across my back, shoulder blade to shoulder blade.

I continued trailing him and I felt the ghost of an itch creep up my bare leg and hoped it was just a figment of my imagination. Most of my irrational fears usually were.

"You might not be cut out for it, but I am. You're lucky you were paired with me." Torin pushed the hair off his brow with his hands this time and smirked, one dimple piercing his cheek. "Must be the whole Irish thing."

"You kinda point out I'm Irish a lot." I paused, planting my hands on my hips, my palms dripping sweat. It was considerably warmer now and hiking only added to the heat.

"Because that's really all I know about you." Torin stayed up ahead of me a few paces and didn't turn to look at me as he spoke. The leaves crunched under his shoes and the sounds of the forest were quiet and hushed, except for our occasional conversation and the popping echo of our feet along the path. "That and you have a boyfriend you've been with for six years. And you're a little crazy, like to use profanities, and are slightly immature."

"Sometimes it doesn't seem like there's much more to know." I shifted the straps on the backpack and sweat slithered down my spine. It pooled at the waistline of my jean shorts, dampening them, making me just uncomfortable enough that I wished I'd brought a spare to change into.

Torin gave me a soft, thoughtful look and I realized my last statement made me appear really depressing, which I never liked feeling. Before I could come up with something to make me seem a little less pathetic, he said, almost as a consolation, "Let's rest when we get to the top of that ridge." He lifted his head up the path to a clearing at the crest of the hill and drew his hand across his forehead and said, "You're not just some half that makes a whole, Darby. I'm pretty sure even if you're in a relationship, you still have an identity, right?"

"Yeah, I guess," I said with a shrug, but didn't really believe my own words. "What about you? You have a girlfriend?"

"Nah. Haven't for a few summers now. I used to hook up with a different counselor each year, but that got old quick. Everyone continues on with their lives after they get down from the hill. But I'm still up here." I didn't think he meant to let it, but a sigh slipped in between his words. "It's kinda lame to be the one left behind."

"Yeah, it is."

I found myself frustrated with Lance for leaving me behind. For taking my life with him and leaving just the shell of me in its place. After I got past that feeling, I moved on to the one that made me feel like a complete idiot for being so torn up about a guy leaving for six weeks. A guy who had cheated close to that many times, and one who I'd forgiven an equal number of times.

And this was just six weeks. I wallowed in how depressing that was for several minutes until Torin motioned toward a large granite rock. I sat down and slipped my arms out of the backpack straps as I took up residence on the boulder. Setting the pack down next to me, I drew out my water bottle from the side pouch.

"It must be nice to have that sort of commitment to someone. My longest relationship was six weeks. Can't imagine six years."

"Six weeks is a long time," I suggested, because to me, right now, it felt like an incomprehensible, infinite length of time. I took a swig from the container and swished it around in my mouth, the cool liquid swimming over my tongue. "And really, I just don't know any different."

"Is that because you want it that way?" Torin unscrewed the cap to his army-green canteen, tilted his head back slightly, and poured a bit over his head. The water beaded in his dark blond hair and slipped down the strands onto the back of his tanned neck. He shook his head like a dog after a bath. I looked away, because something about watching him made my stomach feel like I was about to sail down the zip line again.

"Yeah, I guess. I like commitment. I like feeling safe."

"Is that why you're an architectural design major?" Torin tossed his water bottle back into the bag and pulled out a slightly bruised, red apple. He bit loudly into it, then talked around the pieces still trapped in his mouth, like manners were something that only belonged at tables with cloth napkins and silverware, not out in the wilderness when sitting on a slab of granite with a girl you hardly knew. "Because you like structure? For things to be concrete?"

"I don't like *actual* structures and concrete, if that's what you mean." I smiled and fished through my bag, looking for some sort of snack, but nothing sounded good, despite the rumble growing in my stomach.

"That's not what I meant," Torin said, rolling his eyes in a deliberate motion. *"Obviously."*

"Really? Was it that obvious? Because it sounded like that's what you might have meant." Torin made it way too easy to tease.

"I'm not some ignorant backwoods kid, you know." He laughed, finished eating his apple in corn on the cob–like fashion, and chucked the remaining core at a nearby tree. It ricocheted off of the bark-crusted trunk and wobbled onto the ground before it settled into place.

"I wasn't implying you were." Well, maybe a little. I honestly didn't know his story, and I wasn't sure I wanted to. Point A to point B. No detours. And definitely no picking up stray hitchhikers along the way, no matter how cute or endearing they might appear.

"I just figured with a mind like that, you like things that have reason and purpose. Left-brain thinker and all."

The rock we sat on sloped at an angle that allowed for us to lean on it like it was a bed, so Torin did just that, propping his arms up behind his head as a literal man-made pillow. The sun bathed his face and he closed his eyes, soaking up the warmth on his tan skin. I didn't want to look at him, but I couldn't help it, considering he was the only breathing thing within a five-mile radius, and considering how good he looked with the light falling across him that way. His cheeks were even more flushed than normal, and I assumed the effort from the hike drew the extra pink to his face.

"You're right," I answered, but just enough time had passed that my reply felt disjointed from his earlier statement. "I do like routine. Reason. Purpose. That's why this honestly really scares me, Torin." I played with the end of my braid, the auburn streaks glistening under the summer light as I coiled it around my fingers.

"'This' meaning camp or 'this' meaning the overnighter?" Torin didn't open his eyes to ask.

"'This' meaning all of it. Totally out of my comfort zone here."

"That just goes to show how much your relationship means to you—that you'd be willing to put yourself out there just so you can save money to visit Lance." Torin angled his face in my direction but still didn't open his eyes, and I wanted to look away because I worried if he suddenly did open them, I wouldn't be able to hide the fact that I had been staring. That I was *still* staring. "It would be nice to have someone hold that much meaning in my own life."

"I'm sure you have something," I said, slipping farther down on the rock. And I really wasn't even sure Lance was the real reason I was stepping out like this, either. I thought my need to have a plan for my life had taken over and maybe it didn't even really matter who I shared that plan with. Lance had been there for six years; he seemed like the obvious and logical fit.

"I do have some*thing*, but not some*one*." Torin rolled his head back the other direction, probably to even the exposure of the sun on each side of his face. His voice was fainter now that he spoke into the air away from me. "Sometimes it takes another person to take you past your self-made limitations and discover who you truly are. Sounds like Lance did that for you."

"So philosophical, Torin," I teased, propping my arms behind my head just like he had done.

"Not necessarily," he said. "Just something I think about."

I heard him shuffle around next to me, but I waited a few moments before opening my eyes. When I did, he was settled back onto the rock, but his shirt was tucked up under his head, his carved chest bare. My pulse quickened, mostly because it embarrassed me more than anything, being completely caught off guard by him lying half-naked next to me. I tried to command my eyes shut, but I couldn't. I was wrong in thinking he wasn't as toned as Lance. Lance was tall and bulky with the solidity of a football player. But Torin was every bit as fit, just leaner, with his muscles more toned, stretched across his frame. I let out a breath and tried to shake the vision from my head. This altitude was affecting me more than I'd originally given it credit for.

"How did they die?" The sudden startle of his voice made me jump, my shoulders arching off the slab of stone underneath. "Your sibling. . . . How did they die?"

It took me by surprise because we had been silent for a few moments, and I knew he was thinking during the quiet that hung around us, but I just didn't know about what. I hadn't figured that was it.

"She died unexpectedly."

"Isn't it always?" he agreed, nodding, his eyes still closed. "My brother, too. I mean, I guess with suicide they say there should be signs, whatever that means. Like there was supposed to be some huge billboard announcing, 'Randy is going to kill himself' that I had completely overlooked."

"Yeah." I slid my head back and shut my eyes against the glare of the sun. I could still see its glowing red outline through the sheer skin of my eyelids. "Death sucks."

"What did she like to do?"

I didn't talk about her much anymore. No one really did. But I hadn't forgotten her. I remembered her in everything I did. In every choice I made. In every thought that traveled through my brain. I remembered her. Because if I didn't, then who would? And what would that mean if I didn't include her anymore? If Anna didn't exist in my life, then she wouldn't exist at all. I felt like I owed her at least that much, to help her keep existing, even if only as a memory.

"She liked to draw," I said softly, because somehow my vocal cords couldn't push out any more sound. "She was really smart. Sarcastic and witty, funny."

"Was she your twin?" Torin asked, nearly interrupting. "Because she sounds an awful lot like you."

"No." I laughed, thinking it was funny because I would never really use those words to describe myself. "And I'm probably the one who takes after her. She was a year older."

"Randy and I were nothing alike." It felt like he was opening up to me, like we were developing some kind of camaraderie over dead siblings, however morbid that was. It honestly didn't feel morbid. "He was always so 'fly by the seat of his pants.' Mom called him the impulsive one and me the thinker."

"You do like to think," I agreed, because I had experienced this side of him firsthand already. "You did a pretty good job analyzing me yesterday on those ropes. Trying to figure out how to get me to take the step with your counseling wizardry."

"It's not really magic, Darby. It's just making you realize what you're actually capable of. And I think you're capable of much more than you think." I heard Torin rotate to face me and when I opened my eyes, his eyes nailed into mine, the green intensity sending a wave of heat through my stomach. It forced me to swallow hard. "You keep saying you're not good at doing things on your own, but I don't think that's true at all."

I didn't know how much I believed him, so I opted for a subject change. "How much more will we hike?"

"Okay, I'll stop." Torin shot me a dimpled grin, blinking rapidly, the eyes and the smile all working together. "Sorry—I just really like to figure out the way people work. What motivates them, what drives them. I'll stop, though."

"I don't mind," I said, rolling onto my back. The stone felt hot against my skin, and I soaked it up the way cats do when they lie on hardwood in strips of window light. "I just don't think like that. Concrete and structure, remember?"

"Right. Things you can feel, see, and touch. Just like the rope."

"I thought we were done, Oh Analytical One."

"Right, sorry. I just find you sorta interesting."

I didn't know why his words had the effect they did, but my entire body shivered, and he'd only called me *sorta* interesting. Had he said I was even *a little* interesting, I probably would have broken out in a full-on sweat. I concentrated on the heat of the stone underneath me, but my fingers and toes tingled against my will. And I assumed the reason the response was brought on had a little something to do with the fact that I felt exactly the same way about Torin. I couldn't make heads or tails of him, and that completely piqued my interest. I liked things I couldn't figure out because after all these years living a life of monotony, everything about me had become pretty darn predictable.

"Don't get me wrong, you're a little odd . . . but also equally interesting."

"Thank you?"

"You're welcome. It's a compliment. I like a little crazy in my women." His mouth stretched into a grin and those chills surfaced on my skin once more. Before I could shoot back the fact that I wasn't actually his woman, he said, "Tell me more about Lance."

"Like what?"

"How does it feel to know that you're so sure about something that you plan to spend the rest of your life doing it?"

I couldn't help but laugh at his choice of words, and I sort of snorted through my nose.

"Wow." Torin blushed, then corrected himself. "That came out wrong. Not *doing* it. Spending your life *with* it."

"It feels comfortable."

"I can't imagine making one decision that would impact the entire course of my life." He pulled himself into a sitting position, and I suddenly felt awkward that I was sprawled across the rock next to him, though I'd felt quite awkward since I set foot at this camp. I slid up to sit, too.

"Not a fan of the institution of marriage?" I continued to flick the end of my braid, and when I glanced in Torin's direction, he was staring at me with an intense look that caused my already empty stomach to roil. I broke our gaze quickly.

"No, I definitely am. My parents have been married for thirty years. I'd love to have that someday. Just can't imagine being nineteen and being *that* certain of something—of someone—you know? Don't get me wrong. I want it. I'm just not sure I'll ever find it."

"I think sometimes all those little decisions make the big decisions for you." I dropped my hands from my hair and knit them together in my lap, needing to keep them busy because they really wanted to reach across and tuck his loose hair behind his ear. And how creepy would that be? If I just stretched over and ran my fingers through his hair? Holy heck, that might be enough to justify sending me straight to the loony bin, because seriously, who does that to a practical stranger?

I squeezed my fingers tighter together and said, "Like how the last six years with Lance have been preparing me for this next step with him."

"Yeah, I get that." He tugged at a piece of grass that skirted the edge of the stone and lifted it to his mouth to bite down on the end of it, then nodded thoughtfully. "I wonder what my past decisions have been preparing me for." Torin twirled the straw back and forth between his teeth like a toothpick, the way I imagined a cowboy would in the bed of his old Ford truck. "And by the way, what you just said is the exact opposite of your whole 'means to an end' thing." The way he leaned toward me and cocked a brow pulled all the air from my lungs, like his words had fingers and were capable of stealing my very own breath from me. "Just so you know."

"Maybe I'm not all concrete and structure after all," I teased with too many nerves in my nearly quivering tone. I played with the same patch of grass next to us and slowly drew in the air that escaped me.

"No, maybe there's room for a few flowers and trees in there." Torin jabbed at my stomach with his finger and I coiled away from his touch. "Come on." He pushed off the rock, stretching out a hand to me. I took it hesitantly, embarrassed by the sweat that so obviously coated my palms. "We have several more miles to go before sundown. Let's continue our journey."

"Okay," I said, slinging my pack over my shoulder. I could handle continuing the journey for now. A small stepping-stone.

It was the longer journey that really worried me.

Chapter 6

"You've got this, Darby." Torin jogged to my side, his feet meeting the ground in alternating claps. His breathing was ragged and uneven, and he folded over and pressed his palms to his kneecaps as he caught it. "This is way thicker than those ropes yesterday."

I gulped down the tight ball in my throat. I wondered if he had known we would encounter this when he chose to let me lead the way. There was a fork in the road a mile or so back. I opted to go right. I swore I had seen him smirk when I arbitrarily made the decision, but I thought nothing of it at the time. That smirk didn't feel so innocent now. I bet he knew this was on our path. He knew this forest like the back of his hand, which I'd spent way too much time thinking about holding.

"You're not going to fall." He jutted his chin toward the log. The branch was about a foot wide and stretched at least two yards over a river that rushed below. Cragged rocks peeked out through the deep water, taunting me like hungry sharks breaking the surface with their gray vertical fins. "You've got this."

And I thought for a moment he could be right. If I was able to suspend a hundred feet in the air the day before without killing myself, I could definitely do this.

I put one foot confidently in front of the other, biting my lip as I willed myself not to look down. There was a bush decorated with tiny pink flowers just on the other side of the gulf and I zeroed in on it, forcing my focus onto the petals that popped off the greenery. Like a gymnast on a balance beam, I stepped forward without falter.

That was, until Torin's fingers brushed my waist. I didn't know what he was doing and I wasn't sure why I reacted the way I did. But any authority I had over my feet and legs was yanked from me, and I wobbled back and forth like a spinning top, teetering precariously on edge. I curled my toes to reclaim some steadiness, but the inflexibility of my tennis shoes prohibited the attempt from doing any good. Like I was in slow motion, my right foot gave up its position and slipped off the log first, then my left, and I clawed and grabbed at the branch—flailing with my arms and legs—but I failed to get a grip and splashed into the water below, breaking the surface with a scream that was quickly sucked up by the water that poured into my open mouth.

It was cloudy and murky and I blinked rapidly to regain my bearings, but I couldn't tell which way was up or down. The tug of my backpack pulled me, swaying me side to side, and I fought to slip it off of my shoulders, unable to manage it free. I was disoriented and dizzy, and took longer than I should to compose myself as I struggled against the backpack and the surprisingly fast current. Unfortunately, my lungs paid the price, hardening in my chest and begging for air. Just a few seconds passed before the water broke again, and just as quickly I was being jerked upward by two strong hands wrapped around the straps of my bag, my body trailing languidly behind. I crested the surface and dragged in the breath my body so desperately craved.

I'm sure I looked like a drowned rat. I felt just about that good, too.

"You okay?" Torin gulped, sliding an arm around my waist as he pulled my pack off with a free hand. From what I could tell, it didn't take much effort for him to do it.

I nodded, treading water. My sneakers didn't serve well as flippers and I trembled back and forth with my legs unsteadily. "Lost my balance there."

"I think I had a little something to do with that." That guilty smirk from before reappeared. "Shouldn't have distracted you. You're a bit jumpy today." He glanced toward my forehead while kicking against the waves, angling toward the direction of the shoreline. I swam with him, and when I felt the rocky ground under my feet, I pushed up out of the water. My shirt clung tightly to my chest and my jean shorts sagged, sodden with the muddy liquid that dripped down my legs.

Torin looked me up and down, his eyes trailing over every inch of me. "We need to get you out of those," he said, pointing a finger at my waterlogged outfit.

"Huh?" I twisted my braid out like a dishrag. Water puddled around my feet and it looked like I was standing in an inch of chocolate milk. "Why?"

"Because they will dry a lot faster *off* of you rather than *on* you." He unzipped my backpack and rummaged through its contents like he was some TSA agent and I'd smuggled a bomb into an airport. He didn't appear satisfied with whatever he discovered—or didn't discover—inside the pouch and let out an irritated huff that I couldn't help but notice. "Everything in here is soaked. You'll have to wear your swimsuit."

My jaw dropped. Like, came completely unhinged the way they do in cartoons. I never thought it was actually possible, but came to find out, it definitely was.

"My swimsuit?" I forced the pack out of his hands, taking it back into my possession. "Not very practical, Torin, walking around the forest in a bikini."

"It's more practical than walking around in soaking wet clothes that will freeze to your skin come sundown." Without permission, Torin snatched the bag from my grip, grasped my swimsuit, and shoved it into my chest. "Put this on."

"Where?" I squeaked, reluctantly taking the red-and-white polka-dot two-piece from his hold. Our fingers brushed and his eyes caught mine in an unsure glance.

"I don't know, behind a tree or something." He continued digging through my backpack, pulling out all of my clothes and the blanket crammed inside. He took them to a nearby rock and spread them out onto its surface like he was a maid with a clothesline and a load of laundry to finish.

"I'm not changing out here." I wrapped my arms across my chest, humiliation spreading throughout my body. Usually people's cheeks turned red when they were embarrassed. I was fairly certain every inch of my skin was blushing bright pink, rivaling the reddened hue of Miss Piggy.

Torin cocked his head and thumbed his chin—something I was beginning to notice he did a lot of—and his dimples eased into his cheeks. "You do realize this is a *survival* overnighter, don't you? There are some things you need to let go of for survival's sake. Modesty is one of those things."

"If I remember correctly, yesterday you pretty much promised me that you'd keep me alive. And I'd like to keep my modesty. I really don't want to change into this, Torin."

He dragged his hands through his hair and sighed in my

direction, sensing the sincerity in my plea. "Darby, it may currently be blazing hot out, but tonight it will get down into the forties. And as of right now, you have no dry clothes to sleep in and your overnight blanket is full of about ten pounds of water. You've run out of options."

I pinched my lips together. What I wouldn't give to be lounging on the couch back at the rental with Sonja, getting fat by binging on Cheetos and other junk food. Even the hope of visiting Lance didn't make any of this worthwhile. I sort of wished Torin would have just let me float out there in the river a bit longer. Maybe I would have passed out and drowned. That would be slightly less humiliating than what I feared was in store for me at the summer camp.

"At least turn around."

Torin looked up at me from the granite slab where he'd arranged my clothes. "What?"

"Please turn around. No peeking."

He shook his head and returned his focus to his work. "I'm not gonna peek. Off-limits."

"I'm off-limits?"

He stepped back and surveyed the spread of fabric, then moved a pair of my socks so they didn't overlap with the T-shirt underneath. "Off-limits. Taken." His pale eyes pulled up to mine. "And even if you weren't, you're not really my type, Darby."

Insult sucker punched me in the gut. "Jeez," I murmured, feeling the hurtful sting of his comment. "Then by all means, please stare away. Take pictures if you like."

"That's not what I meant." Torin stepped back from the rock and fiddled with his belt. Before I could register what he was doing, he'd unzipped his fly and was down to his boxers, pulling one leg, then the other, from his cargo shorts. My throat went dry and I tried hard to swallow, but my mouth was all sandpaper and it scratched my tongue. Where did his pants go? And why was I staring at his underwear, which was covered in hundreds of yellow smiley faces, repeated over and over in a dizzying, disorienting pattern? Seriously, why were his boxers smiling at me?

"Lookswise, you're all right," he continued, twisting his shorts between his fists to squeeze the water out of them. He laid them across an empty space on the granite rock. The smiley faces continued to mock me with their oversize grins. "But you're too stubborn. I don't like that in a girl."

I stood there—speechless—for longer than I should have, but the shock that Torin had stripped down to his underwear like it was a totally normal thing froze me in my place. I literally had to shake my head to toss off the gaping expression draped across my face. Nothing about this was normal. It wasn't often that I saw guys stripping down to their skivvies in front of me.

"Okay. So I'm decent looking and stubborn."

"Pretty much."

I balled up my swimsuit and flipped around to face the river. "Well, you happen to be really blunt." Recalling the murkiness of the river, I slipped into the water until it came up to my shoulders. With my back turned, I pulled my top over my head, and then tucked it between my legs to keep it from floating away as I fastened my bikini top.

I stole a glance over my shoulder. Torin wasn't even looking in my direction. It shouldn't have bothered me, but it did. Wouldn't every normal nineteen-year-old guy be tempted to check out a half-naked girl just twenty feet away? But then again, I'd already established that nothing about Torin was normal. He didn't even have a normal name. (In all fairness, neither did I, but this diatribe was directed toward him, not me.)

Maybe he wasn't into girls. Maybe that was his deal. It actually made me feel a little better to think that. Honestly, whatever it was, it shouldn't have had any effect on me one way or the other. Who Torin was—or wasn't—interested in did not involve me in any way, shape, or form. I tried to feed myself the lie, but it truly tasted awful.

I pulled off my shorts and slipped my bottoms on, then resurfaced and walked toward Torin with more movement in my hips than I displayed during our hike earlier this afternoon. He was still completely unfazed, and I blushed at my failed attempt at mild seduction. I seriously sucked at this.

"Are you gay, Torin?"

"Excuse me?" He angled his face up toward mine, the sunlight streaking his blond hair.

"Are you gay?" I chucked the remainder of my wet clothing at him, and he caught it against his stomach like a football. "Because I was just naked out there in the water and you didn't even so much as glance in my direction. I thought you wanted to see my colorful body art. Totally missed your chance, dude."

Torin placed my shirt and shorts on the rock and then strode over to me, stopping just inches from my face. His lips were pressed tightly together, pinching something back that I figured he wanted to say but knew he shouldn't, and he propped both hands on his hips disapprovingly. "You gave me very clear instructions not to look. And, like I said before, you're off-limits."

His breath swept across my cheek and I found myself averting my eyes, trying not to make contact with his. Unfortunately, they were this unique green color with flecks of gold in them and unlike any I'd seen before, which sort of made me inherently unable to avoid them. "I make it a habit to not tempt myself with things that can get me in trouble," he continued to explain. "A wise man never plays leapfrog with a unicorn."

I ignored the last offbeat remark (I assumed it was another infamous quote) and said, "So you were tempted?" I had no idea where all of this boldness came from, or what I was doing exactly.

Maybe this was flirting. It felt like it might be. But it had been so many years since I'd flirted with anyone that it just felt awkward and unnatural. And wrong, because even though Lance hadn't always been faithful, that didn't give me the green light to start interacting with other guys this way. I'd never believed in an eye for an eye, even when Lance's eyes had done too much wandering.

"Just like I'm not attracted to stubbornness, I'm not especially attracted to brunettes."

"But I'm a redhead."

"No," Torin said, his tone riddled with condescension. "No, you're not."

"Yes," I tried again, "I *am*."

"Darby, you're definitely not a redhead." He slunk his arms across his chest. He was still just in his smiley-face boxers, and I forced my eyes to stay focused on his actual face and not the rest of him, no matter how much it felt like everything was pulling my eyes down. I wasn't sure if it was sweat or leftover trails of water that slithered down his chest to the ripples of his abdomen, but it was there and it made me sweat, too, but not at all in the sexy way he was sweating. My feet and armpits and hands were all coated with an embarrassing amount of perspiration. "I'll give you auburn, but that's it."

"I'm a redhead, and I've got the freckles to match," I asserted, tugging my hiking boots onto my feet and tossing my tennis shoes aside. I tightened the laces around my ankles with angry effort, binding them like a corset onto my legs.

"Since when?" Torin scanned me up and down, his eyes dragging over my body. "Maybe when you were twelve." He leaned his upper half forward and squinted as he transferred his gaze to my face. "But I can hardly see any freckles and your hair is definitely more brown than red." Dropping down to where his bag rested, Torin pulled out a pair of jeans from within it. It made me just as uncomfortable watching him dress as it did watching him undress, and I pinned my eyes to the ground while he zipped and buttoned his pants. They settled low on his waist, but the muscular curve of his hip peeked out the top, distracting me with its perfect definition and tone. "I'm not sure where you get your self-image," he continued, "but it needs to be updated. Along with your maturity. Because the girl I'm looking at right now clearly isn't the same one you see when you look in the mirror."

"You think there's something wrong with my self-image?" My feet felt heavy and my ankles were tight, the bulk of the boots unnaturally disproportionate to the lack of weight of clothing on the rest of my body. I slung the backpack over my shoulders again, grateful for what little odd balance it provided.

In one swift gesture, Torin tossed his bag over his shoulder, too, and stepped back onto the trail, a cloud of dust billowing around his feet. "I think you're lost and I think you've become someone else's creation." He took over the lead, commanding me to follow not with vocal instruction, but with his no-nonsense stride that confidently navigated the dirt path. He was definitely the lead dog.

"You mean Lance's creation."

"I mean whoever it is that makes you believe you aren't capable of creating your own identity."

There was a time when a statement like that would have readied me for combat. When such an accusation would have ignited a defense to spew out through aggressive words and justifications. But I had nothing. I opened my mouth to contest his assertion, but I was firing blanks. I prayed for an original comeback, some thought that was my own, but the abyss that held my repertoire of retaliations was empty. Which could only mean one thing.

He was absolutely right.

After trailing him like a sad little puppy for the following ten minutes, I finally gained the courage to speak. "I'm not interested in reinventing myself."

"Whatever, Darby." Torin's feet fell in heavy steps. I was beginning to think they should have labeled this a survival marathon rather than overnighter, because all we'd truly done was walk up and down the wilderness trails with absolutely no purpose in our actions. I was going to pay for this day in the form of ugly blisters on my tired feet. "Sometimes things are set in motion and it's too late to stop them from continuing, from perpetuating. It's called inertia."

"Inertia, huh?" I knew what inertia was. And I knew what he was insinuating. That this trip would change me. That I would somehow come out different on the other end. That the Darby who signed up as a counselor would not be the same woman who would leave the mountaintop. My reinvention was well underway.

I got it. But what I didn't get—nor remotely understand— were the other things that were set in motion, the ones that I seemed to have no control over: my fluttering heart, my flustered mind, and my wandering eyes. But I wasn't about to admit to those, wasn't about to admit to the separate ball that he had somehow set rolling.

I had to find a way to stop it in its tracks.

Unfortunately, I was beginning to think it had already gotten away from me.

Chapter 7

"I'm cold," I murmured, rolling onto my side. The blankets bunched up under my legs, tangling with them like a fabric web.

"C'mere." Lance curled an arm across my chest and hooked me toward him, just like every other night when I stayed over. I never knew why he wouldn't let me run the space heater. He had mentioned once that his grandma's house caught on fire, so he was constantly touting how unsafe they were. But honestly, even the warmest evening on the peninsula still called for heat during the cold hours of night. Luckily, Lance's body served as quite the sufficient blanket.

He pulled himself playfully over me, pressing down so our hips met and our chests were merely inches apart. This was so like him. "I can think of another way to get warm," he crooned in my ear. Middle-of-the-night make-out session—totally Lance's thing. While I was usually up for it, for some reason that night I was more exhausted than usual, like my body had already spent its quota of energy for the day and I had nothing left. I was on empty.

I pressed a hand to his arm. "Not tonight, Lance," I said quietly. "I'm really tired."

"All right." He planted a chaste kiss on my forehead and I instantly knew what it meant.

That this was all a dream.

There was no way Lance would be that easily satisfied with my request. He'd push to the point of begging, and I'd end up surrendering because in reality, making out took less energy than trying to argue my point with Lance.

"G'night," he slurred against my cheek, his lips wet. I pulled back to slide toward my edge of the bed, but, knowing that this was a dream, I decided to steal one more kiss before this fabricated reality was yanked away with the rising sun. I hadn't seen or talked to Lance in days, and though dreaming wasn't the same, it temporarily filled that gap. The withdrawals had been too much; I needed another fix.

I dragged my fingers across his jaw and took his chin between my palms. He was completely asleep, breathing heavily against my mouth, warm air rushing steadily in and out. I was surprised by how solid he felt, how my fingertips sensed his skin just under them. Though the outline of his face and features flashed across my mind in hologram-like form, he physically felt real and tangible. I slid closer to him, hauling myself over his body to straddle him. Lance loved when I took charge, but he rarely let things stay that way. He was a control freak in every area of his life. Our relationship being a very large area.

But since this was *my* dream, I decided to play it out the way I wanted. That meant having the upper hand, so I did just that. Still sitting on his waist, I bent over and brought my mouth to his, stopping just before our lips met, hovering an inch over him.

I pressed both palms to his chest and Lance brought his hands to my arms, stroking them up and down with slow, deliberate movement. The fine hairs on my skin rose as he swept gently toward my elbow.

I liked this Lance of my dreams. He was so much more aware and responsive than the one that existed in reality. But I guessed that was to be expected—that my subconscious would create the perfect fit, the perfect version of my already near-perfect boyfriend.

I lessened the space and surrendered my mouth to his. At first he acted surprised, which I guess was fitting since I had just denied his earlier advances. After a moment's hesitation, his lips softened, the firm pressure receded, and they became putty against my own. Putty that I had the ability to mold and shape through pressure and guidance.

I pulled his bottom lip into my mouth, surprised when I felt the effects of the act deep in my stomach. My breath and heart rate spiked, and I assumed Lance heard it because he reacted noticeably, pressing against me, deepening the connection.

It was all so vivid, so real, yet at the same time, so dreamlike because this wasn't how Lance typically acted. This was how I'd always *wanted* Lance to act. I'd wanted him to take things slow and to read my cues and respond. But that wasn't Lance. It never had been, and after six years, I was fairly certain it never would be.

Sliding off him, I kept my mouth on his until the last moment when I pulled away to creep to my side of the mattress. A cold gust of air swept across my face and I reached to tug the covers closer, tucking myself under the fabric until just the tops of my ears were exposed.

It was freezing. Lance must have left the window open again; the frigid chill that skated over my skin felt just like the night breeze that rolled in off the misty ocean. He loved to fall asleep to the distant sound of the waves crashing against the rocks, but I found it almost impossible to sleep when my body temperature was equivalent to the actual temperature outside.

Annoyed, I pushed the sleep that hung over my eyes and fogged my brain, and shook my head, forcing the lingering effects away. The bed was firm. Hard, not like usual. I ran my hand across its surface and felt the bumps under my fingers. Rocks.

Oh, God.

My heart propelled against my ribs, vibrating more than beating, because the pulse was so quick there was no way individual beats could even be detected. It was just a fluttering, racing mess.

I glanced over my shoulder. Torin's dirty-blond hair peeked out above the nylon edge of the sleep sack. His chest rose and fell steadily. Trees climbed skyward around us, outlined by the white glow of the full moon that hung with the stars above.

Shoving a hand through my hair, I tried to remember how I got there. We'd hiked for more hours than I could count, ultimately ending up back at our makeshift clothes-drying station. Luckily, nearly all of my belongings had a chance to dry. All except for my sleeping bag. *Of course.*

Torin was right. The forest did get noticeably colder once the sun went down. And while he'd offered me his bag, I couldn't take him up on it with a clear conscience. He'd made dinner— rainbow trout caught in the nearby stream—set up our campsite, and pretty much did everything while I trailed quietly behind him like a sheep following her shepherd. I told him we'd share, but only under the condition that he'd join me once I was fast asleep. Something felt wrong about lying down with another guy, even though Lance had done the same with a girl named Lindsay just a few months back. But I didn't want to be like that, so I determined that falling asleep on my own and then having Torin slip into the sleeping bag later made sense. It didn't feel like cheating; it seemed innocently necessary.

But nothing was innocent about the tingle that pulsated on my lips. I dragged my finger across them, and they were still swollen and tender. I knew I'd had some pretty darn realistic dreams in the past, but usually the feelings they evoked disappeared the moment my eyes flickered open. They didn't hang around, and even when I had tried to fall back asleep to continue the dream, I'd never been successful. Dreams didn't last. They got sucked away into the void of night where illusions and fantasies existed.

Torin shuffled and rotated over in one swoop, his face inches from mine. Though the sleeping bag was big—definitely made for two people—there was no denying the fact that we were zipped up in the same space, and even if I had wanted to gain some distance, I wouldn't be able to.

But what confused me the most was that I didn't want to at all.

"Darby?" Torin murmured. I trapped in my breath and clenched my eyes, wondering if his voice was a figment of my imagination. There were a lot of sounds in this forest: owls hooting from their perches overhead, squirrels rustling in the brush nearby. For all I knew, that could be a mountain lion crunching down the leaves under his paws just a few feet from us. Somehow, even that was less scary than the thought that Torin was aware of my presence in his sleeping bag. I wondered just how aware he actually was.

He shifted closer to me, the bag buckling between us. I pulled the fabric to my face, covering my mouth up to my eyes the way I did with my blanket when Sonja and I watched horror films. "Night, Darby," he murmured again.

"Night," I croaked, still not resuming my normal breathing pattern. And when Torin's lips met mine, I knew my breathing wouldn't fall back into its usual rhythm any time soon.

I wanted to pull back—I knew I should pull back—but I didn't. And the fact that I didn't made something in my gut twist with a guilty sickness that threatened to eject from my lips. I bit it back.

Torin's mouth was soft, warm, and familiar. Without a doubt, I knew I'd felt it before and that my dream from earlier wasn't all an illusion. Half of it might have been, with the thought that those were Lance's lips tangled with mine. But the other part— the very real, physical part—was in no way fabricated. It was acted out like a play, however unintentionally, and Torin was Lance's understudy. I really wanted him to take center stage.

I closed my eyes. I needed to stop. But I didn't. Instead, I willed myself to sleep again, willed myself back into slumber. Because that was the only thing about this that would make it okay—if I was still sleeping, unconscious of the things my body was doing.

But I wasn't asleep. I was wide-awake and aware. Hyper- aware, in fact, of all of my senses. Torin's mouth continued to press into mine, and his palms lifted to cradle my jaw. He was so gentle and so cautious that the "mountain man" term I'd used earlier to describe him was a total misnomer.

His lips pushed in and his leg wrapped over mine, so we were scissored together within the sleeping bag. I knew I shouldn't want this, but everything in me did. Maybe because it had been so long since I'd seen Lance. That had to be the reason. But as Torin continued to kiss me, his lips sliding over my own, I knew it wasn't Lance I craved. It never was. It was Torin. I didn't just want *a* kiss; I wanted *that* kiss.

Though I had been frustrated with Torin from the moment I met him—how he made me do that terrifying high-ropes course, how he had to come to my rescue when I fell into the river, how he even challenged the color of my hair—nothing about kissing him frustrated me.

I felt his chest rising against mine, and our body heat stole away any of those chills I'd had earlier. I melted into him, wrapping my arms under his, feeling the damp sheen of sweat from his palms across my neck as he swept my hair back to trail light kisses there. A warm shudder drew up my shoulders, and when Torin's lips returned to mine and coaxed them open and his tongue slid in, the ache in my gut intensified.

I didn't know how he did it, how he stayed controlled and collected, because I was bordering on ravenous and wanted to tear and claw at him. Maybe it was because he was still asleep—still in that dreamlike limbo—so his movements were light and airy just as they should be. I clenched my fingers, curled my toes, and regained my bearings.

Drawing back slightly, Torin pushed his full lips to mine again, and whispered, "G'night, Darby," softly against my cheek, his light breath caressing my skin.

In what I hoped would be my most convincing act yet, I muttered, "Good night, Lance," and rolled to my side of the bag.

Chapter 8

"I have something to confess, Darby."

It was early—like butt-crack-of-dawn early—but Torin had obviously been up for a while. The fresh fillet skewered over the fire kind of hinted at that. He must be a morning person, and a cook at that.

I, on the other hand, had just emerged from the sleep sack, my hair ratted and tangled around my shoulders like a lion's untamed mane. I finger-combed it wildly, ripping my hands through the frizzy strands. But the fact that I was going on day two without a shower, good toothbrushing, or deodorant application defeated any attempt at making myself presentable. I was an utter mess that could probably be smelled from a mile away.

"Sleep well?" Torin glanced up at me from the fire as he rotated the fish like a rotisserie. His hair was tousled and unkempt, strands jutting every which way, but it looked good on him. In fact, the more time we spent out there, the better looking he got. Maybe that's what happened when you were in your element. If that was the case, I probably looked about as good as Medusa and her snaky mess of twisted hair.

"I slept okay." I dropped down onto a log across from him and swiped the back of my hand across my eyes. Sunlight filtered through the hedge of evergreen around us, creating starlike bursts that twinkled into the morning atmosphere. It was a gorgeous dawn, but one I would probably have appreciated more if I wasn't so tired, disoriented, and completely confused.

"You have a confession?" I asked, hoping with all my being it didn't have anything to do with the previous night's sleep kiss. There were people who talked in their sleep, people who walked in their sleep, and even people who snored. Making out was not something I'd heard before. We just might have made up an entirely separate category of embarrassing sleep issues.

"Yes," he replied, stoking the fire with a pointed stick he had probably whittled by hand. The embers glowed against the charcoal-colored logs that hissed and popped as he poked at them. "I lied to you yesterday." His green eyes lifted to mine, hovering once they met. "When I said you had to wear your swimsuit."

I stared at him blankly through the screen of smoke between us.

"Your clothes probably would have dried just as well on you as off of you."

"You perverted little creep," I teased, folding my arms across my chest in false disgust, because I really wasn't disgusted at all. In fact, it made everything that happened the night before start to make sense. "So you just wanted to get my clothes off?"

Torin smirked, then averted his eyes. "Um, yeah," he conceded. I'd have thought he was blushing if I didn't already know that his cheeks were typically that rosy. "Of course. I mean, seriously, a girl in hiking boots and a bikini? That's like teenage-dream material right there. I think I may even have had a poster like that pinned to my wall when I was younger."

"But I thought I wasn't your type." I dragged my fingers across my scalp again, loosening the knots that tangled at my hairline. "I thought I was . . . what did you say? Crazy and off-limits?"

"You are," Torin said, nodding his head swiftly. "But I mentioned before that I kinda dig crazy."

"Just to be clear, what about me is crazy? Not that I don't feel that way sometimes," *always*, "I just didn't know it was so blatantly obvious to the casual outsider." I played with my cuticles, pushing them back nervously because, for some reason, talking to Torin had started to make me nervous. The day before had been fine, but things had changed. Like somehow even talking was dangerous because it also involved that dangerous mouth of his. I got myself into quite a lot of trouble with that mouth last night. I really needed to watch myself today.

"First off," Torin started, raising his index finger. "I'm not a casual outsider. I slept with you last night, Darby." I knew what he meant by his statement, but the innuendo was all too clear and made me giggle like I was in junior high and wasn't mature enough for the conversation. Maybe I wasn't. I covered my mouth to trap the laughter in. "Second, it wasn't entirely obvious."

"I assume an answer detailing my craziness is forthcoming," I interrupted.

"You're an impatient one, aren't you?"

"All of us crazies are. It adds to the crazy—the nervous impatience. Foot-tapping, nail-biting, pacing. I'm well practiced in all of those. Bolsters the whole shtick."

Torin laughed and dropped his head in a way that I found incredibly adorable, which made me mad because I didn't want to find him adorable. I was still holding out hope for the whole jerk thing to come to fruition.

"There are three reasons why I think you are a touch crazy. In the past, I've found that if you have three facts of supporting evidence, your theory usually holds true."

"Your first piece of evidence." I waved a hand toward him, motioning him to begin laying out his body of proof.

"You have been with the same guy since you were thirteen. *Thirteen*, Darby. That is insane on multiple counts. I mean, seriously, I cannot name one thing I liked when I was thirteen that I still like now."

"Posters of hot girls in bikinis," I interjected. He blushed.

"I had that when I was fifteen. And I don't like the posters anymore. I prefer the real thing."

"Gotcha." Was it weird that I sort of hoped he considered me the "real thing"?

"So the fact that you're still in love with someone that you fell in love with when you were a mere adolescent makes you a tad bit crazy, sorry to say."

"Noted. And your other evidence?"

"You don't act like a college chick, let alone a chick that goes to one of the most prestigious schools in the nation. In all honesty, you talk and act like you're still thirteen. Like you're stuck in some immature space of time when Lance—or someone—took over your life."

I wanted to be mad at him for making such an all-encompassing, flippant observation of me. But he was kind of right in his assumption—at least half-right—so being mad felt like an unfair expression, just like calling him a jerk was an unfair label. And he didn't know the whole story. It felt wrong to be mad at him when he didn't have all the facts.

"To be honest," I began defensively, "I don't always act that way. Around Lance, it's all keeping up appearances and playing the supportive-girlfriend part. I've been primed to be the perfect politician's arm candy." And it was true; my soon-to-be sister-in-law had already given me several extensive lessons on this. "I've never been on my own adventure without him. The last time I was by myself was when I was thirteen. Thirteen wasn't a good year for me." I toed at the dirt with my shoe, drawing lines and circles in the dust underneath it.

"Don't get me wrong. I really like Darby WL."

My curiosity was plain on my face as my eyes lifted to his.

"Without Lance," he clarified, smiling. His green eyes were playful and looked way too alert and awake for as early as it was. "She's a bit crazy and immature—"

"And stubborn."

He smiled again. "Yes, and stubborn. But I like her. But I think I'd like the nineteen-year-old version of her, too."

"I think this *is* the nineteen-year-old version. Believe me, the thirteen-year-old prototype was incredibly flat chested with bad teeth and knobby knees. They've made some major improvements to the body and frame of the latest model."

Torin chuckled while shaking his head. "You're only adding to my case, Darby." Which I was, however unintentionally. "Talking about yourself like you're a car."

"Is that your third piece of evidence?"

"No. There's more." Of course there was. "You said being one of eight kids was like having eight television shows playing all at once."

"Right, and I'm still proud of that analogy. It's a pretty darn good one."

"As you should be," he agreed, "but it's weird to describe your life as something that's scripted. Life isn't scripted, Darby. Life is fluid. It's changing. It fluctuates."

"Maybe your life, Torin." Because I was sure his was. I bet every day at Quarry Summit was a new adventure waiting to be written. "But mine isn't anymore and that's how I want it." *That's how I need it.* "I can tell you with certainty exactly how my life will play out. I've got a plan."

"And that is crazy point number three: if you really do think life is scripted, you've given someone else the pen to write your own story." He was still crouched down by the fire like a catcher waiting for the pitch. He balanced on his toes and tipped his head toward his right shoulder. "How can you give up authorship to something so important? Don't you regret doing that?"

I fidgeted on the log, not out of physical discomfort, but because the words he spoke felt like fingernails scratching up my back and made it impossible for me to sit still. "Do I regret letting Lance become part of my story—"

"Not part of your story, the *whole* story."

"I'm not sure I think he is the whole story. I'm here, aren't I?"

"You're *here* so you can go *there.*" Torin replayed my lines from the day before, the word thief that he was.

"I think it's inertia, Torin. Like you said. I think when you're with someone, something gets set into motion and your lives move forward together. There's really no way to stop it, even if you wanted it to." And more often than not, I did want it to, I just didn't know how.

"Of course there is. You take the pen back. You say, 'Thank you for the chapters you've written, but I've got it from here.'"

"I think Lance is a decent enough author," I admitted, staring down at my nails. I had pushed all of my cuticles back as far as they could go, and then I moved on to picking at hangnails.

"I think Lance writes mediocre, predictable jargon. I'd much rather read something penned by the brilliantly peculiar Darby Duncan. Now that could be a *New York Times* bestseller."

"She's retired."

"Yeah." Torin chuckled. "I heard. Ran out of ink at the ripe old age of thirteen."

I pulled at a piece of skin a little too forcefully and blood pooled at the base of my nail. I thrust it into my mouth to suck it off and to buy some time before answering, "Why do you care who writes my story? In six weeks I'll be out of here and done with this chapter."

Torin pushed his hands to his knees and rose to stand. The smoke from the fire danced between us, curling around him as he looked down at me. His eyes lost that playful gleam and embodied an intensity that drew the hairs on my arm to stand up on end. "I care because I'd like to be more than just a few pages in your book, Darby."

I didn't say anything for a few minutes. Neither did Torin. He rotated the fish more times than necessary. I figured he was banking on the fact that I didn't know anything about cooking food over an open flame, but I was pretty sure you didn't have to spin it quite that vigorously. I didn't say anything, though.

"I told you I had a confession."

I looked up at him, startled by his words because it had been quiet long enough that I'd almost forgotten what his voice sounded like. "Another one?"

"Yeah. I'm on a roll, huh?"

"You should totally title your own biography *Confessions of a Mountain Man*."

"Funny, Darby." Torin shot me a contrived smile. "I wanted to apologize for thinking the things I did about you."

"About how I'm a crazy, stubborn, failed author?" Among other things.

"No, about how you're hot and intriguing and how I totally wanted you." My stomach dropped out of me completely. Good thing I never felt like eating, because it was completely gone. "Seriously, like, I even dreamed about you last night." I could see him faintly pull his bottom lip into his mouth, and I knew exactly what that dream involved. It had been a reality for at least one of us. "You said you wanted to hang on to your modesty yesterday, and I basically made it so you couldn't. And then I totally thought things about you that I would never want some guy thinking about my girlfriend. That's completely wrong and I'm sorry. I probably owe Lance an apology, too."

I tucked my chin into my neck and tightened my brow to the point where it started to impede my vision. "That's not necessary," I said quickly, knowing that his confession to Lance would likely result in Torin's broken jaw. And he had a pretty nice jaw. It should stay intact. "Just so you know, Lance has thought those things about other girls, and acted on them, too."

"And you've stayed with him?"

"Yeah." I'd never been insecure about that fact, but the way Torin looked at me with such questioning eyes made me second-guess myself and my decisions.

"Why would you stay with someone who could do that to you? And please don't say 'because I love him,' or 'he said he was sorry,' or something equally self-demoralizing."

"You lost your brother, right?"

"Yeah." Torin's eyes slivered.

"So you know what it's like to lose someone you love, not by choice."

"I suppose."

"I chose to forgive Lance because I'm not ready to lose him. He's become family, and family makes mistakes. The ones you're closest to are the ones who have the ability to hurt you the most, right?" Wasn't that how the saying went?

"I can't decide if you have a really big heart or just a really small brain." Torin rotated his face and looked directly at me. "But since you go to Stanford and I have to assume the admissions department that reviewed your application wasn't a bunch of mindless monkeys, I'm going with the former."

"Lance isn't the kind of guy you break up with." The edge of the butterfly bandage fluttered from my forehead and I lifted my hand to secure it back into place. Unfortunately, all the stickiness was completely gone and it peeled away almost entirely. Fantastic. I had Medusa hair and bandages falling off my scabby body. Not to mention I didn't get any sleep the night before. Unless Torin had a thing for zombies, I didn't think I'd run the risk of him ever "wanting" me again.

"What does that mean? That he's exempt from being dumped because it's not kosher to break up with a guy like him?" Torin sounded frustrated. "I'd like to learn how to achieve that elite status because it sounds pretty nice to get a free pass to do whatever you want and still have an amazing girl at your side."

I didn't know what to think about that because it was an insult and a backhanded compliment all wrapped up in one punch.

"Listen," Torin continued. "I get that relationships are complicated. Life is complicated. I just want to make sure you're not selling yourself short, Darby. Because I don't know Lance, but the fact that he's cheated on you pretty much makes him an ass in my book."

Torin noticed me fiddling with the bandage and walked over, lowered his stance, and pulled his hand up to my face. His eyebrows lifted to ask permission and I nodded slightly. He tugged the remaining portion of the Band-Aid from my forehead and ran his finger over the scab, the fresh ridge of it under the pad of his index finger. We were inches from each other, and his eyes secured onto mine in a way that made my entire body buzz just under the surface of my skin.

"This looks good," he said, his gaze lifting to the injury above my brow. "I think you should leave the bandage off and let it get some air today." I nodded again, still fixated on him. His gaze briefly trailed down my face to my lips, and it held there long enough that it made me uncomfortable, light-headed, and slightly giddy. "I'm sorry if I overstepped my bounds; I just want you to know that you're worth more than being someone's backup, Darby."

"I don't feel like his backup. I feel like his constant. And in truth, I'm too afraid to be anything else."

"We need to work on your fear of the unknown."

"I've had the unknown happen, Torin. And it was more terrifying than anything I could have ever imagined."

"I know." His voice trailed off and so did his eyes. "Me, too."

Still kneeling in front of me, he took hold of both my hands, pulling them close to his chest, the beat of it vibrating against them. "And I think that's something we should work on together."

Chapter 9

"When we get to the end of this trail . . ." Torin called out over his shoulder, motioning with a stick toward the base of the trampled path, "we'll need to stop."

"You finally getting tired?" I was hoping beyond hope that I wasn't the only one on the brink of passing out. I'd reached that stage where my heartbeat flooded into my eardrums and the echo of my pulse didn't just reside in my wrist and my neck, but strummed all over my body.

"Not at all."

"Oh." Shoot.

"We gotta do a tick check."

"A what-what?" Of course that rock had to be precariously placed right in front of my left shoe, and I stumbled forward, my gangly arms flailing on either side as I awkwardly skip-jumped before rebalancing back into an upright walking position.

"You okay?"

"Yup." I totally almost ate it.

"A tick check. I need to check you for ticks."

I went more bug-eyed than the literal bugs Torin was talking about.

"You do know what a tick is, right?"

My eyes rounded and I held up an impressively unfazed front, but the thought of a bloodsucking parasite burrowing into my body sent waves of panic through me that I could hardly contain. I loathed insects to an unhealthy degree.

"There are ticks here?"

Torin pulled his backpack off of his broad shoulders and tossed it to the ground, then grasped the hem of his T-shirt between his fingers. In one fluid movement, he lifted the fabric from his torso, a sheen of sweat glistening across his tanned chest. "Now you do the same," he said monotonously.

"Wha—?"

"Totally kidding." A playful smile burst onto his face. "Just take off your backpack."

I did as he requested and the tick inspection began.

Lowering into a squat, Torin started at my ankles, carefully surveying the bare patches of skin up to my shins. He grazed across my flesh with the palm of his hand, running it up to my knees with the lightest amount of pressure. I wasn't sure if this was actual overnighter-survivor protocol, or if he was pulling another bikini prank on me, but I honestly didn't care. I felt too good to be angry.

"All clear. Turn around." I rotated 180 degrees and his hands dragged across to the backs of my thighs, his thumb brushing against the soft flesh at the base of my jean shorts. The pit of my stomach felt heavy as I trapped a breath in, hoping my body wasn't as shaky as my breathing. "This looks good, too."

With his hands on my hips, he swiveled me around to face him, guiding my body under the intense scrutiny of his eyes.

Torin coursed his hands up my arms, to my shoulders, then to the slope of my neck, every area that my tank top didn't cover. I could see his midsection flex out of the corner of my eye into six distinct ripples and I thought maybe for a moment he was trying to control something in himself, too. But I didn't let that thought get too comfortable in my head. I shouldn't be thinking things like that about Torin.

"See anything?" My loose hair tumbled across my shoulders and Torin scooped it into a ponytail to survey the skin underneath.

"Nothing so far," he said, his mouth so close to my skin I could feel the air behind his words. "But you'd be able to feel them, too. They pinch."

That was a relief to hear because it terrified me to think that I could have a foreign bug feasting on me without even knowing it.

"Almost done."

I felt his fingers skimming my shoulder blades, and in the same moment that he said, "Uh-oh, wait," I felt the prick of something at the base of my neck, a piercing sensation that completely freaked me out.

Unfortunately, my freak-out wasn't limited to just my thoughts, and it burst through my body, too. Swatting at my hairline, I batted Torin's hand away, using my own to claw and scrape at whatever had stung my neck.

"Get it off, Torin!" I shrieked, beating his bare chest with my palms. "Oh my God, get it off of me!"

"Hold still."

"I can't!" I screamed, jumping up and down and shaking my head with the force of a heavy-metal headbanger. "Seriously, Torin!"

"Let me see," he said way too calmly. "You have to hold still."

But asking me to do that was like asking a sugar-loaded toddler to sit through an opera at the Met.

"I can't!"

"You *have* to." Torin grabbed me by the shoulders, bracing me tightly as he said, "Stop moving."

"Get it out! I can feel it crawling into my neck!"

"No, you can't."

"Yes, I *can*, Torin!" Visions of me laid up in a hospital bed with Lyme disease and Rocky Mountain spotted fever cartwheeled through my head.

"Did it feel like this?" With the tips of his thumb and index fingernails, he grabbed a section of skin on my forearm and squeezed down, leaving two crescent-shaped marks in their place.

"Exactly like that."

An innocent couldn't wear the grin that crept onto Torin's face, so mischievous and coy. No, he was guilty—incredibly guilty of making me just complete the biggest freak-out session anyone this side of the Trinity Alps Wilderness had ever witnessed.

"You," I snarled through gritted teeth, slugging him solidly against his chest again. I wasn't expecting my knuckles to actually sting from the punch.

"I'm just trying to keep you prepared, Darby." He coiled back from my fist against his shoulder, but I could tell that I wasn't hurting him in the slightest. "I had to prepare you for what it might feel like to have a tick on you. Helping you with your fear of the unknown and all."

"You're terrible." I rubbed out the soreness from my fist, flexing my hand open and closed.

"I'd like to prepare you for a few more unknowns, too."

I twisted my fist in my palm. "And what would those be?"

"This."

Torin took one quick step forward and suddenly we were face-to-face, his mouth inches from mine. His lips were slightly parted, and the tingle of air that rushed in and out through them grazed over my wet lips. His eyes lingered on mine, blinking softy with fluttering movements. I could see his chest rising and falling again, reminding me of the night before, and I could feel it as it pressed against mine while he drew in a trembling inhale. Snaking his arm around the small of my back, he hooked me closer to him until I was pressed fully up against him. Fireworks went off in the pit of my stomach, the igniting spark of some sort of passion that was nothing short of explosive.

I almost readied myself for the kiss, slipping my eyelids closed, but Torin didn't lean in any closer just then. He held me there, in this intense space where his lips hovered just over my lips, in this pause of anticipation, like the moment at the starting line before the gunshot rings into the air.

Every millimeter that he drew closer was a vast expanse of measurable depth. I'd never been so aware of the proximity of anyone to me ever before. I could sense his breathing, his heart rate, even the damp moisture held on his full mouth.

"A man had given all other bliss, and all his worldly worth for this, to waste his whole heart in one kiss, upon her perfect lips."

The words tumbled out from him and I swear I could taste them on my tongue, like some sweet, forbidden fruit.

"Tennyson," he explained, shaking his head as if to snap himself out of the trance he was under and had sucked me into. Just as quickly as he'd drawn toward me, he circled away, his back to me, a shield between us. "I can't waste my heart on you, Darby. As much as I may want to."

Knotting my fingers together, I asked in an insecure, frustrated voice, "Why would it be a waste?"

"Because I can't have yours."

. . . .

We stopped for lunch after the impromptu bug inspection and I tried to fill my stomach, but I couldn't; the ball of guilt was so large, it seemed to expand and take up every square inch of my gut, leaving no room for anything else.

Torin was honest with me, even if his honesty was coated in the form of Sir Lancelot's poetic declaration to Lady Guinevere. I owed him that same honesty. I needed to tell him about our late-night make-out session, even if he didn't remember it as vividly as I did. I owed him that. He confessed his feelings to me. Now it was my turn. Spill my guts. Let it all out.

I readied for the admission, but I couldn't do it. I went about my morning, pretending nothing had happened. I seriously could have gotten an Oscar for outstanding female performance based on the act I tried to maintain. Things were different, and even if Torin didn't consciously know the reason why, I'm sure he sensed it. He'd wanted to kiss me but wouldn't allow himself to, and I wondered if he'd felt the familiarity in that hesitant restraint. It was definitely like déjà vu for me.

I'm sure he also sensed the way my breathing changed when he got close to me. I'm sure he noticed the way my eyes fastened on his lips when he talked, not at all interested in the words that spilled out of them, but focused on their texture, shape, and form. I'm sure he saw that I took a few seconds to respond when spoken to, distracted by the memory of the night before on my lips. Things were different, and all it took was one little mistake. One omission of truth. One little regret.

"I have something for you," Torin said as we cleaned up our lunch. I had my pack hitched over my shoulders, ready for our trek down the hill toward our cabins. Five more days until the campers arrived. I could really use the extra people and bodies as a buffer and distraction. One-on-one with Torin wasn't proving so good for my sanity, or my hormones.

"I made this for you last night when you were sleeping, hogging that bag all to yourself." Torin dug his hand into his front pocket and pulled out a bracelet made of thick thread, woven into an intricate pattern with a charm dangling from its middle.

He thrust it toward me and I clumsily wrapped my fingers around it. "Thank you," I muttered, rolling it over in my palm. "You made me a . . . um . . . friendship bracelet? How very endearing in an elementary school sort of way. Does this mean you *like*-like me or something?"

"It's a survival bracelet," he explained with a laugh, fingering a similar one bound around his wrist. I flipped it onto its side to examine the copper-colored charm. *Quarry Summit* was written in raised, hollowed-out lettering, pressed deep into the back of the metal. "It's made of five-hundred-pound paracord—basically fourteen feet of rope that you can unravel within seconds if you're ever in a situation where you might need it."

I unclipped the clasp and fit it onto my wrist.

"I made yours red since you go to Stanford. That's your school color, right?" I nodded and twisted the bracelet in circles, rotating it against my skin. "And your swimsuit is red, and your hair—supposedly—is red, too."

"I'm Irish, I've had the same boyfriend for six years, and I like the color red." I hooked my thumbs under my backpack straps and slid them up and down. "Yep, that pretty much sums me up."

"You forgot the part about buildings and concrete." Torin sidestepped around me and I fell in line behind him as we started our descent down on the mountain trails. He really did enjoy being the leader of the pack. "I know that about you, too. But not much more."

"Reminds me of that game I used to play when I was a kid." I spoke over his shoulder as he kept just two feet ahead of me on the path. Bits of light stretched through the rows of tree trunks that rose out of the ground in our periphery. I could see the dust that our boots kicked up, shimmering in the morning air like speckles of golden glitter. "Remember?" I continued, trying to jog his memory. "I think it was called MASH or something."

Torin acknowledged me with only the shake of his head, still facing forward. "I'm nineteen, remember? Not thirteen, sorry."

"Oh, come on, you remember. Same era as the cootie catcher?" I prodded, moving my hands in the motions of the game, opening and closing the imaginary paper origami between my fingers, even though he couldn't see me.

"Not a clue."

"That's unfortunate, because MASH was this game that predicted who you were going to marry, where you would live, and other amazing stuff like that," I explained, making cootie-catcher motions with my hands. *Open, close. Open, close.* "Anyway, that's what your little summary reminded me of: I'll be married to a guy named Lance and will live in a red, concrete house in Ireland."

"Sounds like an incredibly riveting game, and an equally riveting future for you."

"It's just something we did for fun, Torin," I justified, probably a little too quickly. So what if I ended up in Ireland with Lance in a concrete house? What would be so wrong with that future? At least it was a future. Not everyone got to have one. "What did you do for fun, mountain man?"

He didn't fire back to deflect my name-calling, and instead just said, "We played Over the Edge."

"And what was that? Like, some game where you tried to push someone to their limit by getting on their nerves or something?" If it was, then that definitely explained the overnight success he'd had in forcing me dangerously close to my own metaphoric edge.

"No." A laugh caught in Torin's throat. "We cliff jumped. Like, dove off of cliffs into the water."

"Oh." Torin totally confused me. One minute he was deep—reciting the famous words of philosophers of old—the next he was talking about leaping off cliffs. I just didn't get him, how he could have so many layers. Even I only had two: my thirteen-year-old version and the nineteen-year-old update. And even those versions weren't entirely my own.

But it was like Torin embodied the sensitive, emotional side that all women inherently desired, yet at the same time he was wholly masculine, to the point of cliff jumping and killing and cooking his own food. He was a complete conundrum.

"Have you always been outdoorsy?"

"Yeah," Torin started, just as we came up on a fork in the road. There were lots of forks in this utensil-filled forest, it seemed. Without hesitation, he veered left, like he could do this in his sleep. "I've always loved the wilderness. I'm at home here. This is where I'm comfortable."

"If you hadn't grown up here—if you had the chance to go to college and have a career—what would you do?"

"I did have the chance to go to college, Darby," Torin corrected smugly, his blond hair glinting under the morning sun that pierced the leafy greenery overhead. "And I would have majored in religious studies."

I hiked the straps higher on my pack and shifted the weight on my shoulders, one to the other. Torin spied me and said, "Need some help with that? I can carry it for you if you like."

"I got it. Thanks, though." I shook off his offer with my head. "So how come you chose to stay here instead of get your degree? If you had the opportunity, I mean."

"Because I'm a lot closer to God here on this mountain than I could ever be in the confines of a college classroom."

Sonja's parents had been missionaries, and I remembered hearing stories about when she was little and they lived in Peru.

How they would visit people in remote villages, converting them at a high rate. I wondered if Torin had that same experience—if some missionary ventured out to his corner of the wilderness and shared the gospel with him. It felt remote enough that I wouldn't have been surprised if that were actually the case.

"How do you even know there is a God?"

"Just look around, Darby." Torin's feet planted underneath him and he fluttered a hand skyward. "The heavens declare the glory of God; the skies proclaim the work of his hands." He was doing it again, reciting some verse in an attempt to bolster his case. But this time it felt different, not like the movie quotes, or even the philosophical notions he'd rattled off earlier. Something in him changed when he said this one, like this was his truth while the other quotes were maybe just things he thought about.

"How do you know?" I followed his eyes toward the hundred-year-old trees that climbed into the sky, reaching so high that they nearly made themselves at home among the clouds. "How do you know that God made all of this?"

"How do you know he didn't?"

"I'm not necessarily saying he didn't, I just don't know." I shrugged, but as I looked at our surroundings, at the intricacies and beauty of it all, I could see how Torin would come to that conclusion. "In some ways, I consider myself religious, too, I guess."

"There is a difference between being religious and believing in something greater."

When he said it, it all made sense. His concern over using people as a means to an end. His interest in all the little steps along life's journey. His belief that something bigger was at work in the details. I'd thought he was an enigma—some indefinable sort of person who just clung to a bunch of random beliefs and principles like so many of the people I knew. People who were searching to find themselves. People who pulled bits and pieces from different ideologies, hoping they fit together in a believable, workable way. People sort of like myself.

But Torin was already there. He seemed to think he had it all figured out. Or maybe that was just his truth. Maybe truth was different for everyone. I had always assumed that was the case because I didn't know how there could be just one path that would lead to our ultimate destination. Just like these various paths that crisscrossed through the forest, maybe there were many options that would take us where we needed to go. It had to be that way, right?

One thing I was certain about was that I wished I'd taken a different path in making my way to Lance.

"I haven't always believed." Torin's voice cut through our silence and my reverie. "In fact, for a long time I was a total atheist." He turned to look at me, his green eyes pulled tight and haunted. "My brother's death changed things. I didn't understand how a supposedly righteous God would allow that to happen." I swallowed and listened intently as he spoke, but my mouth watered with that familiar acidic bitterness that I'd been biting back for as long as I could remember. "I was angry at the idea of God and at my parents. Because they seemed to think that this God not only existed, but allowed for what happened to Randy to actually occur." He shook his head violently and strained his brow, dragging his hand down the length of his face like he could sweep the emotion from it into his palm and keep it there, tucked away, rather than vulnerably exposed for me to see. But I was glad to be able to see it, because looking at him felt like looking into a mirror.

"I didn't want to be part of anything that would allow Randy to die." Torin gazed into the forest like he was watching a movie played out in the distance, a movie I felt like I'd seen one too many times. "But then I saw how my parents used Randy's choice to change others' lives—how out of his death, they could somehow impact people that were in his same situation," he continued, threading his fingers together at the back of his neck and craning his head upward. "It made me realize that maybe there was something out there that could take even the bad in our lives and somehow use it for good. I don't think people are capable of doing that on their own. Something greater has to give us the strength to do that, right?"

I figured I was staring—probably gawking—and the fact that my jaw was unhinged made that pretty obvious. I didn't really have a response, but I wasn't sure he was looking for one. I was just amazed by the person standing before me, amazed in more ways than I could count. And that frustrated me because, in all honesty, I really wanted to dislike him. He was doing such a good job helping me get to that point with the ropes course and the swimsuit debacle. But now I couldn't. His beliefs sort of ensured my admiration. It was hard not to admire someone who believed so strongly in something, even if you didn't necessarily agree. Conviction was attractive because it hinted at a passion not all of us had.

"Anyway," Torin continued, swiftly waggling his head, "to answer your original question, I did have the chance to get an education. I just don't necessarily think higher learning occurs exclusively on a college campus."

Before coming to camp, I probably would have disagreed with that statement, but the more time I spent out in the woods, and the more time I spent with Torin, the more I learned about myself. But unfortunately, I didn't really like the assignment I had been given, or my current performance. And I figured I was getting a little too friendly with the teacher. Either way, I was pretty sure I was getting a big, fat *F*.

But I was learning, all right. I was learning that coming to Quarry Summit just might be my biggest regret yet.

Chapter 10

"Take my hand."

There was no way I was touching his hand again. I didn't even like standing that close to him because I was sure he could hear my heart ramming loudly against my chest. It rang in my own ears like the methodic rumble of a freight train barreling toward me. He had to be able to hear it—it roared down the rickety tracks at breakneck speed. *Chugga-chugga, chugga-chugga.*

"Darby," Torin instructed, impatiently fluttering his hand in my direction. "Take it."

"I feel like this is one of those 'been there, done that' scenarios."

"And that's a problem how? Because in the past, girls really haven't complained about doing me more than once."

"Yuck, Torin." I grimaced and Torin laughed outright.

"I'm completely kidding, Darby. Just take my damn hand, will you?"

Reluctantly, I grabbed on to his fingers, and they immediately tightened around mine, yanking me with him without a second's hesitation.

We slid down the ravine.

Well, Torin slid, the tread of his shoes somewhat gripping the dirt underneath, while my shoes more like skated over the surface. I felt as though I was hydroplaning down the dusty embankment as my weight pushed forward onto Torin and he leaned back into me with the pressure necessary to keep us both upright. So much for walking the trails. This was definitely off the beaten path.

What felt like our equivalent of skiing down the hillside suddenly came to a halt when Torin hooked his arm around a nearby tree.

I slammed into his back, ramming into him with full force.

"Hey now," he teased. "It's really not necessary to throw yourself at me."

"Sorry, Torin, but you're not my type." I stole his words from the day before and righted myself, dusting off my palms, flashing one of the widest grins I'd ever smiled. "I prefer guys that are much more civilized."

"Ouch," Torin said, clutching his chest with his one free hand. "Low blow."

"And educated."

Torin threw his head back like he'd been severely injured.

"And good looking."

His eyes grew wide. "Hold up," he interjected, hand raised. "I might not be as smart and sophisticated as your Lance is, but I haven't heard any of the campers or counselors complaining about my looks." A devious smirk broke across Torin's lips. "Just the opposite, in fact."

"I'm not into blonds."

"Well, good thing I'm not blond." Torin wove his arms over his chest, his shoulder pressed into the tree trunk, the only thing keeping us from slipping and sliding our way down the nearly vertical slope.

"You are definitely blond," I retorted, my limbs shaking. "Okay, maybe dirty blond, bordering on light brown, but still blond."

"My hair is as blond as yours is red."

"So you're totally a blond, then. Now that explains a lot."

"Do you honestly think I'm stupid, Darby? Because it's starting to get a little insulting. First mountain man, now dumb blond."

"I don't think you're stupid," I said just as Torin snagged an arm around my waist, noticing my body's nervous tremble. I sucked in a breath, because his body this close felt amazing. "But I do think you're amazing."

Torin's head whipped toward mine.

My face heated a thousand shades of red at my slipup. It was like someone singed my cheeks with a lighter and then left it there, just inches from my face so I had to endure the burn. "Annoying," I corrected hurriedly, but it was too late. "I meant annoying."

"You said amazing."

My eyes rolled to the back of my head. I wished they would get stuck there just so I didn't have to look at him. "Amazingly annoying." I hated that I had to hang on to him—that I was literally clinging to him—in order keep from sliding to my humiliating death. And I hated that my mouth emitted words that my brain didn't give it permission to. "It's *amazing* how *annoying* you are."

"Not what you said." In one sudden swoop, Torin flipped around and swung me onto his back. "Hold on," he instructed, forcing me to wrap my legs around his waist. But I was grateful for the help. Aside from Torin making me feel weak with those smirks he kept firing my way, my muscles were dangerously close to shutting down completely from trying to keep upright. I gripped him like it was a piggyback ride as he sort of jogged and slid down the steep mountainside. The pace was fast enough to keep us from slipping, but slow enough that it wasn't a full-on run. I imagined him losing his footing and both of us tumbling snowball-style to the bottom of the ravine, our bones cracking and twisting the entire way down. I had only a small ounce of confidence that this wasn't actually going to happen.

My shirt slipped between my skin and his bare back, the thin layer of fabric between us sliding in a way that made me want to grip on tighter to avoid being so turned on by it. The gorge ahead crept closer with each movement he made.

He kept his hands tucked under my thighs until we safely reached the flat surface of the valley floor and I could slide off of him, my feet meeting the dirt.

"Wanna play a game?" He picked up the pack that he'd earlier launched down the hill. It no longer looked black; at least an inch of dirt coated its canvas surface. In an effort to shake some of the filth free, Torin thumped on it a couple of times with a balled-up fist, punching it like he was a boxer during a workout session.

"I don't know."

"It's called Ten from Now," he continued, slinking his arms into his backpack, apparently satisfied with its appearance. Dirt clung to the rivulets of sweat on his chest and it looked a little like war paint, marking his body in an almost barbaric manner. "This way." He nodded toward the carved-out path. Apparently, the hill sliding was some planned shortcut.

"I said I don't know."

"Oh." He sounded surprised. "I'm sorry. I thought you meant you really didn't know if you wanted to play. I figured I'd make up your mind for you."

"Saying 'I don't know' is sometimes a polite way of declining." I wiped my palms on the thighs of my shorts. It was hot—sticky hot—where everything on you perspired. I was pretty certain even my toes were sweating, the balmy temperatures affecting every crevice and patch of skin.

"No." He shook his head at me. "A polite way of declining is to say, 'No, thank you.' Saying 'I don't know' just makes you indecisive."

"No, I don't want to play a game with you."

"Oh, I see. Completely drop the polite part altogether." There was a clearing up ahead and I thought for a moment that we would stop to rest there, but we walked right through it, picking up the trail on the other side.

Torin continued, "So, what do you hope to be doing ten hours from now?"

"Is this the game? Are we playing a game now?" I asked, chewing on the inside of my cheek and pinching my lips together. "I see how you did that, just barreled right into it."

"I hope to be sleeping in my bunk, dreaming about hot girls in polka-dot swimsuits and hiking boots." He barreled right into his answer, too.

"I hope to be in my bed, dreaming about political galas and soirees," I said, deciding to join in on the barreling.

"No one dreams about that."

"Lance does."

"So you guys dream the same things? Like some magical, synchronized dreaming?" He pulled his hair back into what I figured was going to be a ponytail, but the length of it just stopped a bit short and he tucked it behind his ears instead. "You don't have your own dreams, Darby?"

"This is a silly game."

"Ten months from now. What do you hope to be doing?"

"Ten months . . ." I thought for a moment. What was on the calendar ten months from now? "Lance's mom's campaign will be in full swing. I'll most likely be working on that. Pounding the pavement. Handing out fliers. You?"

"I hope to break ground on a new center we have in the works for the camp. So I'm hoping I'll be putting my skill-saw and nail-gun expertise to work." That sounded only slightly more exciting than my plans, but only because it hinted at danger, and dangerous things were, by default, more exciting than nondangerous things. "Okay, ten years."

"In ten years, I'll probably be married with at least two kids." One boy and one girl, if Lance got his wish. "We'll probably be living in the Bay Area, or D.C."

"Ten years for me: I hope I'm still involved with the camp here. Probably running it since Mom and Dad will be close to retirement. Have a family. And a hot wife who walks around in bikinis." His eyes glazed over in a far-off stare. "Yep, that's my dream."

"All of that sounds realistic, other than the 'wife in a bikini' part. Good luck with that." I delivered an audible snicker, just for the effect.

"Don't need luck. I've got a twinge of Irish in me, too. Luck is in my blood." Luck, as I'd discovered, wasn't in mine. "By the way, Darby, you do realize that everything you said involves plans with Lance, right?"

"He's pretty much my plan." I couldn't foresee a future that didn't involve Lance in it. Even with our mistakes, it felt safer to keep him in my life than to let him fall out of it.

I realized that maybe made me seem pathetic to the outside world, but the outside world hadn't seen how dark my inside had been. Lance was the light that I'd needed at a certain time in my life, and even if that light had dwindled to the point of a dim flicker, it was still there. In the darkness, he still provided some guiding illumination that I really was afraid to snuff out completely. I didn't want to be left alone in the dark.

"You must have missed the part where I said, 'what do you *hope* to be doing.' If you were listening, all of mine were hopes, all of yours were plans," Torin continued.

"I think it's good to be prepared."

"I think it's foolish."

"How so?" I questioned him, cocking my brow. "It's kinda foolish to be caught off guard."

"It's kinda prideful to have a plan."

"Once again, Torin, you've talked me into circles with your philosophical ramblings."

I wasn't trailing behind him anymore, but was at his side, and our hands did that awkward thing where they would nearly brush against one another, but not quite. There were moments that felt like maybe they should be holding, but not really. The inch of space between them buzzed like the air was alive.

"To have a plan is prideful because it's saying we think we have some control."

"If you're trying to convince me of some greater power, I'm not sure you'll be successful," I warned.

"I'm saying it's fruitless to plan. A waste of time. We can't control our future any more than we can guarantee our next breath."

Because his statement made me nervous, I took an extra long time inhaling, just to be sure to fill my lungs to full capacity, before I expelled, "That's really depressing."

"Maybe." He lifted his shoulders in surrender. "Or maybe not. I think it's nice not to have all that responsibility. All that planning takes work, and life hardly ever turns out the way we plan," he continued. "I like adventure. Starting each day as a new one. Keeps things exciting."

"Then what's the point of your Ten from Now game if you don't plan?"

"I hope."

"Plan. Hope. Isn't that the same?"

"No, one involves expectancy. The other involves optimism."

Though it was really all semantics, he was right. It made me think for a bit, and the quiet that fell between us should have made me uncomfortable, but apparently Torin and I had reached that point in our new relationship where we could be silent in the other's presence without the awkwardness. That was about the only thing about us that *didn't* feel awkward.

"I think maybe you should come up with a new game," I said finally.

"Come on. Has to be better than that *mush* game you played as a kid."

"MASH," I giggled, cupping my mouth with my hand. "And it was seriously fun, but cootie catchers were better." I pulled on the straps of my bag until they were so tight that they almost cut off the circulation in my arms. Why did being around Torin make me do these awkward things where I practically inflicted pain on myself? "We'll play once we get back to camp."

He smiled his "okay" and then said, "You did really well, Darby," nearly congratulating me, catching me off guard. "You survived." He slapped my shoulder and unbearable heat swept through my veins as his palm stayed there just a few moments longer than it needed to.

"Just barely," I muttered, crumpling my shoulder straps between my tense, nervous fingers.

"Just barely is loads better than not at all." He stood directly in front of me, and when he playfully brushed the tip of his finger across my nose, my legs dropped out from under me and I went all boneless. "Which is good, because you're kinda growing on me. So I'm glad you're still alive and well."

Though I might have physically survived the overnighter, it sure didn't feel like the Darby who came to camp two days before was alive and well at all. She might not have been dead, but she was definitely lost. Total missing-persons status. Unfortunately, it seemed as though Torin had made it his mission to find another missing person. I almost hoped he failed, because I couldn't even begin to think what it would mean if he succeeded.

Chapter 11

"Now pick a color."

"Yellow." Torin tucked his legs up underneath him so they crisscrossed in a knot. The mattress jumped a bit with his movement and I almost wanted to duck to avoid cracking my head against the rails overhead again.

"Y-E-L-L-O-W," I said, opening and closing the cootie catcher, alternating with each letter. "Now pick a number."

"Six."

"One, two, three, four, five, six." My fingers opened and closed along with my mouth. "Another number."

Torin scrunched up his face playfully like he was deliberating, wobbled his head back and forth, and after a long, overstated pause—the ones that aren't necessary for anything other than dramatization—said, "Four."

I peeled back the tab with the 4 scribbled across it in black ink. "'You will do something that terrifies you.'"

"False!" Torin blurted loudly. His voice cracked, and though it probably embarrassed him, as it rightfully should have, I found it quite endearing.

"It's not true or false. And it's not even a question. It's a fortune."

He pulled his shoulders up to his ears, his blond—definitely blond—hair coiling around the curve of them. "I'm not afraid of anything, so it's not doing a very good job predicting my future."

"Oh, come on!" I leaned closer and wagged a finger in his face. "You're seriously not afraid of anything? Everyone's afraid of something."

"Try me."

The cocky quality of his tone posed his statement as a challenge, so I took him up on it. "All right." I thumbed my chin and tightened my brow, scrunching my lips as I racked my brain. "Snakes."

"Kill an average of six a summer."

"Okay," I said, running down a list of common fears in my brain. "Bears."

Torin chuckled and buckled at the waist in an exaggerated fit of laughter, wicked witch–cackle style. "Oh, please, Darby. At least *try* to be serious."

"Falling."

"Have you completely given up?"

"Flying." No readied comeback sailed from Torin's lips and I thought for a moment I might have touched on something. "You're afraid of flying?" I held my eyes wide-open, awestruck.

"Not necessarily afraid," Torin said hesitantly. He looked a little irritated, like I might have discovered some weakness in his armor. "I subscribe to the belief that it's impossible to be afraid of something you've never done."

"You've never flown on a plane?"

"No," he retorted. "I've never had the need or the opportunity."

"We need to see what we can do to change that." I'd flown in planes more times than I could count. I couldn't imagine being nineteen years old and never having seen the earth from a bird's-eye view. Torin was seriously missing out; from what I knew of him so far, flying would totally be his thing. Maybe it was my turn to help him with his unknowns.

"Anything else you've never done?" I jeered, intentionally trying to rile him up because I liked what it did to him when he got flustered.

"I've never had sex," Torin shot out, "but I'm fairly certain I'm not afraid of that, either."

Record scratch.

Wait . . . *what*?

I tossed the stare from my face quickly and attempted to reclaim my composure, but it was completely lost. My eyes dropped to my hands, which had totally mangled our poor cootie catcher. It was nothing but a crumpled wad of paper in my clenched grasp. Torin pulled it from my fingers to smooth it out, grinning widely like he was proud that he caught me off guard, like maybe that was his plan.

"Excuse me?"

"Don't worry." He smiled, his dimples deep set, making something within my stomach flip-flop. "Unlike the flying, I'm not expecting you to 'see what you can do to change that.'"

I tried to swallow quietly, but I was certain he heard it. Like that awkward moment when you'd watched a movie with your parents and a full-on sex scene started on the screen. All you wanted to do was hide.

"Okay." He reassembled the cootie catcher and slipped his thumbs and third fingers into it awkwardly like he was holding a grenade that was about to detonate. "Your turn."

"That's not how you hold it."

"Show me, then." Torin thrust his hands toward me.

I pulled back, the rickety bed frame rattling underneath me.

"Show me, Darby."

"Like this," I said, holding up my index fingers and thumbs to illustrate how to correctly do it, but they were stiff and hesitant and took more effort to move than usual.

"I don't get it," he said, but he couldn't be serious. Five-year-olds had mastered cootie catcher. "*Show* me."

I wasn't about to slip my hands over his to teach him some playground game.

Totally ignoring my falter, Torin grabbed my hands within his, his knuckles brushing the backs of them. "Show me how to do this, Darby." I felt my pulse slamming in my wrists against his warm skin. A sheen of sweat swept across my upper lip. "It's only fair, since I taught you how to survive in the wilderness and all. An actual *skill* you might use someday." He pulled my hands tighter. "The least you can do is teach me how to play this juvenile game."

"I don't think the wilderness thing will ever come in handy," I breathed, my words so light and airy, it made me dizzy to say them. "Fortune-telling seems a bit more useful than wilderness training."

Torin continued cupping my hands, and I slipped them out to rest on the outside of his. Taking his thumbs and index fingers, I positioned them in the slots in the origami. "Okay." His eyes drilled into mine and drew the available breath out of me, which wasn't much to begin with. "Now what?"

"Now you pick a color," I instructed, but the only color that registered was the intense green that stared at me, flooding my veins with fire. I take that back. Red. I could picture red, too, because my cheeks had to be the darkest shade of it. If you could literally feel a color, I was in the midst of being red. Hot, fiery red.

"Blue," Torin answered. He still hadn't blinked.

"B-L-U-E," I spelled, moving our hands to motion each letter by rhythmically opening and closing the folded paper. By the time I got to the *E*, I was going to pass out. How on earth could playing a game like cootie catcher feel like foreplay? "Now pick a number."

"Three."

"One, two, three." Our hands glided again in synchronism, the paper rustling between us. "And one last time."

Torin's eyes remained pinned on mine. You'd never even know there was anything in our hands because he hadn't bothered looking down at them once. That was, until he gave up his intense stare for a brief second, his eyes sliding down to my mouth, pausing a moment before they snapped up again. I licked my lips because they were incredibly chapped, but that was probably from all the air I had been panting in and out. Seriously, what was happening to me?

"One."

Grateful to be done with our game, and with our handholding, I peeled back the triangle and read, "'You will learn something new.'"

Like he couldn't believe it, Torin shoved my shoulder and I nearly tumbled all the way back onto my pillow. "You totally set that one up, Darby!" he playfully accused, his eyes slivered and his lips pursed. He jabbed at me again.

I caught myself on my elbows and pushed back up to sit, shaking the cootie catcher at him. "No I didn't. It's your fortune. I told you these things were useful."

"I've learned a lot today," Torin admitted, nodding. He stretched his hand across the space between us, and when it settled on my own, my mouth went dry, like a hundred cotton balls were stuffed into it. I couldn't form any words, and even if I could, they wouldn't have had any room to make their way out. "You're a good teacher, Darby. You'll make a great counselor." He bit his lip sharply between his teeth. "I should head back to my cabin. I'm really not supposed to be in your room, let alone in your bed."

"You're not *in* my bed, Torin. You're *on* my bed."

"Same difference." He perked up, straightening his spine to its full length. His head was just an inch shy of hitting the bars, which supported the top bunk overhead. "See . . . *on*." Then he slid his legs down, pressing his hip into the curve of the mattress as he reached for the crumpled-up quilt at the foot of the bed to draw it up to his shoulders. Looking like he was preparing for a nap, he snuggled his head into the feathery cushion of the pillow. "*In*. Same thing."

"That is not the same thing at all." I laughed.

"Yes, it is. You try."

I was already sitting, so he curled his hand around my elbow and tugged so it buckled, then gave out from underneath me. Our heads at eye level on the pillow underneath us proved without a doubt that *on* and *in* were essentially opposites. I could (almost) handle having Torin on my bed. But having him in it brought me straight back to the sleeping bag and straight back to the familiar ache that swam in the pit of my stomach. Without realizing it, I rubbed my fingers over my abdomen, trying to calm the eager rush that tugged at my gut.

Torin took notice. "Stomachache?"

"Nah. I'm fine."

"Butterflies?" He smiled.

"What?"

Yes, there was a growing swarm of butterflies ramming about in my ribcage, but I hadn't expected Torin to not only acknowledge it, but point it out, too.

"Do I give you butterflies?"

"No, Torin," I lied through my teeth. "You don't give me butterflies."

"You sure? 'Cause you give me bumblebees."

"Bumblebees?" I angled my head in his direction, but we were close and if I moved any farther, our noses would touch.

"Yes. Butterflies are too light and fluttery." He must have moved, because suddenly that gap was nearly nonexistent. *In* was definitely not the same as *on*. "You make me feel like I have a freaking hornet's nest buzzing and stinging at my insides."

"That's a weird thing to say."

"But it's true. It's practically painful to be around you."

"And that's a mean thing to say."

His hand dropped onto my cheek and I went instantly rigid, like there was some electrifying jolt that spread out from his fingertips. "It's not a bad kind of painful. It's a good kind."

"How can any pain be good, Torin?" But the searing heat of his palm on my face answered the question. The physical contact was extreme in a way that bordered on painful, but that had to be because it was something that couldn't be realized, something that couldn't come to fruition. The fact that things would stop at just this—that was what caused the bittersweet intensity. It was the absence of what we wanted to happen that truly brought about the real pain.

"You tell me. How does this make you feel?" He inched his face closer to mine, his hand still laying against the slope of my jaw. "When I do this . . ." He tilted his head just slightly, his lips lined up with mine. "When I get this close, but stay this far away . . ." Not moving another millimeter, he spoke softly, "does it give you butterflies, or does it give you bumblebees?"

I gasped, then became overwhelmingly embarrassed by the fact that I'd just literally gasped at the thought of kissing him.

"Right," he said coolly, running the tip of his tongue across his bottom lip, leaving it there in the corner edge of his mouth, nearly biting down on it. "I thought so." Then, like the sudden torrential downpour of rain that comes without warning, the serious gaze snapped from his eyes and he rammed his index finger into my stomach, blurting, "Buzz, buzz, buzz!"

I swatted him with the fury of a thousand angry queen bees. "I really do have to go, as much as I want to stay and poke you."

I gulped even louder than my inadvertent gasp. "You did not just say that."

All color drained from Torin's face and his swallow was louder than my gulp and gasp combined. "I did. Reason number two why I need to go: I'm speaking in innuendos. That's never a good thing."

"I might disagree with you on that."

"I think we'd need to go deeper in order to know for sure."

The giggling had already started with his first remark, but that one sent me over the edge into certified hysteria. I buried my head in my hands and tucked my legs to my chest to absorb some of the laughter. "Knock it off, Torin," I shouted between cackles.

"I can't. It's really hard."

"Seriously!" I practically screamed, worried that I was nearing the pee-your-pants stage of laughter. "I can't take anymore."

Torin nodded, pulled both of his legs over the edge of the bed to stand, and said, "I should probably get off."

"I'm *so* serious right now." The tears streamed full force down my cheeks and I could feel the snot start to drip from my nose, collecting above my upper lip. I'd officially reached the ugly, utterly uncontrolled point in my fit.

"I'm finished, don't worry." Torin gave me the most incriminating smirk I'd ever seen him muster, and without saying another word, slipped out of my cabin. Even after the door had shut fully into its frame, I continued giggling, unable to get Torin, his lips, and his words, out of my mind.

Chapter 12

Three weeks later

"Time to go," Ran said, resting his hand on Maggie's shoulder affectionately. He looked over at me, his blue eyes warm with sincerity, as he tossed the last of their luggage into the bed of their blue truck. "Take care, Darby. I'm glad we got to know you a bit during our time here." Ran held out a hand to me, shaking mine firmly, and Maggie wrapped an arm over my shoulder. "We'll keep in touch."

I nodded my agreement, and within minutes they'd loaded up the vehicle, backed out of the lot, and were headed out of Quarry Summit, leaving summer camp behind in the dust that kicked up off their tires.

Two loud footfalls blended in with the dissipating roar of the engine, trading places in volume and intensity.

"Did they leave already?"

I didn't have to turn around to know who it was. I didn't even have to hear his actual voice, either. That scent—that familiar faint spice that reminded me of home—instantly clued me in to the boy standing at my side. My body acknowledged him, too, as a wake of goose bumps crossed over my skin. His breath rushed out of him in pants, like he'd been running to make it in time to say his good-byes. But he was too late.

"Yep. Just left."

"Damn it!" Torin bent at the waist and pressed his hands to his jeans, dragging in air in shallow, uncontrolled pulls. "I wanted to say good-bye."

"I hate good-byes. Good-byes suck."

"I'm good at them." Torin swept his hand across his sweat-beaded forehead and smirked before wiping his palms on the front of his pants. "When your friends come in six-week waves, you get very good at good-bye." He looked up at me and my stomach did that awful falling thing where it dropped out. Why did I feel like I was on a roller coaster every time I was with this guy? "This summer has been weird. I didn't get a chance to say good-bye to you, either."

"I'm still here." I kicked around a rock with the tip of my shoe. "You've got three more weeks of me."

"But I haven't really *seen* you for the past three, Darby."

"The campers came." I rolled the stone under the tread, running it up and down so it made a gritty nails-on-a-chalkboard sound against the crunchy gravel.

Though I never would have admitted it could ever have happened in the beginning, our time at camp had really flown by. Part of this was due to the fact that the actual campers arrived, bringing with them their own drama, emotions, and responsibilities. Focusing on a cabin full of girls somehow forced my issues to the backseat position, a place where I'd securely seat-belted them and hoped they would stay for the remainder of the ride.

Since the overnighter, I hadn't had nearly as much one-on-one contact with Torin, though that wasn't saying a lot considering the amount of actual, physical contact I'd had with him during that night.

For all intents and purposes, the camp really was divided between the girls and the boys. The male counselors focused on their own campers, while the rest of us interacted mainly with our cabinmates. Surviving the heartache and the trauma that each of my girls brought with them to camp was somehow—even all compiled together—unbelievably easier than surviving that one night in the woods with Torin. Three more weeks. Halfway there. I had this. I could do this.

"I've been busy," I offered.

"Get lunch with me."

"What?" My shoe stopped in its place and I pinned him with a stunned glare. This chapter didn't involve lunch. It involved me going back to my cabin and wallowing in the fact that two of my main characters were yanked from the script. I needed someone to fill that supportive best friend role. Torin should not be that person.

"Let's get lunch. I'm starved." He snagged my hand and threaded his fingers through mine so swiftly that I didn't have time to shake it free before he was yanking me toward the dining commons. "You got a good cabin?"

"Um, yeah. I guess." I willed the sweat to stop pooling in my palm, but it didn't do any good. I tried willing Torin to let go of my hand, but that didn't do any good, either. He gripped on tighter. I needed to work on my willing. "They're okay."

"I've missed you."

"What?" I choked—literally choked—on the word. I'd never

realized syllables were physical things, but that one lodged in my constricted throat. I tried again. "Why?"

Torin leaned forward and shook his head condescendingly. "Because I haven't *seen* you in three weeks."

"You haven't seen the other counselors, either," I teased, searching for some sort of defense. It wasn't like I was the only one he hadn't been in contact with.

"Yeah, but I haven't shared a sleeping bag with the other counselors." He propped open the dining hall door with one hand but didn't break his grip on the other. "You heard from Lance at all?"

I didn't want to answer his question, because it really hurt that the answer was no. No, I hadn't heard from Lance. Though I hadn't honestly expected to communicate with him regularly while we were both away, I'd at least hoped for a message—a note—some sort of confirmation that we were still, you know, *us*, whatever that even meant anymore. But that hadn't happened. Nothing had happened. Total radio silence.

"No, I haven't."

"You should check at the front office. You know they keep the messages there, right?" Torin guided me toward the line of staffers at the buffet, their plastic plates perched in their hands as they loaded up on carbs and sugarcoated sweets. Diabetes on a platter. Camp food left much to be desired for my poor taste buds.

"I didn't know that," I said, grabbing my own tray, fork, and napkin. I followed him down the line, transferring deli meat and fruit onto my tray, but none of it looked all that edible. I was still trying to find my stomach again after that free fall from earlier.

"I'll go with you after lunch. I bet there's something there from him."

I nodded gratefully and deposited another slice of ham onto my plate. "Thank you. That would be nice."

"You on the Atkins diet?" Torin's eyes narrowed as he pointed to the pile of meat grasped between the metal tongs suspended between my fingers. I had mindlessly stacked more slices than I could possibly eat onto my tray, completely covering it, leaving no inch of it empty.

"No."

"It looks like you're hungry."

"I'm not really." I unloaded some of the food, dumping it into a trash can near the end of the buffet line, feeling a little bad to be so wasteful and feeling a little embarrassed to come across so out of sorts.

"Could've fooled me." Torin's smile was huge. "Let's eat outside."

There was a picnic bench just outside the dining commons door, and Torin settled his tray onto it, the metal soda can clacking against the surface as he placed it on the wooden planks. "Have you missed me?"

"What?"

"Have you missed me, Darby? We did share a pretty intense twenty-four hours together."

"I have." *Did I really just admit that? Out loud? With actual words?* "My girls have kept me busy," I backpedaled, pushing around the food on my tray with my fork, shoving all the fruit to one side, all the meat to the other. "I'm pretty focused on them."

"That's awesome," he said around a mouthful of raspberry Jell-O. When he chewed, his dimples pricked his cheeks slightly and pulled in my gaze like a magnetic field. I'd always assumed magnetic fields to be much, much larger, but apparently they were just the size of a dimple pressed into a cheek. Go figure. "I told you you'd make a great counselor. Especially with them being thirteen and all." He winked at me, and that sucked me completely into the vortex.

"I don't know about great." I poked at my food, stabbing a slice of bologna with my fork so it left a row of four tiny pinholes. "But I'm trying."

"That's all that matters." With a flick of his wrist, he plopped a purple grape into his mouth. "I've got an interesting batch this time. Two former meth addicts and one kid who tried to kill his mom."

My utensil dropped from my fingers, clanking loudly against the plastic plate. I scooped it back up, but my shock was already made embarrassingly, and loudly, evident. I felt the eyes of a few nearby counselors but kept my head down like a scolded dog's. Unfortunately, I couldn't avoid the stare from the boy across the table. Our eyes collided.

"I know, right? Serious stuff," Torin agreed, nodding. He chomped down on another bite of his lunch and that dimple reappeared. "I'm glad they're all out on their canoe trips for a few hours. As much as I love what I get to do and who I get to be in their lives, I need something a little less intense for a few hours." He smiled, his cheeks puffed up like a chipmunk storing nuts for the winter. I wanted to pinch them. He pointed his fork in my direction and muttered around his food, "You are less intense."

But I found it crazy that he could say this was less intense than what he'd been experiencing, because for me, this was over-the-top, about-to-explode intense. Like a balloon inflated to its bursting point. Maybe because I'd replayed everything that happened between us over and over like a movie during our hiatus. Maybe because every night as I was falling asleep, it was Torin's lips on mine that flashed before my closed eyes, his scent that filled all of my senses like a toxic vapor. Maybe because for the past few weeks I'd thought—fantasized even—about what our next interaction would be and even prayed for a tick just so he could remove it. Maybe that's why this was all so intense.

"I think I have to go."

I pushed the tray away from me, extending my arms as far as they could go, until it almost collided with Torin's. My glass teetered precariously and soda sloshed over the side, pooling in my fruit salad in a fizzy, carbonated mess.

"Why?"

"I just have to." I rose to stand, but he caught my wrist. "I really should go, Torin."

His hand cuffed my arm and didn't let go even when I tugged it away. I turned, still keeping up my stride, and pulled him behind me until we were around the corner near the side wall of the dining hall, out of sight from the other counselors consuming their lunches at the tables that lined the decking.

"Torin," I said firmly, though my voice was weak and betrayed my oath to stay strong. "I have to go."

"Really?" Torin scooted closer. I pushed up against the wall to reclaim some distance, yet he followed my movements and pressed in even more. The breath in my lungs spilled out in a quiet, shaky rush. "Where do you have to go, Darby?"

"Somewhere not here."

His eyes roved over my face and a familiar throbbing filled me, tugging at my stomach and sucking the air out of my chest. He looked from my eyes down to my mouth. "What did I do? Why are you acting like this?"

I swiped my forehead with my hand. "This is painful."

"The camp?" Torin tossed his head, his hand sliding down the outer curve of my body, just far enough away that he wasn't actually touching me, but close enough that it was unbearable. "The camp?" he repeated. "Or me?"

"Yep. Gotta go."

"What's going on, Darby?" Torin demanded again, his voice equally as assertive as it was pleading. "What aren't you telling me?"

Um, that we made out three weeks ago during that stupid overnighter and since then it's all I've been able to think about. That I can't be around you without wanting to launch at you and do it all over again. How about that for starters?

"Nothing. Please just let it go, Torin." I pushed past two counselors who were headed toward the dining hall for lunch, chatting about what they planned to do with their free time that afternoon. I knew exactly what I planned to do: get out of Quarry Summit. Page break. End of chapter.

Torin shouldered them out of the way as he raced to catch me.

"I don't think I can." I heard his shoes as they clapped loudly against the ground. "There's something you're not telling me."

"I'm going to go see if I have any messages." *There.* Change the subject. Avoid confrontation. Act like a total coward and run like hell.

Torin pulled back a little as though he was going to allow me to behave like a child. He was quiet for so long that I felt like he was going to retreat, like he was going to give up the fight, like maybe my mule-like ways had finally gotten me somewhere. I was about ready to puff up my chest with stubborn pride when he blurted, "Fine. I'm going with you."

Chapter 13

"I'm going with you." Torin stated it again.

"I don't think you're invited," I said in a controlled, purposefully calm voice.

"Yes, I am." He scanned the message once more, flipping it over to continue reading the message scribbled on the back. With a loud flick of his index finger against the paper, he said, "See? Right here. It says to bring a friend."

"I'm not sure that means you."

"Are there a bunch of other friends you have here that you're keeping hidden?" He rotated at the waist to scan the room. "Because as far as I can tell, I'm it, Darby. Maybe you have some little leprechauns you're hiding in your pockets?"

I ripped the note from his hands and ran my eyes over it. "I don't think Lance's idea of me bringing a friend involves someone like you."

"Someone like me . . . please elaborate on that elusive statement. Because it could mean any number of things." Torin's lashes lowered as he rested against the receptionist's table, one leg propped up on its surface. He looked so casual and at home, and I hated that I was turned on by his relaxed pose. I hated even more that I was analyzing the fact that I was turned on. "Someone as annoying—or was it 'amazing'—as I am?"

Of course he remembered. I was hoping three weeks was enough time to erase that statement from existence, but it was still there, apparently tattooed in his brain. It's lovely how the mind chooses to imprint the embarrassing moments, while the nonmortifying ones fall by the wayside. Why couldn't that one have disappeared from his memory?

"Someone as male as you," I answered finally.

"Maybe we can find someone a little less male, then. Patrick doesn't seem overly masculine—I think I saw him rearranging one of the floral centerpieces in the dining commons. Would you like for me to see if he is free to accompany you?"

"That's not really what I meant."

"It says to bring a friend. I am a friend." Torin pulled the paper out of my hand, crumpled it up, and tossed it into the wastebasket across the room in three-pointer-like fashion. "Problem solved."

I hauled myself to the trash can and fished out the memo. *My* memo. My memo from Lance. This piece of paper wasn't meant for Torin, but he'd tossed it aside like it actually had something to do with him.

"I don't have a problem to solve."

"Okay, maybe not *that* problem, but you are going to have to figure out how to convince me to let you fly across the continental United States all by yourself. That seems like a pretty big problem to me." Torin sounded serious. "Because that's not gonna happen on my watch." I honestly thought he might actually be serious.

"News flash: I'm not on your watch." The room felt small—much too small—all of a sudden, and I pushed on the wooden door to escape the confines of the claustrophobia-inducing space.

"Where are you going?"

The wind rushed at me as I opened the door, and I filled my lungs to the brim with the crisp air until they couldn't expand another millimeter, and then I loudly exhaled, closing my eyes. "Whew. I had to get out of there."

"You mean, you had to get out of the building?"

"Yeah." I opened my eyes to look at him. "It was getting too hot and stuffy in there. Too confining."

The dimple appeared before the full-on smile burst across his lips. "You mean you had to get out of that *building* and get into *nature*?"

My therapeutic breathing halted immediately. "No, I . . . I just—"

"You turning all trees and flowers on me? No more buildings and concrete?" His taunting voice irritated me, mostly because it made my gut do these cartwheels that forced my food to flip-flop within it. I hadn't eaten much lunch. I'd like to keep what little I did consume within the confines of my stomach.

"Correction: I thought I had to get out of there"—I thrust a finger toward the reception hall—"but it turns out I still can't breathe, so it's obviously you I need to get away from."

"That's not going to happen." Torin dropped his hands onto my shoulders, two palms cupped on my skin. "So you're going to have to get used to the whole 'not being able to breathe' thing. I'm not going anywhere."

"Guess it's a good thing I am, then." I gripped the memo between my fingers. For a moment I contemplated folding it into a cootie catcher, but instead I shoved it into the depths of my jeans pocket.

I think Torin stepped forward—he must have—because we were suddenly closer than moments before. I felt the heat of his body; his chest was a few inches from mine, and my brain went back to the overnighter when I straddled him, thinking he was Lance. Goose bumps flared up across my skin and arrested my breathing.

Reminding myself to breathe wasn't something I was used to doing. Reminding myself to take out the trash, to email my college professor about office hours, and to remove the laundry from the dryer were actual things that required real reminders. But breathing was sort of a gift that was given to you—one thing your body knew how to do without thinking. Instinct just took over and completed the work for you. But suddenly, in my case, instinct had something against me and decided to add one more task to my to-do list. *Remember to breathe: check.*

"Did you miss the part where I said I'm not letting you get on that plane alone?" Torin was talking softer; his voice didn't quite sound the same. It was deeper but smooth, and made me shudder, which drove me nuts because he still gripped me by my shoulders and I knew he felt it. "You cold?"

"No." I shook his hands off. *Breathe again.* "I need to pack."

"Good plan. Let's go pack."

"You're not coming with me, Torin." I clomped toward my cabin. I wondered how long I could lock myself in there before someone noticed. I had two Tic Tacs and a stick of gum in my pocket. That might buy me six hours. I wondered if that was enough. Probably not, because three weeks had gone by and he appeared more attached than ever.

Despite the rules to stay out of the female cabin area, Torin stayed right behind me.

"What's the weather like this time of year in D.C.?"

. . . .

"You have to take your shoes off."

Torin dropped his eyes to his steel-toe boots. They were coated in dust, the yellow laces tangled haphazardly into two messy bows. "Why?"

"Because you might be hiding a bomb or something in them."

With the toe of one shoe, Torin pushed the heel off of the other and tossed it into the empty tray that crept slowly down the conveyer. "A bomb in my shoes?"

"You know . . . you're pretty much Unabomber material, Torin. Raised in the wilderness, totally reclusive."

He emptied his pockets, depositing his keys and wallet into a plastic container before unhooking his watch and tossing it in. "I'm not a recluse, Darby."

"Oh, that's right." I slipped my flip-flops from my feet and placed them into the tray, along with my purse and carry-on. I really wished I'd worn shoes with socks. My bare feet stuck to the gritty airport floor, trapping who knows what against my sweaty soles. "You actually have some weird attachment issue and won't let me travel to see my boyfriend by myself. I take back the recluse comment. You must have abandonment issues."

An annoyed TSA officer waved Torin through the X-ray machine. It didn't buzz, but for some reason he was still pulled aside after he exited it. Another officer mumbled something into his ear and patted Torin down, his hand pressing lightly over the surface of Torin's chest, arms, and thighs. I tried not to watch, but I couldn't help it. Kind of like the way you can't help but watch a car crash or a train wreck—you know you shouldn't, that rubbernecking will likely only lead to another accident, but you can't avoid the pull.

I slipped through the detector and joined him next to the conveyer where our belongings popped out like items on an assembly line.

"Well that was an experience." Torin slung my bag over his shoulder as he slid his things back into his pockets. "Would have been more fun if someone else were patting me down, though." I didn't dare look at him this time. "So, what do we do now?"

"We find our gate." I slipped my feet back into my shoes and pulled my boarding pass from my pocket to figure out just where we should head. Gate B19, the opposite end of the terminal. "And we sort of need to hurry."

The ride to Sacramento had been long—much longer than we'd anticipated—and I had pretended to be asleep for the majority of it. Fake sleeping was a good option because I could avoid the silence that pulsed throughout Torin's Jeep, surrounding us with heavy, quiet air. I had a sneaking feeling I'd be doing a lot of faking this weekend to avoid all sorts of undesirable things.

"Come on," I said, picking up my speed. "They're probably boarding already."

And they were. In fact, we were the last two on the plane, and the eye rolls and irritated smirks from the passengers already comfortably situated in their seats as we pushed down the aisle indicated we might even be holding things up. Like we had that much power, to keep an aircraft grounded. For a moment, I wished they had taken off without us.

"Please take the nearest open seat," an attendant instructed as she pulled a bag from Torin's hand and slid it into the overhead compartment. She clicked the hatch back into place loudly.

"We really need to sit together," Torin explained, motioning toward me.

"I don't think that's necessary." I shook my head and smiled at the stewardess politely. "It's fine. Any open seat will do."

"No, it won't." His tone lowered, and both the flight attendant and I widened our eyes. "We really need to sit next to each other."

"I can move." A woman, probably in her early seventies, rose from her middle seat and scooted one over. She lifted her purse from the window seat and tucked it under the chair in front of her, sliding it forward with the toe of her brown loafers. "There you go, kiddos."

"Thank you," Torin said as he smiled sweetly and slid in past her, his arms holding on to the headrests in front of him. I dropped down into her vacated seat and it was warm, which kind of bothered me. Like when the toilet seat was warm in a public restroom. I ignored it and focused on the other thing that was making me equally as squeamishly uncomfortable: the persistently endearing blond seated immediately to my left.

"Why did you insist that we sit together?" I asked as the flight attendant began her instructions over the intercom. She was waving some breathing device around that should only be used in the event that we lost pressure in the cabin, but I thought I should probably keep one on hand since I was constantly light-headed and found it hard to breathe on my own. I wondered if it was something I could purchase online or from those *SkyMall* magazines. I really needed the help of that breathing apparatus. "We don't have to sit together. Honestly. I'm fine sitting anywhere."

"I'm not." When Torin clicked his seat belt across his lap, I noticed a slight shake in his hands. Then I looked up at his face, and there was a gleam of sweat that coated it, like he'd just completed a pretty intense workout.

"Are you *scared*, Torin?"

The plane jolted as it pulled back from the gate, rolling on its wheels like a car in reverse. One of the other flight attendants continued rattling instructions, but he did it as a song—almost a rap—so that at least provided a little in-flight entertainment.

"I'm not scared." The vulnerable quiver in Torin's voice did something weird to my nervous system, something that I could feel all the way in my toes. I wriggled them to get rid of the feeling, but it didn't work. It almost felt like they were asleep, but this feeling was much more enjoyable, if tingling in that way could be enjoyable.

"Yes, you *are* scared."

"Remember?" That shake was still there. "I'm not afraid of anything." He thumbed through the seat pocket in front of him and pulled out the white barf bag, fingering its opening.

I yanked it from his hands and tossed it on my lap. "You're not going to need that."

"How do you know?" He reached for it again.

"Because you're not going to throw up, Torin," I assured with a grin. The plane stopped abruptly and someone in a command tower must have given us the go-ahead, because we started rolling forward, the rumble of the runway vibrating the tires below. "I'm here. I'll distract you."

"Darby, what could you possibly do that would be able to distract me from the fact that we're about to be thirty thousand feet above ground in a hunk of oversize metal?"

I bit down on the inside of my cheek. "I don't know. I'll think of something."

But I couldn't think of anything, and poor Torin's anxiety spiked to full panic mode as the wheels retracted into the under-carriage and the tip of the plane angled skyward. All color drained from his face, and I thought he might actually chomp through his bottom lip, he was biting it so hard. I felt like I should tell him to stop just for the sake of saving his mouth, but the dimple that creased his cheek when he did it completely drew my focus and I worried it might go away if he stopped the nervous lip chewing. Selfishly, I kept my own mouth shut.

The jet jerked suddenly and that weightless feeling pulled at my gut as the aircraft tipped to the left, wings tilting, slicing through the sky.

"Darby," Torin stammered. His knees bounced up and down erratically. His knuckles were so white. "Darby, you need to distract me."

I racked my brain to come up with a suitable topic for discussion. But I couldn't think of anything that might distract Torin from the fact that we were floating in the air in an oversize bus. He was right—when I actually thought about it, this was all pretty terrifying.

"Darby," he said again, his voice faltering. "Distraction . . . like, *now*."

So I did the only thing I could think to do in the moment, the one thing that had been a successful distractor for me these past three weeks: I closed my eyes and pretended to ignore the reality of my surroundings.

But that didn't last long.

Torin grabbed both sides of my face and shoved his lips onto mine. A sound rumbled from deep in his chest, not unlike the earlier rumbling of the wheels on the runway. My own breath hitched and I tried to draw back, but he captured my face in his palms and warmth slid through my veins, radiating out into every square inch of my body. I groaned against his mouth, forgetting about the perfume-drenched grandma sitting right next to me, forgetting about the entire plane filled with passengers altogether. I forgot it all—everything but that night in the sleeping bag—as Torin's mouth collided with mine, tugging at my lips in a way that swamped my gut with a dizzying heat.

My lips fell open as a sigh slipped from me, and Torin's tongue delved in, his fingers twisting in the loose curls of my hair. Another groan worked its way up my throat, but I held it back, even though it took a serious amount of effort to keep it from escaping in an embarrassingly breathy growl. Trailing the roof of my mouth, Torin pulled his tongue back, but his lips still glided over mine, making me nothing but a ball of overactive sensation. That tingling was back in my toes and this time, in my fingers, too. It worked its way up my spine and settled at the base of my neck.

Torin's mouth moved steadily with mine, and it felt so good that I wanted to cry or scream or do something to release the pent-up tension that had been filling every part of me since the overnighter. But I didn't do any of those things. Instead, I thought of how everything about this was so horribly wrong, even though it felt all kinds of incredible. That despite the incredible feeling, it actually made me feel equally sick. I wondered if this was how Lance felt when he had been with other girls. Something about it made me think that answer was no.

Just as Torin twisted in his seat to lean into me, his chest hovering over the armrest separating us, I felt everything in me start to rise, creeping through me and spinning my head and my insides in an upward-moving whirlpool. Unfortunately, my lunch traveled that same path, and in one forceful rush, it pressed at the back of my mouth. I yanked my lips from Torin's, ripped open the small, white bag I'd been holding in my lap, and dry heaved into it, sickened by my betrayal, and totally regretting what I'd just done.

Chapter 14

"So, kissing me makes you sick."

I slid farther into my seat and pulled the magazine up above my head like a protective shield of armor. "You have to go back to your own row. He's gonna come back from the bathroom soon."

"I think *you* have to go back to *your* row." Torin pushed a finger into my shoulder and grinned. I walled him off with the pages of the gossip mag in my hands.

"I am in mine."

"You seriously up and moved on me?" He grasped the paper from my grip and threw it to the floor. Those innocent green eyes impaled me. "You're not going to sit with me?"

"You didn't get that hint five hours ago?" I looked back toward the restrooms and the Occupied sign was still lit. How long could it take a guy to go to the bathroom? I really needed my seat partner to come back and reclaim his spot next to me at

the back of the plane. And I needed to get to Washington, D.C.—
I needed Lance to reclaim me, too.

I shifted my gaze toward the window and stared blankly into
the clouds that rested just below the wings. They were fluffy and
white and looked like you could stand on them if you tried. It
was amazing how something that appeared so real and solid
could be so utterly deceiving.

"Are you embarrassed that you nearly threw up in front of
me?" Torin caught my chin between his fingers and pulled my
face in his direction. It was hard not to look at someone when
they were basically controlling the movement of your head, like
a puppeteer and his Pinocchio. "Because I've seen you throw up
before. Remember, in the tree?"

I recoiled and looked back out the smudged glass window
again. "I'm not embarrassed about the gagging, Torin."

"Then what is it?"

One of the flight attendants halted at the end of our row. Her
hair was wound so tightly all her features pulled upward and it
made her look like she was made of plastic, like Flight Attendant
Barbie. "Peanuts? Pretzels?"

I took both packages from her hands and tore them open,
glad to have something to fill my mouth so I didn't have to use it
to answer Torin's questions.

"Why did you leave?" He fumbled to open his bag of peanuts, and when he finally did, it split from end to end and the
contents soared into the air, ricocheting against the seat in front
of him and landing in a lady's Bloody Mary across the aisle. She
shot him an angry glare, but Torin just shrugged sheepishly and
waved. He looked to me again. "Just so you know, it worked."

"What worked?" I mumbled, still loading my mouth with
salty carbs.

"Your distraction." He took a palmful of peanuts and slammed them into his open mouth. "It worked during takeoff, and it's been working throughout the entire flight. I'm completely distracted. Good work, Darby. I've got this flying thing down. Might as well call me Ace."

"We shouldn't have done that, Torin. I mean, seriously, I should swap this stupid Stanford logo out for a scarlet *A*." I waved my hand across the fabric appliqué on my sweatshirt, a frustrated groan following my words.

His eyes went wide like a cartoon character's. "Is that what this is about? Are you worried that you've cheated or something?"

"That's *exactly* what I did." I gulped down the last bits of my snack and used the tip of my fingernail to dislodge a piece wedged between my front teeth. "That was wrong on so many levels."

"Oh, but it was oh so right on so many levels, too." The way Torin's voice crooned out of him made my heart palpitate faintly, like a pitter-patter, which I always thought was just as weird of a word as it was a feeling. Like *twitterpated*. I had totally become twitterpated with Torin. If I had been as into quotes as he was, that would be the one I would recite. Here he was referencing poets of old, and I was thinking about a stupid skunk from *Bambi*.

"Seriously, Darby. You have some incredible distraction tactics."

"I *kissed* you, Torin!" I saw the man in the seat in front of me turn his head in my direction, but he continued reading his book out of the corner of his eye like he wasn't actually eavesdropping at all.

"Yeah, you're right, you did. But it was more like you kissed me back. And I liked it."

"So did I, but that's not the point—"

"You did?" Torin practically gasped. "So the gagging thing . . . that didn't have to do with the kiss?"

"Well, it did—"

"So I *do* make you sick."

"No," I continued, but had a feeling he wasn't going to let me finish my thought. "*I* make *myself* sick."

Torin shook his head, his blond, shaggy hair tossing back and forth. "It's okay, Darby. It didn't mean anything."

My throat went dry. "It didn't?"

"No. It would only be cheating if there was something behind it. In our case, it was purely for purposes of distraction." He fluttered his hand between us nonchalantly. "It was just a kiss, Darby."

I heard the click of the lavatory door behind us and shot out the tense breath I'd been trapping in my chest. My seat partner had finally finished his business. I don't think I'd ever been so happy to be sitting next to an overweight, middle-aged man with sewer breath in my entire life. *Welcome back, buddy. What took so long?*

"But it sorta still feels like I cheated, and I hate that. I hate what that makes me."

"A kiss is just a kiss, Darby," Torin said in a singsong, his voice much better than I'd imagined it would be. It had a soothing tenor to it, one that I could get used to hearing.

The man waddled his way down the aisle and stood over Torin, his Santa Claus–like belly pressing into Torin's elbow. They locked eyes and Torin stood to give up his seat. Before he turned to head back to his original row, he gripped on to the seat back in front of me and leaned forward as he said, "Don't give it another thought, okay? I'm serious."

I bit my lip and nodded, but knew that even the act of bobbing my head up and down was a total lie. Like I wasn't going to give it another thought. It was *all* I'd been able to think about. And apparently, it was all Torin had been thinking about, too. Fan-freakin'-tastic.

As he walked back to his seat, he shot a look over his shoulder and mouthed, "Fuhgeddaboudit," like he was some old cinema Mafia boss. This guy and his impersonations.

I tried to forget, I really did. But I couldn't.

For the duration of the flight, I busied myself by coating my lips in every single tube of gloss I had packed in my purse, like somehow five shades of lip gloss smeared across my mouth could cover up the fact that it had completely betrayed me. Like Lance wouldn't find out. Like it wasn't written plainly all over my face.

I buried my pile of lip-gloss tubes into the depths of my bag and zipped it up angrily.

"Ladies and gentlemen," a robotic female voice recited through the overhead speakers, "as we start our descent, please make sure your seat backs and tray tables are in their full upright position. Make sure your seat belt is securely fastened and all carry-on luggage is stowed underneath the seat in front of you or in the overhead bins. Please turn off all electronic devices until we are safely parked at the gate. Thank you."

I shoved my purse farther under the seat with my foot and pulled the belt strap tight across my lap until it hurt. I deserved to feel a little pain. Someone should probably even slap me for what I'd done. It totally would have been appropriate since this time my lips and brain were working in unison, unlike the dream kiss a few weeks back.

"And to the passenger in row 29, seat B, we ask that you remember this one thing." I peered down the aisle as Flight Attendant Barbie handed over the microphone to a male flight attendant who said, "Play it again, Sam."

There was a short pause as passengers glanced about the cabin, and when all eyes fell upon me, I realized just what was going on, and just who was sitting in 29B.

"*You must remember this . . .*" the attendant crooned, his voice rich and delicate. He obviously had several years of voice lessons under his belt. *"A kiss is just a kiss . . ."*

My jaw dropped to the floor, so much so that I almost thought the flight attendants were going to come around and ask that I stow it under the seat in front of me. I whipped my head and shook the stunned expression from my blanched face. *What on earth?*

"A sigh is just a sigh . . ."

I wanted to leap out of my seat and track Torin down to ask him how I was supposed to forget something he kept bringing up— this time in the form of performing flight attendants—but he had conveniently waited until I was prohibited from leaving my chair before doing something as mortifying as this. Every eye in the last three rows glued to me, like I sat there naked or in my underwear.

Flight attendants serenade their passengers every day, right? Didn't they?

"The fundamental things apply . . ." Several more people joined in, channeling their best Sam Dooley from *Casablanca*. One guy a couple of rows up even busted out an air piano and pretended to caress the imaginary black and white keys as he swayed melodically to the music. *"As time goes by."*

Oh. My. Word. This wasn't happening.

But it was, and the entire plane partook in Operation Humiliate Darby, belting out the final line of the classic song in an impressively loud ending note. I slunk as far in my seat as humanly possible and was so grateful for Santa next to me, who shielded me quite effectively from the stares of the passengers-turned-musical-chorus around us with his gluttonous midsection.

The plane did that dipping thing as it lowered toward ground, and I readied the barf bag . . . just in case. But we managed to land without any more dry heaving on my part, and without any more embarrassing stunts on Torin's. When the seat belt sign went dark, I clicked my belt free and waited my turn to deplane. Powering my phone on, I anticipated the familiar buzz of a text, and within seconds, my phone vibrated in my palm.

Lance: Waiting outside security. See you soon.

The guy next to me took his time gathering his belongings, slinging his carry-on over his shoulder like a giant toy sack. But I didn't mind. In fact, the longer I could dillydally, the better chance I had to shake Torin loose. Maybe he'd get totally lost in the terminal. I doubted he'd ever left that mountaintop of his back home. Sure, he could navigate that no problem, but a bustling airport in the heart of Washington, D.C.? I'd like to see him survive that scenario. Or the scenario in which I confront him about the number he pulled with the whole singing thing. I balled my hands into fists. Yeah, his chances of survival were looking pretty slim right about now.

What the heck? Why had I turned all mean and feisty on him?

I pulled my luggage out from the compartment and fit it to my shoulder, my purse slung over the opposite one. I was literally the last one off the plane and Torin was nowhere in sight.

I walked up the aisle toward the exit, knowing in just a few moments, I'd be reunited with Lance. This was what I'd been waiting for all summer. Forget Torin. Forget Quarry Summit. Back to my ever-consistent, dependable reality.

"You gonna leave me to fend for myself?"

My heels dug into the tattered aisle carpet. I nearly skidded to an abrupt halt.

"What?"

Torin was hunkered down into his seat, looking like a sad, lost puppy, no longer the confident alpha dog that he was back in the forest.

"You weren't even going to wait for me?" He popped up and unlatched the overhead bin to pull out his carry-on. "That's not very nice, Darby, and I actually considered you to be a nice girl." He slid his shoulders into the straps of his backpack and wriggled them until it situated comfortably on his back. In the same, swift motion, he pressed his fingers to my hips to guide me farther down the aisle toward the cockpit. "It's not nice to invite me here and then completely abandon me."

"You told me to forget. And then you dedicated that song to me, Torin. Tell me how that's supposed to help." I nodded a good-bye at the pilot and flight attendants who stood at the front of the plane and Torin did the same. "The easiest way for me to forget you is to leave you behind."

"Wait a minute," Torin said, his hands still planted on my hips. They were a thousand degrees. "I thought that song was perfect! *Casablanca*? Totally fitting since we're heading to the home of the *White House* and all. And 'a kiss is just a kiss'? Come on! I thought it was genius!"

"You use the term *genius* rather loosely." I kept my eyes forward, adjusted my straps, and picked up my pace. "Embarrassing me in front of an entire plane full of people does not help me forget what happened. It brands it into my brain. The easiest way for me to forget is to not be around you."

Torin froze, like I was some ice princess who had cast a spell on him. "I thought we were just trying to forget the kiss." His face fell noticeably and it made me feel absolutely horrible. "I didn't realize you were planning to forget me altogether. That's going to make this a little awkward, then, don't you think?"

"Make what awkward?" I scanned the terminal, looking for the Baggage Claim sign. I located it to the left of us and headed toward the escalators.

"The fact that you dragged me across the country with you!"

I swatted his hand away and dodged the rush of people that barreled toward me like they were obstacles in a video game. "I didn't drag you across the country!" I squawked, pulling down on my volume when the woman in front of me eyed me suspiciously. "You were more of a stowaway."

"No, I'm pretty sure I remember you saying you couldn't survive a mile apart from my presence."

"You're making things up. I don't ever recall saying that, Torin. I can easily survive without you."

With an air of condescension, Torin shook his head and rotated sideways to skirt the cluster of tourists that gathered in front of him to examine their boarding passes. I continued my determined beeline toward baggage claim. "You can't survive one night without me, Darby." My phone buzzed in my pocket, startling me and making me skip a step. Kind of the same way my heart skipped a beat when I thought about that unforgettable kiss *that was just a kiss*. "We've proven that already."

Lance: At the bottom of the escalator. I'm really glad you still wanted to see me.

I ignored Torin and slipped through an opening in the crowd, pushing my way past security. Torin was fast—and determined— because he successfully edged his way around the knots of airport congestion and was at my back within seconds. Lance's text was weird, but I ignored it, because in all honesty, Torin was weirder, and that demanded my immediate attention.

"Is that him?" With the tip of his index finger, Torin pointed toward the landing at the base of the escalator. Sure enough, Lance was there, his eyes wide, his hands holding a bouquet of long-stemmed red roses.

I nodded.

Torin didn't do me the favor of masking his smirk under a false smile, and instead wore it bright and proud on his face, like those maniacal fun-house clown grins. He bent over to whisper in my ear, "And you've been together six years?" His warm breath left a trail of goose bumps along the curve of my neck. "I've only known you a short time and I already know you're all structure and concrete. Definitely not flowers."

I swiftly elbowed him in the gut.

"Babe!" Over the tops of the heads of those who separated us, Lance called out as I stepped off the escalator onto the marbled floor.

"'Babe'?" Torin echoed quietly to himself, but loud enough that I could hear. It was completely intentional, so I intentionally made the choice to completely ignore him and raced toward Lance's out-stretched and open arms.

With a move that rivaled those seen in romantic comedies, Lance engulfed me and swung me around, my legs trailing out behind me as he nuzzled my neck. Those goose bumps were still there and I worried that somehow he'd know what originally triggered them. But he didn't seem to have any clue and continued twirling me, his cologne sweeping through my nostrils. It almost burned and my eyes watered on cue.

"Babe, how was your flight?" He placed the flowers into my grasp. "Any turbulence?"

"Oh, it was pretty turbulent." Torin stepped up to my side and answered for me like maybe I was mute or something and needed his vocal assistance. "Hey, I'm Torin." He jutted a hand toward Lance.

"Hi, Torin." Lance flashed his award-winning, blinding smile. He really was ridiculously good-looking. "I've heard a lot about you. I can't wait to introduce you to my parents—I think you'll really like them."

My stomach tumbled and Torin cocked his brow, trying to figure out what that must have meant, I was sure. I interjected quickly, firing my words into the empty air. "So, the big fund-raiser's tonight?"

"Yes." Lance slipped my carry-on bag from my shoulder and transferred it to his. "And that's why I really wanted you here. It's Mom's biggest one yet. One of those galas that will be heavily photographed. Can't have my mug end up in the newspaper without your beautiful face next to it. You're obviously my better half." He swept a soft kiss across my forehead.

Behind me, I caught Torin's gaze right at the end of his exaggerated eye roll. I had to give it to him; Lance could be pretty cheesy. Either that or hopelessly romantic. I chose to favor the latter description. Unfortunately, so did many of the other girls who came in contact with him.

"Our driver is outside and will take you both to the hotel."

In the distance, the bags from our plane rotated around the luggage carousel, and I spotted my large pink duffel as it dropped onto the conveyer. Lance left us to retrieve it, knowing exactly which one was mine.

"So that's him, huh?" Torin slid his thumbs under the straps of his backpack like he did so often and scanned Lance up and down from afar, giving him a very thorough once-over. "I wasn't expecting him to be so . . ."

"Handsome?" I offered, because that was the go-to definition when it came to Lance. Seriously, both Lance and his brother were Kennedy material with their good looks and alluring prestige. Once, when we were in high school, *GQ* came out with a cover that had a twenty-something actor on it who was the spitting image of Lance, or rather Lance of him. I couldn't even remember what Hollywood icon it was. All I knew was that specific cover propelled Lance from high school homecoming king status to model material. His crew of friends even started calling him "GQ." He was no longer a boy, but a man—and had the gorgeous doppelgänger to match.

"No, not handsome," Torin continued, still trying to find an adequate description for Lance. "So . . . so happy to meet me."

My mouth twitched. "Why wouldn't he be?"

"I don't know." Torin's childlike grin fluttered my heart and made me feel like I was spinning around in circles again in Lance's arms. "I was hoping he would view me as a threat or something. I mean, I did just spend the past three weeks with his girl."

"He doesn't view you as a threat."

Torin worked on a swallow and said, "Why not—"

"All set to go?" Lance returned and fell in step with us, my pink bag adorning his shoulder. The McIversons' personal chauffeur was perched against a black Range Rover just outside the exit doors, the SUV's windows tinted almost as dark as the finish of the paint on the vehicle. "Let's get you both settled in."

Chapter 15

I folded the last piece of clothing into the dresser and tossed my duffel bag into the towering wardrobe, latching the mahogany door back into place.

"I still don't see how this is okay with him," Torin chimed from the front of the hotel room. I heard the slam of a drawer first and then his footsteps as he entered the room. Lance had gotten us a suite, so I took the room in the back and Torin claimed the fold-out sofa as his own. And now he stood in the doorway separating the two spaces, his tanned arms zigzagged over his chest. "I don't get how he's all right with us sharing a room."

"You heard him," I said, taking my toiletry bag to the adjoining bathroom. The mirror stretched all the way to the ceiling and the lights that hung on it glittered against the glass like amber stars. Even the hotel bathroom was excessively ornate. Seriously, all you were supposed to do in there was pee. It really didn't call for gilded drawer handles and gold-encrusted faucets. Oh, the McIversons and their overstated tastes.

I set my makeup bag on the marble countertop and stared myself down in the oversize mirror. I looked sort of awful. That was fitting, because I felt sort of awful. One day of deception (okay, maybe two) and the lying had taken an obvious physical toll. By the end of the trip, I'd look like death warmed over. "We have to share because he said there was only one room available."

"So why aren't you staying with him?" Torin plopped onto the foot of my bed, his legs tucked up under him. He was tense, and the muscle that pulsed at the back of his jaw did this tightening and relaxing thing that made me grit my teeth in an attempt to steady my erratic breathing. I'd never felt asthmatic before, but Torin did something strange to my respiratory system.

"He can't have guests at his apartment. Something to do with his internship. I don't know."

"I know it doesn't bug you, but I'm starting to feel a little insecure about him being *so* okay with me hanging around." Torin flicked his head to shake the hair from his forehead. He was way overdue for a haircut. Maybe I should add that to our agenda: lose the disheveled, untidy mane. "I might not be a McIverson, but I don't think I'm repulsive."

I bracketed my hands on the curved ledge of the bathroom counter and laughed lightly. "You're not repulsive, Torin."

"No. I just make you gag."

After placing my toothbrush in a glass near the sink, I exited the bathroom to join him at the foot of my bed. "You don't make me gag." Well, he did, but not for the reasons he thought.

"That's not true. It's happened twice now."

I dragged in an extended breath and closed my eyes, knowing things were about to get seriously awkward. "I may or may not have told Lance that you might be gay."

There was a long, uncertain pause. Someone just dropped a pin over on Pennsylvania Avenue; I'm fairly sure I heard it.

"That's very confusing, Darby. You may or may not have? What is that supposed to mean?" That muscle along his jaw thrummed again. "Your boyfriend thinks I'm gay?"

I tried to swallow the lump in my throat, but it was the size of a tennis ball and I choked instead. "Lance is not the understanding guy I've made him out to be," I explained, twisting a strand of hair around my thumb until the fingertip looked like a swollen grape. I felt my pulse beating in it. "He's actually sort of the jealous type. He'd never be okay with you flying out to D.C. with me. I had to come up with *something*."

"And telling him I was gay was the only option? How am I going to pull that off?" With an unexpected smile, Torin tapped his fingers on his mouth like he was actually trying to figure out how to make this whole thing work.

"Pull that off?"

"Well, yeah," he said, nudging my knee, giving me a sidelong glance. "It's no secret you didn't really want me tagging along with you, Darby. But for some reason, I'm here, and I feel like I owe you something for that. So tell me, how do I pull this off?"

"Well, for starters, you're going to have to dress a lot better than that."

Shifting his gaze, he surveyed his clothing. His black V-neck shirt was so faded that it looked more gray than ebony, and his jeans had about five holes ripped through the tattered fabric, like he had gotten into a fight with a feral cat in some dark alleyway. "What's wrong with the way I dress?"

"Nothing." I laughed, covering my mouth with my palm, "if you're homeless."

"It's comfortable." With his thumb and index finger, he pulled at the hem of his shirt, exposing his taut stomach slightly, reminding me of the day on the rock when he lay there bare chested next to me. I really wished he wouldn't do that. To go with my recent asthma self-diagnosis, I was about to write myself a prescription for an inhaler.

"It's not presentable. You can't go to the gala tonight wearing something like that, Torin." When I realized I was unintentionally fanning myself with the end of my braid, I dropped it like it was on fire, hot-potato style.

Leaning in closer than he should, Torin said, "Well, then. I think we have some shopping to do."

. . . .

"Your boyfriend is freakin' hot."

I was used to hearing that phrase. If I had even just a penny for every time I'd heard it, I'd likely be able to pay my own college tuition, and my education came with a hefty price tag. The only thing was, this girl was not talking about Lance.

"I think I like this last one on him the best." She smacked a pink wad of her gum between her teeth and swiveled her perfectly curved hips as she made her way back behind the register.

A few feet away, the dressing-room drapes fluttered. Torin reached a hand out to draw the curtain back all the way, and it was like one of those slow-motion dramatizations in a soap opera. Or maybe it was the fuzzy feeling in my head that seemed to slow everything down, like the world spun just a little more lazily on its axis.

I crisscrossed my legs, the sweat on my thighs slipping over them. The East Coast during the summer was hot, humid, and all kinds of uncomfortable.

"Do you know how to do this?" Torin emerged to stand immediately in front of me, outfitted in a tailored charcoal-gray suit, the flat-front pants looking like they were made just for his body and the jacket tapering perfectly over his angular shoulders. A thin, black tie hung loosely around his neck and he flipped the end of it up. "I've never worn one of these."

I peeled myself from the chair and stood on unsteady legs.

Torin looked amazing. It was like one of those unbelievable before-and-after transformations. The only thing was, the before was already pretty incredible, so the after took him to a whole different level. He was all sun-kissed hair, tanned skin, and sleek, tailored lines. Total model status. A status I was completely uncomfortable with, especially when I realized this was the same guy I'd kissed just hours before. I suddenly felt out of my league, which was an odd sensation considering I was actually dating a guy who was literally in a league all his own.

"Can you help me out with it?" Torin flicked the tie, wrapping it clumsily over itself in a pretzeled knot.

"Yeah." All of my syllables got twisted together in my mouth. "I can help."

I'd tied a tie a hundred times at the very least. But as I grabbed ahold of the silken fabric draped around Torin's neck, it was like my fingers forgot how to move, how to function in any sort of manner that would make tying a tie even possible. I was all thumbs. In that moment, I wouldn't even be able to tie my own shoe to save my life.

"It's not a noose, Darby." Torin smiled a lopsided sort of grin. "Try not to strangle me. Though I wouldn't blame you if you wanted to. I probably deserve it after that stunt on the plane."

My eyes lifted to his as my fingers slowly recalled how to work again. I tugged the wider side of fabric through the loose knot and pulled it tight, sliding it up toward his throat, wriggling it back and forth slowly in a rhythm that made the whole thing seem strangely sexual, kind of like the cootie-catcher disaster. A slight sheen of sweat pooled at the divot where Torin's collarbone and neck met, and I fought back the urge to sweep it away with my fingertips. Well, in reality, I fought back the urge to lick it off first. And when I realized how inappropriate—and slightly gross—that was, I fought the urge to wipe it off. Like he could somehow sense this ridiculous internal struggle of mine, Torin's Adam's apple lifted up and down as he quietly cleared his throat, ripping me out of my hormone-driven state of being.

"I don't want to strangle you," I said, reclaiming my right to my own composure, but my voice was too hushed and almost raspy.

Peering down at me, Torin wrapped his fingers over mine on top of the knot at the base of his neck. "Thank you."

"Yeah."

"Yeah." He narrowed his eyes at me, slivers on his face, almost like he was trying to read my thoughts. But even if he could, he wouldn't discover anything. My brain was fuzzy and empty, like I'd been sucking a balloon filled with helium.

With his chin tucked, his head leaned forward an inch. My natural instinct was to press up on my toes to lessen the gap, but I didn't. I fought it; I fought the pulling sensation in me that wanted to kiss him again. And it was so weird, because there was this charged chemistry between us that—under other circumstances—would lead to kissing eventually. In fact, I was sure it would lead us to a lot more than that. There was an undeniable rush of excitement that filled me when Torin was close. I didn't have this with Lance. And it wasn't one of those situations where I used to have it with him and after six years, it slipped away. I'd never experienced this, so it was unnatural to fight it off when it was the most natural thing my body, and my brain, had ever known.

I wet my lips, not intentionally, but it did something to Torin. There was a shift in his demeanor, and a shift in his posture. His fingers tightened around mine, still placed on his necktie, though there really wasn't a need for them to be there anymore. There wasn't a need for me to even be in this dressing room with him, let alone the store. Torin didn't need me, but for some reason, I needed him. Or at least this felt like need.

That pull between us took on an intense electricity. The three full-length mirrors behind him were angled in a way that created an endless tunnel of reflections, and he was all I could see: his image repeated infinitely over and over. It was almost too much, but I didn't think it was something I could ever tire of looking at, because it was mesmerizing.

"Darby," Torin muttered, his tone rough. My body did this weird thing as my pulse strummed brutally under my skin. My ears started to ring and my vision blurred until those reflections began to morph into one solid image. It was almost like I was going to pass out, but it was almost as though everything had finally become clear. Like the blur before the focus. "Dance with me, Darby."

"What?"

"Dance with me," he said again. "I have to see if I can even move in this suit. It sorta feels like a straitjacket." He tugged on the hem of his coat. "There will be dancing at the thing tonight, right?"

Oh, yeah. The gala. The whole reason we were in D.C.

I nodded.

Suddenly, Torin yanked me close so our chests pushed up against one another's, and he hooked one arm around my waist while he kept our hands pressed between us on his tie. For as many times as I'd made fun of him for growing up in the wilderness, dancing with him retracted any of those ignorant comments. Because as his body started to sway, as his feet shifted and his hips moved, there was absolutely no credibility in my past statements. He wasn't some inexperienced backwoods kid. In fact, he was clearly *very* experienced when it came to knowing his body and how to control it. And it appeared he was just as experienced in knowing how to control mine as he guided me softly back and forth, rocking on our heels across the gray dressing-room carpet.

I dropped my head to his shoulder and a shudder ran the length of Torin's body.

"Mrs. Robinson, are you trying to seduce me?" Torin smiled, imitating rather than being authentic, once again. I was beginning to think it was easier for him to plagiarize someone else's thoughts rather than declare his own, because the frequency in which he spoke another's words was much higher than any other nineteen-year-old I'd ever known.

"Please, Torin. I'm only two months older than you. And I'm not seducing you. You're the one who asked me to dance."

He swiveled his head. "Fair enough," he conceded quickly. "Do you like it? The suit, I mean."

"Mm-hmm" was all I got out.

"Do you think I'll be able to convince Lance with it?" He laughed, flicking his head back to toss away the hair that slid into his eyes. I was going to cut that hair of his.

"I don't think I want you to."

Torin's steady movements faltered. "What?"

I backpedaled five thousand feet. "Nothing."

"What do you want, then?"

Silence.

"Darby?" Torin said again, planting his feet. "What do you want from me?" He bit down on his lip and I wished he hadn't because it made me want to do the same to it. "Tell me what you want . . . because I'll give it to you."

I looked up at him and he was gazing at me with an intensity that took me by surprise.

"I want you to say what you're really thinking instead of hiding behind songs and famous movie quotes. I want to know *your* thoughts, Torin, not some line that's been spoon-fed to you."

"You want to know what I'm thinking?" he said, vulnerability rippling out of his tone like a stone thrown into a still pond. It reverberated and rattled in my head and I felt the heat of his stare echoed in my gut. "Do you seriously want to know? Because I'll tell you if you do." I answered with my eyes held to his. "I'm thinking how much it sucks that I'm six years too late."

My hands fell to my side. The room turned into a Tilt-A-Whirl.

"*That's* what I'm thinking." He inclined forward. His chest pushed against mine and it ached, feeling instantly heavy the moment we touched, like heartburn or something that made it impossible for me to swallow without experiencing the pain of it. "So do you want me to go back to my one-liners now?"

"Yeah," I croaked. Yeah, I wanted to go back. I wanted to go *way* back.

Six years, to be exact.

Chapter 16

The walk to the hotel was quiet. The garment bag carrying Torin's new suit swished against him as we traveled down the busy city streets, and I tried to focus my attention on the way it crinkled with the movement, like the sound of someone rustling a newspaper or magazine. It was easier to zero in on that than it was to think about anything else because my brain was a vapid space of incoherent thoughts and hormone-riddled impulses. Garment bag crinkling I could process; everything else was questionable.

"I bet you're loving it here, right?"

My feet scraped along the sidewalk. "How so?" I glanced up at the ominous structures around us.

"This is your mountaintop, yeah?"

"Yeah, actually," I admitted, a little surprised that he could see that deeply into me. "It sorta is."

"I like that about you, Darby." Torin switched the bag from one hand to the other so it was on the opposite side of his body. When it was in between us, it felt like some sort of fabric-laden barrier. But now I was suddenly exposed and closer to him than I should have been. Let's be honest: I shouldn't even be near him at all. I should be on one coast, and he should be on the other. We should have some forty-odd continental states in between us.

But even that didn't feel like it would be enough distance, and I doubted it would change the way I felt right then. Absence made the heart grow fonder, right? Maybe being this close to him would have the opposite effect. Yeah, right. Who was I kidding? My fondness for Torin was reaching alarmingly unacceptable, skyscraper-like heights.

"I like that you and I are so different," he continued, unfazed by my lack of words, which was good, because I was still trying to relearn the English vocabulary since everything in my brain was sucked right out during our impromptu slow dance.

"Me, too. I like that we're different," I agreed. Repeating his words was the safest option.

A man chattering on a cell phone shouldered me as he raced past and I wobbled out of his way. Torin shoved me back to my spot with his elbow and laughed like he thought something about my clumsiness was endearing, which was a first because I'd always thought it just made me, well, clumsy.

"As an architectural design major, I bet you have a lot of places you'd love to travel. Lots of ancient buildings to see, huh?"

"No, not really." I pushed my hands into the pockets of my jean shorts. "You can pretty much see everything on the Internet. Real-time images and all." I shrugged. "But I kinda want to see Boston Light."

"What's that?"

"A lighthouse in Massachusetts. The first lighthouse built in the United States." I found a loose string in the seam of my pocket and fiddled with it between my thumb and index finger. "I don't think it's necessarily anything special, but I remember seeing a picture of it once in a book my sister had about lighthouses. I told myself then that someday I would see the real thing."

"That's a sweet story."

"I know, it's stupid."

"No," Torin quickly said, like he could retract the insulting tone of his previous statement. "Not making fun. I think it's really sweet. Like a world-renowned chef wanting to go to the first McDonald's or something. Simple. Understated."

"I just like what it stands for, I guess." I spotted the overhang of our hotel a block up, the maroon canopy strung above two gold poles that rose out from the ground. We halted at the curb and, once the Walk sign flashed, stepped out into the street. "Lighthouses were used to warn sailors to change their positions so they didn't hit land," I explained, though I was certain he knew the functions of a lighthouse. I just felt like I should explain myself and my weird fascination with them. "I think I just like the idea of having some guiding light to direct my path."

We hopped back onto the curb on the other side and a taxi nearly sideswiped us as it took the corner on two squealing wheels. Torin protectively pushed at my back to steer me out of the way, and when his hand lingered at the base of it just above my waistline, I willed another car to come careening toward us just so his palm would stay put. "Guess you sort of have that already, though," I said. "With your beliefs."

"I do." He nodded. "But I don't always follow those warnings like I know I should." He jogged to catch the door to our building and held it open for me, completely ignoring the bellman, and he almost bowed as I passed through, trying to be a gentleman. "Because with you, it feels like I'm heading into troubled waters. And as much as I see the path I'm supposed to take, I want to veer off course so bad."

That wasn't at all what I was expecting him to say.

But he was right. This *was* uncharted territory: someone being so upfront and vulnerable. Though he'd been honest in the past— specifically when he confessed his thoughts to me after the night in the sleeping bag—this was the most transparent Torin had ever been. The most transparent anyone had ever been with me, in fact. I didn't quite know what to do with it, but it felt like a gift.

"Thank you."

"For what?" He pressed a finger onto the elevator button at the north side of the lobby. The reception desk buzzed with a hum of chatter, combining with the rolling of luggage wheels on the marble floor to create a melodic beat of life carrying on around us. Which felt weird because it seemed like everything in my own life had temporarily come to a stop.

"Thank you for telling me that."

The elevator doors slid open and several businessmen— probably politicians—funneled out, their polished European loafers edging us out of the way. Torin held up a hand, trapped the door open with a tennis shoe–clad foot, and waved me through.

"You're welcome, Darby. I'll tell you anything you want to know, but I don't necessarily see what the point is."

Once inside, the doors closed, making a sucking sound when they did, and then the elevator jolted as it began its climb to our twenty-first floor.

"There's always a point to saying what you feel."

In that moment, it was like my statement lit something within Torin, and without warning, he jammed a finger against the number pad and the elevator jerked to an abrupt stop, practically giving me whiplash as it halted its upward glide.

"What are you doing?" My heart rate kept climbing even though the elevator didn't.

"I need to go find a floral shop," he said matter-of-factly, like I should have known exactly what the cryptic declaration meant.

"What? Why?"

"I need to buy you, like, the fattest bouquet of flowers right now, Darby." He laughed and it echoed in the tight space we were in, bouncing off the gilded walls. "Do you realize what you just said?"

"I said it's good to say what you're feeling."

"Right," he confirmed, nodding. "You're going all soft on me. Trees and flowers. And I kinda like it. I'm chipping away at your structure and concrete." The elevator still hovered somewhere between floors ten and eleven. My stomach hovered somewhere between my esophagus and my mouth. "Don't get me wrong," he continued. "I like that you're hardheaded and stubborn, too."

"That's not true, Torin. You said you're not attracted to girls who are stubborn."

"Normally, I'm not. And I'm not attracted to brunettes—er, redheads—either." He cast a sly grin in my direction. "But I'm attracted to you, Darby. And not just bits and pieces of you, as if I could just take the good and leave the bad."

"Sometimes it feels like there's quite a lot of bad—"

"Don't say that." He silenced me with a shake of his head. "There is not. But even if there were, there's something about you that keeps drawing me to you. And it's incredibly aggravating because I told you I'm trying my best at being a decent guy." Torin took two steps toward me and trailed a finger down my cheek, sweeping a strand of hair behind my ear. "You're like the damn Sirens who tried to crash Odysseus and his men against the rocks. I'm seriously contemplating getting some earplugs and tying myself to the bed to get away from you."

"You want to be tied to the bed?" I gulped, trying not to envision that because it did spastic things to my asthmatic breathing.

"That's not exactly what I meant," he murmured, a rosy blush crawling up his cheeks that made him look nervous, which was sort of irresistible. "I was referencing the *Odyssey*. You know, where Odysseus has his shipmates stuff their ears with beeswax and then has them tie him to the mast as they pass by the singing Sirens?" His finger rested by my earlobe. I didn't know why it was still there. "I'm not sure why I said the bed. There is probably something else in our room you could tie me to." His hand dropped. "Damn, that doesn't sound any better, either."

I laughed quietly and covered my mouth, but Torin pulled my hand back the second I did so, almost frustrated by the unintentional act.

"Don't do that," he said in a soft, hushed voice. "Don't cover up something so beautiful."

I pressed into the elevator wall, my hands wrapping around the gold bar to provide some semblance of stability. I had every intention of leaving what happened between us in the dressing room there and not carrying it with me up to our hotel floor. But it wasn't just those moments that I had to avoid; it was the moments that made me want to trade in everything I ever thought I needed in my life for something as uncertain as this. *Someone* as uncertain as Torin. "Who *are* you?"

"Honestly?" Torin's brow creased tightly and his eyes were almost hidden in the shadow it created. "I'm still trying to figure that out."

"Really?" His swift, unexpected answer surprised me. "Because you say things with such confidence, like you're absolutely sure of yourself."

Torin slid against the wall next to me, his head hanging low, his blond hair tumbling into his eyes. I really wanted to cut it, but I was beginning to think that was due to the fact that it would give me an excuse to run my fingers through the golden strands.

He continued, "The things I've already discovered about life I'm absolutely sure of, you're right. Like family and faith. But the other things—the things that I'm still figuring out about myself— they're not so concrete." Torin suddenly flipped around in front of me, his hands bracketing me on either side with intense control. "Like trying to figure out what to do with the fact that I'm pretty sure I'm falling for a girl who is probably going to end up with someone else." His eyes roved over me and fastened on my mouth, like he was contemplating kissing me again.

I'd kissed Lance literally thousands of times, and I was even up to two shameful kisses with Torin, but the anticipation of kissing Torin again and the way his eyes looked at my lips like he wanted to eat them couldn't compare to any of that. Even if every kiss I'd ever experienced were added together, the weight in this moment would be more than those combined, more than all the kisses I'd ever experienced. Maybe even more than all of eternity's kisses piled together. I didn't think there was ever a moment in history more charged with tension and anticipation than this, because I was certain no one else could survive it. I was surprised *I* was able to. Maybe I did learn a thing or two on that overnighter.

Torin leaned in, his forehead pressed to mine, and I tried not to groan into his open mouth, but it was impossible to keep the sound in. The tips of our noses touched first, lightly, then his hand lifted to my jaw and his thumb ran circles across my chin. He tilted my head up so our lips were an inch apart, lined up, and ready for the other. His breath was warm and sweet and fell on my mouth with light pressure, like a tempting hint at how his lips would feel and taste, too. "Tell me what I'm supposed to do with that. With the fact that you're like this damn mirage and every time I think I'm about to get close to you—about to realize my dream of you—it evaporates and I'm left completely deserted."

My head twitched and I licked my lips nervously. I shouldn't have done that, because it ignited a fire in his eyes and faltered his breathing. "I don't know."

Just as suddenly as Torin stopped the elevator moments before, he pushed off from the wall with one hand and turned toward the doors. Punching a button again with his finger, he said over his shoulder, "And that's a problem, because neither do I."

. . . .

"I'm going to read your book while you shower."

I could hear his voice through the crack in the door, yet the rain of water from the high-pressure showerhead mostly drowned it out. Though I didn't normally leave bathroom doors open—even if only a sliver of an inch—while a boy who I may or may not be falling for sat on the opposite side, Torin managed to convince me. He'd had three bottles of water to drink that afternoon and what if he had to pee while I was showering and primping for the gala? What was he supposed to do? Could I, with a transparently clear conscience, put his bladder through something as traumatizing as that? He wasn't a camel, after all, and couldn't store water for very long. Apparently, I was cruel to think otherwise.

I figured the real reason was that the sounds of me showering only added to the reality that I was naked on the other side, soaping myself up, just a half-closed door barricading the space between us. I wasn't quite sure what I'd do if he actually did have to pee. I had three brothers, yes, but nothing about Torin felt like a brother, and I didn't want to get to know him on that level. The sound of him peeing wasn't something I really hoped to become familiar with.

I ran my fingers through my hair, plopping a dollop of the hotel's shampoo into the palm of my hand. It smelled like lemon and vanilla, and reminded me of a martini my mom used to make. She often drank, and every time she mixed something up, it was a fruity concoction and she'd let me have a shot glass full of my own.

But that hadn't always been the case, and it struck me as odd how things could change so quickly. How just one event, one of life's many circumstances, could change the way you viewed moral issues like giving your underage children alcohol. I guess you picked your battles. I wasn't even sure my mom was strong enough to fight at all anymore.

Tilting my head back, I let the water massage the shampoo out of my hair and run down my backside, pooling into a bubbly froth around my feet. Everything had felt so fuzzy and I'd hoped the shower would bring some clarity. Like I could wash away the feelings I knew I had for Torin; like I could cleanse myself of the cheating I'd done, even if Torin didn't agree with that label.

I was so immersed in my detoxification that I didn't hear the creak of the door, and didn't sense Torin on the other side of the shower curtain, until his voice breached the quiet and nearly sent me slamming into the tiled wall, as if being woken from a deep slumber by the shrill, sudden blast of an alarm clock.

"Darby. Is that picture of her?"

I didn't answer, but knew exactly what he meant.

"Because at first I thought it was you."

With my right hand, I twisted the knob on the faucet to the left, the scalding water leaving piercing beads of heat across my skin. It hurt, and I bit down on my lip to endure the pain. I'd become a master at that—at replacing one pain with another. Usually, it was the empty growl that eroded my stomach that I preferred. That was my go-to. For now, I'd settle for the burn.

"Darby, can you get out of the shower and talk to me?" He thrust a white, fluffy towel into the gap between the curtain and the wall. "It's time you talked about this."

"I don't know if I can, Torin." I grabbed the towel from his grip, but didn't dry off. I held it to my face, the bleached cotton billows enveloping my small yelp of a cry that I knew he could hear. Even above the water. Even through the towel. He heard me.

"Darby, please. Please talk to me."

I didn't talk. I just cried, and I hated how weak it made me sound, because I didn't like crying, and honestly, I didn't do much of it anymore.

"I'm coming in there with you, Darby," he warned, and I didn't doubt for one second that he wouldn't. I'd learned that Torin was both a man of action and a man of his word. If he said he was going to do something, then it was a certain fact that he'd do it.

Taking the towel from my face, I twisted it around my body, securing it under my collarbone above my chest. The shower curtain rings slid on the rail, and just like in the dressing room, Torin's hand pushed the curtain back all the way. With his clothes still on, he stepped into the shower, wrapping his arms around me from behind, tucking his chin onto my shoulder. The way he held me and let me face the water so I could at least pretend to camouflage my tears in the streams that trickled down made me feel anything but weak, and I was grateful for it, and in awe of the sensitivity of this guy who I'd only known a few weeks.

"Are you ready to tell me about her?" he asked again, his question taking on the form of gentle pleading. "Because your tears tell their own story, but I want your words, too, Darby."

His shirt clung to my back, to the bare skin above my towel, and his breath fell softly against my neck. It should have struck me as weird—there we were, Torin fully clothed and me with only a terry cloth wrap covering my bare body—but nothing about it felt weird, or even remotely wrong. I'd kissed him and that felt all kinds of inappropriate, but standing together in the shower—that was right. At least, in that moment it was right.

"Do you want me to tell you my story first?" When his mouth moved with the words, his chin pressed in and out of my shoulder, and he didn't lessen the grip he had around me, but pulled me tighter.

I nodded.

"I was the one who found him," Torin started. "It was in between camps. I had been gone all day cleaning the dining commons—that was sorta my task, and I liked doing it. Mom said I was good at it, but I think that just meant she didn't want to do it. Whatever. I felt useful, so I didn't mind. I mean, honestly, how well could a twelve-year-old kid clean an industrial-sized kitchen and a two-thousand-square-foot eating area?" The question was rhetorical, so I just listened and let him continue. "I'd always figured Dad went back in after me to do the real deep cleaning, because they totally would have shut down our camp if we operated it the way I'd left things. But that day I saw him sweeping up after I'd finished up, and for some reason, it totally pissed me off. Like I wasn't responsible enough to handle a real job. Like I was just going through the motions and still needed Mommy and Daddy to come to my rescue and clean up my mess."

The towel around me began to sag, laden with the water that continued to flow from the showerhead. Torin twisted his arms tighter to keep it in place—not what a typical nineteen-year-old boy would do, but Torin wasn't typical. We'd established that from the get-go.

"I went back to our cabin and Randy was there, dangling from the exposed beam in the ceiling. And, God, he'd used my belt, Darby. *My belt.* He couldn't have used his own damn belt?"

I turned my head slowly, angling into his to offer some sort of comfort, but I doubted it helped much. Gestures like that had never helped me much.

"You hear these stories where someone is charged with a crime because they left their gun out without a lock on it and someone else fired it. Didn't matter that the owner had nothing to do with the actual incident. That's how I felt. Like somehow leaving my stupid belt lying around was the same as handing Randy a loaded gun. 'Here you go, bro. Feel free to take your life with this thing that I use to keep my pants from falling off my ass.'"

"Torin—"

"The worst part?" he continued as though he hadn't heard me interject. Maybe he hadn't. "He left me the letter. Like, addressed to me and all. As if I didn't already feel responsible enough, now I had to be the one to share his suicide note with our parents. And you know what it said?"

I shook my head.

"That he decided to clean up his mess so Mom and Dad didn't have to. The irony wasn't lost on me, Darby. That just moments earlier I'd been so angry that my dad was literally cleaning up after me. Stupid worries of a twelve-year-old. And here was my brother, literally terminating his own existence, like that would clean up the 'mess' he'd made. He'd slept with some camper and apparently she was saying he'd raped her. She was going to go to the police with it. Press charges. Threaten to shut down the camp. So instead of telling anyone, he just killed himself. Like that was the best option? Like it would clean up his 'mess'? No, it just created an entirely new one. One *we* had to live out, not him."

As he spoke, Torin reached around me to twist the faucet off. My body went instantly cold as the towel hugged my skin, water collecting at the hem of the cotton, trickling down my legs. I turned around to face him, and he drew me in to his chest, his fingers tangling in my knotted wet hair.

"I saw her picture in your book, Darby. I wasn't trying to snoop or anything. It just fell out when I opened it up," he confessed quickly. "I want to know everything about you, and she seems like a pretty big part." With his thumb and index finger, he pulled my chin up, and in that instant, the notion flickered through my brain that I might actually love him.

No one asked about Anna anymore. No one cared. Not even Lance. No—no one cared except for Torin. So in the hotel shower, wrapped in a towel, streaked with tears, I thought I loved him, because he tried to see me, he wanted to know me. Even if he was right, even if I was just a mirage to him, he tried so hard to make me real. And I needed to be real. More than he knew. "She was a redhead, and she had freckles, but she's not you. Is there a reason you are trying to be her?"

I shook my head like I was saying no, but I wasn't saying no to him. I was saying no to the past six years, to the life I had created, to the identity I'd stolen. He couldn't have been prepared for what I was about to say, because hell, I wasn't even prepared to utter it, but when the words tumbled from my lips, he didn't falter even slightly, almost as though he knew it was coming. As if he knew all along.

"She was my sister. She's dead. And she's sorta the reason I've stayed with Lance."

Chapter 17

Reporters had been camped out in front of our house for three weeks. But once her body was found, all of that disappeared—the media, the spotlight . . . Anna's memory. The case went on for over two years, but it didn't bring me any comfort in hearing the final verdict. Of course he was guilty. He'd kidnapped, assaulted, and killed three other girls before Anna. The mountain of evidence was stacked so high against him that he could have suffocated under the crushing weight of it. Too bad he didn't.

"She ran to the store two blocks away to grab some poster board she needed for her history project." We stared up above us, both of our ankles crossed, our hands stacked on top of one another behind our heads like we were looking up at the stars rather than a hotel room ceiling. I focused on the intricate molding around the fan, how the wood coiled and twisted on the circular medallion ornamenting it. My hair was still damp from the shower, but the pillow soaked up much of the moisture. "Dad would have driven her, but he was at my brother's soccer game."

Torin nodded and the mattress jolted a bit underneath us.

"But we did that—fended for ourselves. There were a lot of kids in my family, so we learned to be self-sufficient. We also learned to look out for one another. Anna and I always did. You're not supposed to have a favorite sister. But she was my favorite. Hands down, Anna was my favorite."

Because I was sure he sensed I needed it, Torin slipped his arm out and slid it under my shoulders, so that his hand and fingers curled around to the other side.

"Anna asked me to leave the porch light on, and I totally forgot. Lance had called her to ask about the project—mistaking my voice for hers at first—and I got stuck on the phone with him. We talked for two hours—all the way into dark—and I didn't think about her once. I forgot to leave the light on and I didn't even realize she was missing until my parents woke me up in the middle of the night. She never made it home."

My lips didn't tremble, my breathing didn't change. Because it wasn't like this was some emotional confession. These were the facts. The irrefutable facts about the night my sister died.

"You weren't supposed to be her lighthouse, Darby. It wasn't your responsibility to keep her safe."

"I'm not saying—"

"You think I don't see that? That you think it was your fault?" The bed dipped as he rolled onto his side. His green eyes were wide—huge—and he faced me like he wanted me to look into them. Like somehow he could shake me out of this with just his stare. But I'd been trapped for six long years, and it would take more than a convincingly warm look to pull me out. I loved him for what he was trying to do, but the reality was that not much else could be done. "This was not your fault. Forgetting to leave the light on was not your fault."

"She didn't know her way home. We'd just moved to the peninsula. What if she'd wandered all those hours trying to find her way back in the dark?" I fired my responses at him because these, too, were facts. "She was last seen two miles away from home."

He shook his head hard, like he was angry, but not with me. Maybe with the situation. Maybe with the facts. Whatever it was, the emotion it drew out of him made me feel less alone, because no one had experienced my story for quite some time, and I liked Torin being a part of it, even if it was a terribly depressing, hopeless story.

"The porch light was not your fault," he said.

"The belt was not your fault," I replied.

Silence, minutes of it, fell around us like flakes of snow, drifting down, coating us with a chilling cold that drew up the fine hairs on my skin. Torin used his arm underneath me to roll me up onto his chest, and I locked my fingers together behind his back, his heart sandwiched against my ear. I listened to it—listened to the way it kept a metronomic beat—and in that moment, it felt like it belonged to me. And when I felt my own beats slow to match the consistent rhythm of his, it felt like it became a part of me, too.

Lance always said I had his heart. But I didn't anymore. That was just something he began reciting when we were young, but it was nothing I'd felt recently. You couldn't just declare something like that and have it stay true forever, especially when he'd given pieces of it to others along the way.

There was more to love than words. A relationship had a pulse, a pattern, like the heartbeats recorded and written on an EKG—ups and downs, but consistencies nonetheless. Falling out of that pattern, that was when things got dangerous. The flat line was the killer, and my relationship with Lance had already died many deaths.

What I'd recently found to be true was the idea that giving away your heart was a steady process, one that occurred gradually until all the beats morphed together. My beats. Torin's beats. They were suddenly the same percussion ramming inside our beings. And so was our guilt. And so—I'd also discovered—were our stories.

"She'd said once that she would give anything for the chance to date a guy like Lance. All through junior high, he was all she ever talked about. 'Anna plus Lance' in big, puffy cursive all over her notebooks and inside her locker." Torin craned his neck up to look at me as I spoke, his eyes straining against the dark to meet mine. "And he'd called for her that night. After two years, he finally noticed her."

"So you fell in love with him as what? Some type of tribute to her?"

"I fell in love with him because he was there for me at a time when I needed love. And Anna never had the chance to fall in love. I guess I wanted to experience that for her."

Torin's heart picked up speed, and for a moment, we were out of sync.

"You can't live someone else's life, Darby," he said in a hushed whisper.

"I owed it to her."

"You are not Anna."

"I know—"

"But you *don't*," he interrupted, placing a lot of emphasis on that last word. "Because if you did, things would be completely different. You wouldn't be stuck in this emotionally stunted realm where your sister's life ended. You wouldn't have dated a guy that couldn't be any more wrong for you—like, seriously, Darby, *he's all wrong*. And you wouldn't be trying to keep her memory alive by making up some sordid alternate ending to her story," Torin said, lifting up off the bed to sit. He'd changed into dry clothes just as ratty and worn as before: a pair of flannel pajama pants and a navy-blue shirt that read *I Survived the Summit* across the front. I joined him, cross-legged, face to face, no longer heart to heart. "Her story—however tragic—ended that night. Randy's ended at the cabin. That was it for them. They are done. End game."

"But she's still a part of mine. Even if she's gone—she's still a part of mine, Torin. She's still a part of me."

"Of course she is, but she's not *it*, Darby. You are your own person. Honestly, it's a little creepy to think that you could take over her existence."

"I didn't start off trying to do that—I just wanted to keep her memory alive. I joined the basketball team just like she had. I listened to the same music she did. I felt close to her when I was doing the things she loved, you know? Don't you get that?"

"Completely. But did you ever begin to love those things on your own? Like, apart from loving the idea that she loved them?"

I didn't answer.

"Being with Lance made you feel close to Anna." Torin sighed. He raked his hands through his hair, like saying the statement was exasperating and he had to slough off some of that exhaustion.

"But being with you makes me feel close to *me*."

Eyes flashing, Torin's head snapped up with such force that it had to have hurt his neck, even just a little. He paused deliberately and then said with an apologetic tone fastened to his voice, "He broke up with you, Darby."

"What?" I'd busied myself with the mindless task of picking my nails, but my hands fell to my lap as soon as he spoke. "What? When did . . . ?"

"Lance broke up with you," Torin continued, pressing up onto his knees. "You'd gotten mail from him before, back at Summit, back in the office. There were a few letters." My mouth was dry. My tongue felt like it ripped against the inside of it as I forced a swallow. "I kept them from you because keeping Lance from you felt like the best thing to do at the time."

The hotel room blurred around me like the dressing room's Tilt-A-Whirl antics from earlier. These rooms and their spinning axes . . . I needed everything to slow down and lock back into place.

"I realize now that was wrong, I do—"

"Yes, because stealing someone's mail is illegal in nearly every state, I'm fairly certain—" I had to search for the humor in this.

"But stealing someone's girlfriend," he interrupted, "though maybe not illegal, holds a certain moral debasement that—turns out—I'm not entirely too concerned with."

I shook my head and a clump of wet hair stuck to my cheek. "What does that even mean, Torin? The letters—when did they come? What did they say?"

Hearing that my long-term relationship had supposedly ended in the form of a Dear John should have shocked me. At the very least, it should have produced a tear or two, some slight mourning over the unexpected loss. But the only thing that coursed through me was relief. Like someone had pardoned a life sentence. Like I'd done my duty. I finally felt free.

"It came the first week." *Wow.* Lance hadn't wasted any time. "It said that maybe this time apart was a good opportunity to 'find himself.'" Air quotes.

"And?"

"And by letter two, someone named Clara helped him do just that."

I wanted to be angry that there was yet another girl involved in whatever this was that Lance thought he needed, but all I could focus on was the sophisticated sound of her name. Clara. A beautiful name—one that fit the McIverson facade so absolutely perfectly. It was like that name had been created and reserved just for their family's use. Clara and Lance. It rolled off the tongue with a royal intonation.

Darby and Torin. Honest to God, we sounded like a pair of leprechauns.

"So why did he invite me here?" The text at the airport suddenly made sense. *I'm really glad you* still *wanted to see me.* Because had I actually received those letters, chances are I wouldn't have. Oh my word, I looked like a total, ignorant fool. "If he wanted things to be over, why invite me here?"

"The last letter I commandeered . . ." He seriously just said *commandeered.* I smirked. "Said something about a huge mistake. That he knew he'd called things off, but his parents loved you. He loved you. You know, that common, sentimental 'I've just given up the love of my life and I'll do anything to get her back' crap. It was honestly a steaming load of shit, if you ask me— vomit-inducing material. I didn't bother showing you that one, either, because I respect you and your stomach too much. You hardly eat—what little you do choke down, you should be allowed to keep there."

"So you kept it from me," I began, grateful for the lighthearted turn our conversation took. Lighthearted, I supposed, in contrast to our earlier dead-sibling discussions, because the termination of a six-year relationship didn't feel altogether lighthearted when I really considered it. "You kept Lance's letters from me because you were worried about me maintaining a reasonable weight."

"It was purely a health concern."

"Then in that case, I forgive you." I smiled at him, grinning a little and slivering my eyes the way I did when I attempted to flirt, for reasons unknown. "Had you kept this life-altering information from me for your own selfish gain, then I might have to deliberate a bit longer." I smirked again and Torin returned it instantly. "But what you did sounds absolutely selfless, so I think I should actually be thanking you."

"I know you're joking," he began, slipping back down onto the mattress, propping his hands behind his head, "but I know a part of you is mad at me for it. You should be. In fact, I demand that you be."

"Why would you demand that?" I bit at my thumbnail, pulling it back and forth between my teeth until a small piece of it broke off. I spit it over the side of the bed and pushed my thumb back in my mouth again.

"I want to be that finger of yours, Darby."

"What?" I yanked my finger out quickly, totally embarrassed.

"Was that out loud?"

"Yes," I said with a laugh. "Yes, it was."

"I love you." Torin closed his eyes. "Was that out loud, too?"

"Is there an issue with your hearing?" I couldn't think of what else to say, though I knew in most instances an "I love you, too" was the appropriate response.

"The issue lies not in my hearing," he explained, sounding once again like some ancient thinker. "The issue lies in my censor. As in, I don't have one when it comes to you, Darby." Again, he pulled at his hair with frustrated fingers. "I do things like fly all the way across the country to be with you, join you in the shower fully clothed, and admit to loving you after we've just discussed the death of siblings and relationships." His eyes were still held shut. "There is no censor. Not when it comes to you."

I pressed my thumb back to my lips, mostly just to see what it did to Torin when he opened his eyes and glimpsed me. I liked what I saw. "What is my official status with Lance?"

"He broke up with you. He wants you back. But as far as I can tell from the letters, and from his behavior at the airport, he still thinks you're broken up. I foresee some serious attempts at wooing over the next couple of days. Be prepared to be smothered with roses, chocolates, and poorly written poems. But yes, you guys are broken up."

I nodded, satisfied with that answer. "That's a relief. I'm not fond of red capital letters on my clothing."

"Huh?" It took him a minute to process, but he got it. "You're not a cheater. Honestly, Darby, the whole time you were at camp, you were technically single. And I'm the one who kissed you."

"I'm not talking about the plane. I'm talking about the night in the sleeping bag."

His eyes narrowed. "What about it?"

"You don't remember?" I asked, knowing full well that he didn't, but holding out hope that somehow what we'd experienced transcended his state of unconsciousness. "Like, you seriously don't know?"

He shook his head, hesitantly. "No, I don't, but sounds like I might have missed out on something pretty monumental. Why don't you remind me? And I'm all for reenactments if you happen to want to test out your acting chops."

"No joke, your censor's MIA."

"I just admitted to loving you and I want to make out with you, Darby. What's so wrong with that?" His eyes crinkled playfully around the corners and his lips tipped up, making me really want to feel them on mine.

"Why do you think you love me?"

"Why does anyone think they love anything?" he asked, squinting past me. I almost wanted to move to the left a little bit to position myself in his line of sight.

"Why are you answering a question with a question?"

"Why are you answering my question with a double question?" I opened my mouth to reply, but he continued before the sentence could work its way out. "We can talk in circles if you want, with our questions to the nth degree, or we can make out. I'm a guy. I opt for making out."

"I just really want to know why you think you love me," I said. "That's a statement, not a question. See how I did that?"

"I love you because, as far as I can tell, I'm the first person you've ever felt safe enough around to just be *you*," he said. "That's an incredible honor, and so, it is also an incredible honor to get to love you for that. I told you I get attached easily, Darby, and you've made it beyond easy for me to not only get attached to you, but to wholeheartedly love you." He rolled onto his side. "You gave me a gift: the real you. I'm giving you a gift: my heart."

And that, I realized as I stared at this philosophical, complicated boy draped across my hotel bed, was exactly how love was supposed to be done. After six years of searching, it finally made sense.

Chapter 18

We didn't make out. Which was a bummer to say the least, because making out with Torin could quite possibly have been the best way to commence this new chapter of my life.

Instead, Lance, a character that—in my mind—had already exited the scene, showed up for an encore performance. He'd knocked loudly on our hotel door three times, and when I answered, the plastic white bag that fluttered between us obscured my vision. When he lowered it and my eyes locked with his, I realized Torin's analogy was way off.

Life was not a book.

It was not made up of chapters and we did not get to write them. How ridiculous to think that we could end one part, tie it up in a neat little bow with perfect shifts and transitions, and then move on to another section. For as often as he joked that I was crazy, the more I thought about it, the more he earned that title.

Life wasn't scripted—he'd said it himself. If it were, Lance wouldn't be standing in the threshold of my hotel room. I would have found my happily ever after with Torin. I could have edited out the parts that I didn't like. But you couldn't do that. How stupid to think that we had any control over any of it. If it was any book at all, it wasn't our own to write.

"I bought this for you." Lance thrust his hand into the room, the hanger jutting toward me. "For the gala tonight."

Over my shoulder, I heard Torin whisper, "Wooing attempt number one." Luckily, Lance was oblivious, which I realized was a good word to describe him as he pressed his way into the room and took up residence on the fold-out couch. He was an unsuspecting, oblivious man who assumed Torin was gay, that we were still broken up, and that somehow—beyond all reason—we'd end up back together. Just like we always did.

Lance didn't look at all at ease as his legs jumped up and down and his hands wrung, one over the other, twisting skin in a violent manner. His shifty gaze also made him look a little maniacal, which was alarming because he'd mastered the cool, collected thing long ago. He still appeared a polished politician, just one who was in some serious hot water. "Just so you know, Clara will be there."

"Oh." In that moment I was so grateful for all that had just transpired between Torin and me, because had it not, I'd have no clue who Clara even was. It was nice to be able to save a little face. "Okay."

"There's nothing going on between us now, Darby."

"Okay." I said it again because that's what it was. It was all finally okay.

I saw Lance's jaw tighten like it was almost wired shut, and when he opened his mouth, I was surprised the words even fit through the small space. "She thinks she's pregnant."

"Hold the phone," Torin, who had been silent up until that point, blurted into our tennis game–style conversation. "You got Clara pregnant?"

Lance's eyes narrowed. "Can Darby and I have some privacy?" He cocked his chin swiftly, indicating the door.

"No."

I tried to stifle a nervous laugh, but I failed to keep it contained. Torin obviously wasn't aware of the well-established fact that no one ever told Lance no. Ever.

Like he could somehow move Torin's body with his eyes alone, Lance drilled an impressively intimidating stare in his direction. But Torin didn't budge, not even to flick away the lock of hair that had slipped to his brow. Though much less menacing, Torin could hold his own, and I thought for a moment I might have even seen a slight cower in Lance's frame.

"You're sort of a bastard, you know that?"

I figured it wouldn't be long before Lance would rise from his position on the couch, because no one talked down to him, physically or figuratively. And right now, Torin was doing both. I found myself starting to worry about that really nice jaw of his, because I was fairly sure if he kept it up, it would become acquainted with Lance's fist at any moment.

Lance sprung to his feet.

"Excuse me?"

He took two measured strides toward Torin. I slunk into the wall that divided the suite into two rooms, pressing my back against an oil painting that hung there, wishing I could be swallowed up in the serene landscape drawn onto the canvas.

"I said you're sort of a bastard," Torin reiterated. "But I take that back."

Lance nodded knowingly. "Then you're a wise man—"

"Because you're a *complete* bastard."

"She's pregnant?" I uttered through a hand cupped over my mouth. He'd said it several minutes ago, but it was as though the words took their time traveling through the air and space to get to me because they were so heavy, so much weightier than any of the other words he'd ever spoken. They took even longer to register in my brain. "You got some random girl pregnant?"

"She's not a random girl," Lance quickly defended, but it wasn't the defense I was hoping for. "I wasn't the one who got her pregnant" or "It's not my baby" would have been nicer to hear. Not the confirmation that wasn't quite a yes or a no, but every bit as definitive. "She's Congressman Reynold's daughter."

I almost threw up. "You slept with your boss's daughter?" The words spewed out of me like verbal vomit.

"I don't know much about politics, but I'm pretty certain knocking up the boss man's daughter must be considered a conflict of interest."

"Why are you still here?" Lance growled, whipping his head around. His chest puffed up like he was collecting all of his anger, ready to hurl it forth in one irate outburst. "Why the hell are you here at all?"

Torin crossed his arms over his body, an air of condescension seeping through his mannerisms. "I'm Darby's plus one for the gala."

"No," Lance breathed hotly. "*I'm* her plus one. That position has been taken."

"Buddy." Torin outstretched an arm to rest his hand on Lance's broad shoulder. The smirk he added was a nice theatrical bonus, but one that would probably cost him greatly. "You already have a plus one. Actually, it sounds like maybe even a plus one and a half."

I should have expected it because everything was building up to this inevitable moment, but nothing could have prepared me for the sickening crack that was Torin's cheekbone nearly splitting in two as it collided with Lance's fury. All of that pent-up aggression was loaded and fired through his right hook, and Torin's face didn't stand a chance against the fist that catapulted toward him, narrowly missing his eye socket, striking the bone that stretched from his temple to his nose.

I thought for a moment that Torin was literally turning the other cheek when he tucked his chin to his left shoulder, wincing from the pain. But when Lance's body flew back several feet and his shoulders curled over as his spine arched out in my direction, I realized Torin's fist connecting with Lance's stomach proved he was the first to ever challenge Lance—because Lance wasn't prepared. He wasn't prepared for the retaliation in the form of a slug to his gut. And when he righted himself, shook off his surprise, and smirked at Torin, whose face was bloodied and already starting to bruise, the look he held—the look of disbelief and arrogance smugly mixed together—made me despise him.

Because I think I did. At least I felt like I had to. I had to feel something toward him because it wasn't appropriate to feel nothing. After all these years, I had to feel something. But the reason I was feeling—the reason I wasn't just completely numb anymore—was because he'd hurt Torin.

Yes, he'd hurt me, but I could handle that. He'd cheated (again). He might have gotten some girl pregnant (again). That should have devastated me. But it didn't, because it didn't feel like he was actually doing any of that to *me*. The girl who had been in that relationship with him wasn't me anymore—she wasn't Anna, either, I knew that much.

As Lance stared at Torin's face, instead of looking like a proud fighter who had significantly marred the physical appearance of his opponent, he looked horrified. He lifted a hand to his own cheek and cupped it in his palm. "All right," he said, stepping back from Torin, who had a look in his eyes like he wasn't about to give up. If anything, it looked like he was readying for the next round. "Let's be men about this."

Torin took a breath and Lance flinched, and I suddenly realized the real reason for his abrupt stop. Torin looked like hell. Like, he literally looked as though his face was split in two with a dull carving knife, and the blood that leaked out of it stained his hands and shirt. And Lance, though he'd sustained a punch to his stomach, was unblemished. He had stopped fighting, not because he cared about protecting his ego, but because he cared about protecting his face. In true McIverson form, Lance was keeping up appearances, even in the heat of battle. He was a coward—but remained a beautiful, twisted coward—one who couldn't physically be linked back to this altercation at all.

But there was one thing that he was still linked to.

"She thinks she's pregnant?" I said it again, and I realized I sounded like one of those windup dolls, because nothing out of my mouth was new. It was all on repeat.

Lance's blue eyes softened slightly, like remorse was pulling at their corners just enough to provide a hint of transparency. He truly did wear the look of regret. "Oh my God, Darby. I'm so sorry." He reached out for me, but I pressed into the wall even harder, though there was nowhere else to go. "You have to understand how sorry I am."

"I understand."

His head snapped up like a rubber band. "You do?"

"We weren't enough."

"Darby—" Torin called out from his corner of the room. He had his hand on his face, and blood coated it as though he'd been finger-painting with only red paint. Though Lance's eyes appeared mildly expressive, Torin's were completely readable. "Stop, Darby."

"No, I get it." I shook off Torin's attempts to come to my defense. "We never were. I don't know who I was kidding. . . . I'm not right for you and the life you want to lead."

"Darby, you're everything—"

"No," I reiterated, "I'm not. I wasn't the right person to pick up the phone that night. I wasn't the one you were supposed to fall in love with. It never should have been me. The fact that there have been all of these other girls over the years should have been proof of that. You've always been searching for something more, because we weren't enough."

Lance finally looked like he'd been slapped in the face, and the way he drew his chin back made me realize he felt the impact of my statement as much as I felt the weight of it as it fell from my lips. "Is this about Anna?"

"It's always been about Anna."

His brow strained painfully. "We were kids, Darby. *Kids.*"

"And what are we now? Because I don't feel like an adult. But I don't feel like a child, either. I'm stuck in some weird in-between and I don't know how to get out." I breathed in deeply through my nose, feeling the air finger out into my lungs. "And I think I've spent too long hoping you were going to be the one to pull me out. Like, I could cling to you and somehow be able to move forward with you because you seemed to have a path you were on." I swallowed and pinched my eyes together, not wanting to cry. Lance would interpret that one way; everything was always about him. But these tears that pressed the back of my eyes—they weren't for him. They were for me. He could never understand that.

"But you didn't help me move forward," I continued. Torin sat down on the couch, his elbows digging into his knees, his head in his hands.

Lance's mouth hung open, like somehow it helped him process the words. "I don't understand."

"Of course you don't. Because it's not about you. It's about me. And you don't know me."

"But I do." Lance's tone took on a pleading. He walked the path across the room to get to me and placed his hands on my hips, pulling me to him. Torin kept his head in his hands and I was grateful because I didn't want him to see this. Even though there was nothing intimate in it, I didn't want him to see Lance with his hands on me. It would provide a visual, and I didn't want him to have that image to build upon. "I know how you hit the snooze button three times every morning before finally rolling out of bed. I know that you like one packet of sugar and two spoonfuls of honey in your tea. I know that you like sleeping with the window open at night but hate what the salty air does to your hair. I know that you want to have two kids—a boy and a girl—and you want to name them Jacob and Abigail. I know you, Darby. You can't tell me that I don't."

Torin didn't lift his head, didn't even make eye contact with either of us, but his voice startled the silence and drew our attention when he said, "But did you know that she blames herself?" He finally looked up, his hands still fisted over his mouth, his eyes straining with anguish. "Did you know that she's carried a burden that wasn't hers for the past six years?" He shook his head. "And did you know that she's incredibly brave?" I felt the memory of the wind on my face high up on those ropes in the tree. "That she puts her fears aside to do what is asked of her? She doesn't like letting people down, most of all herself. But she's completely fine— to a terrible fault—with others letting her down. And she's had a lot of practice in that with you." Torin and Lance exchanged a heated glare. "Did you know that she has been living her life as some sort of guilty tribute to her sister? That she's *that* incredibly selfless that she would give up on her own dreams in order to keep Anna's memory alive—however crazy that made her? And do you know what you've done with that? You've completely hijacked her. You let her take on your own dreams, never once thinking she might have her own somewhere deep in there." Torin rose to his feet. His face was mottled with gashes and blood, but he was beautiful. In fact, he was stunning. "Because you didn't take the time to look. You didn't take the time to look for her."

Lance's jaw pulsed and I could hear his teeth grit together. He dropped my hands and twisted at the waist to face Torin in aggravatingly slow motion.

"I *looked* for her." Torin thrust his index finger into his own chest. His eyes welled. He pressed his finger in harder. "I found her."

My own tears spilled down my face so freely—so fast—that I couldn't sweep them away quickly enough. I was grateful Lance's back was to me, and even more grateful that Torin's eyes were locked with mine. That the "I love you" I'd failed to speak earlier was now pouring out of me so visibly. He said it back, too, not with words, but with the understanding expression cloaking his bruised face.

"This is ridiculous." The comeback was weak and empty, but I realized that's exactly what Lance was. I'd always thought he was this strong, larger-than-life figure. But life—I came to find out—was pretty damn large. It coiled and wove and spun its own story, threading together tales to create an intricate, confusing saga. We didn't get our own book. We were all part of the same infinite one. My story didn't exist apart from Lance's. His didn't exist apart from Clara's. And now she was a part of it all, and so on and so on. We weren't chapters. We weren't even sentences. My part in it was as insignificant as a letter on a page. I'd contributed to humanity, but not much. I wanted it to feel like more. I wanted my life to be worth reading.

"This is completely ridiculous," Lance said again.

"Maybe, but so is trading in someone as incredible as Darby for what? A one-night stand?"

"I didn't trade her. I've never traded her. I've just made a lot of mistakes in my past. I'm not proud of that." Lance ran his hand over his mouth, then ripped his fingers through his dark, gelled hair. "It wasn't like I meant to get Clara pregnant."

"Of course you didn't. But you might have. And now what? Do you honestly think you and Darby can go anywhere from here?"

My stomach rumbled, but not because I was hungry. Just empty, like always.

"She's not saying it's mine. If she really is pregnant. We have it all figured out," Lance retaliated, like it even mattered anymore. "My parents have talked to her parents. She has a boyfriend and he's agreed. It all works out fine. Everyone is fine with it."

"As in," Torin began to clarify, "you've paid off her boyfriend to keep his mouth shut and say it's his."

"Do you even know what this would do to my family?" Lance's voice boomed through the hotel room. "Do you have any clue how this could tarnish everything?"

"I think I have an idea."

"I don't think you do." Lance shook his head with a force that I could actually feel as the air whipped past me. "It would *ruin* us. It's a scandal that could take down everything my family has ever worked for. And Congressman Reynold's family. There is no choice but to do this. I have no choice."

"Wrong," Torin interjected like a buzzer. "You had a choice. You chose poorly. And now you're saying Darby is the one who doesn't have a choice. And now she's supposed to what? Just accept it and move on?"

"We have to. It's what needs to be done."

"To protect your family's name."

They still faced each other. I still slumped against the wall. "Everyone has a role to play in this, and I need her."

"You don't need her," Torin spat, angered by Lance's words. "You just need her compliance. That's completely different."

"I need Darby. I can't do this without her."

Torin nodded and thumbed his chin in that dimple. His cheek had started to swell, and it made his right eye smaller than the other as the scarlet inflammation crept up his face. "You can't pull off this lie without her, you're right."

"We can't live the life we've always dreamed about if we don't do it this way."

"I don't dream about us anymore."

Lance spun around so fast on his heel that he had to catch himself before he completed another rotation. I wanted to see hurt in his eyes because it would make what we had feel like it was worth something, but only anger came through.

"I don't dream about us anymore, Lance. I haven't for a while now." I was pretty certain I said the words, but they were so quiet even I had a hard time hearing them. "You are not part of my dreams."

"And what? Torin is?" Lance flicked a glance over his shoulder. His eyes slivered. "You're not actually gay, are you?"

"No," Torin said, "I'm not. And I'm pretty sure I'm in love with Darby. And I'm pretty certain she's in love with me." My head felt dizzy. My legs went all Jell-O. "And even if she isn't, it doesn't change things for me. Because unlike you," Torin continued, tilting his upper half into the space between the two of them, "I'm still capable of loving her even if she's not physically in my life. Even when she's not around. Even if she chooses you and only becomes a memory to me." Torin was talking to Lance, but his eyes didn't falter from mine. "Even if that was all I had, I would love that memory of her. She taught me how to do that—to love the memory of someone like it's a real thing." Torin swallowed quietly. His voice became even quieter. I knew he was talking about what I'd done with Anna, and it made me feel less crazy than I probably deserved to feel. "If that's what I was left with—with only our brief story—I would love that time when we were together with all I had. Because those memories are real and tangible to me, and if loving them was as close as I ever got to loving her again, that would be enough."

I shook my head in disbelief, in the disbelief that someone like Torin even existed in the world. And that somehow—by some intervention I could only consider divine—I'd been lucky enough to find him in a corner of mine.

"If Darby ends up with you, that's fine," Torin continued. "I can live with that because you won't be getting the same Darby I had. If she picks you, then she's gone again. And I'll know I'm the only one who ever got to *really* have her. And I'll hold on to that knowledge for the rest of my life and feel honored that I was that one person she briefly let in." Lance didn't say anything, but neither did I. We waited for Torin to finish, because his soliloquy had us both drawn. And I realized that out of all the words he'd ever spoken—both his own and the borrowed ones—these held the most truth for him. These held the most truth for me.

"But if she chooses me—she chooses herself." He shook his head and closed his eyes. "And, God, I hope that she does. I hope, for once, she chooses herself over everyone else."

There was no use fighting back the tears anymore. No use because it was a battle I wasn't strong enough to fight. I sniffed an ugly-cry sniff, shoving the heel of my hand against my nose to try to hold it back, but nothing worked. Every emotion I had for this boy came out of me with uncontrolled abandon.

"There was a time when Darby needed me and I was there for her. I need her now." Lance finally turned toward me, speaking these words to me rather than to me through Torin. "I *need* you, Darby."

Standing in front of two people who claimed to love you should make you feel, well . . . *loved*. But it didn't. Because I only felt it from Torin, and what I felt from Lance, though existing in a separate space than those feelings from Torin, pulled down on everything. It was like my reality was crashing around me and there I was, standing among the rubble. Lance had demolished it all, and Torin was trying to build it back up.

"I needed you once, too, Lance." I felt the sweat slipping down my back. Everything was hot. Stifling. I needed to get out of this building. I needed some air. "I honestly don't know what I would have done if you weren't there when everything happened with Anna." The tears had stopped, thank goodness. Those I had under control—at least when talking to Lance. "But I needed you because something I could have never expected— something I had no control over—happened. I needed you to help me navigate through it all." I tossed my hand skyward. "But this? This thing with Clara? This was not out of your control. You controlled every aspect of it, but I can't let you control me anymore. I can't let Anna, either. I have to take control. I have to do this for me."

"But there are other people involved in this, Darby. My parents? Oh, God, my parents. Do you have any idea what this will do to them if you don't go along?"

Lance started to pace, not in an orderly pattern, but one that zigzagged across the room with frantic motion. His breathing picked up speed, and so did his feet.

I caught his eyes as he strode toward me and swallowed before saying, "But do you have any idea what it will do to *me* if I do?"

After that, no one said another word.

Chapter 19

We didn't go to the gala, though I was pretty sure we didn't even have an actual invitation to go anymore. We really didn't have a reason to stay in D.C. at all. But Torin was there. To me, that felt like reason enough.

By the time Lance had left, I'd wondered if he would even make it before the festivities were over. But that wasn't my problem anymore. Lance needed practice in the art of truth telling. If anything, I'd given him another opportunity to perfect those very rusty skills.

It was late. The time indicated that to be the case, but the three-hour difference made it feel weird to be going to bed so early. Nine o'clock was really our six o'clock and that was more like dinnertime than bedtime. Even still, I slipped out of my clothes and into a spaghetti-strap tank top and flannel pants while Torin brushed his teeth in the adjoining bathroom.

I listened to the rhythm of the bristles scraping his teeth, the back and forth of a sound that felt intimate on some level. Because doing commonplace, routine things with someone held a certain sense of intimacy that wasn't at all sexual or sensual, just intimate. There was a difference. To know someone intimately was to experience these little, daily consistencies with them. And as insignificant as toothbrushing could be, it felt entirely significant.

"Ahhhh," he proclaimed as he propped open the door. He didn't have a shirt on; his pajama pants were slung low on his hips. "Minty fresh." His dimples pulled at his cheeks, though the one on the left was harder to see under the swollen flesh. "Want a taste?"

Yeah, I really did, but instead I just laughed it off, thinking it might be a joke, but realizing (and hoping) it probably wasn't.

"I'm starved." He yanked the room service binder off the nightstand and crashed down onto my bed. I really liked the sight of him on my bed, and liked what it did to my stomach. Instead of the hollow growl, a swarm of butterflies and a nest full of wasps filled the typically vacant space. "Let's order in, shall we?"

We talked over our options, noting room service practically cost the equivalent of our plane tickets home, and both of us settled on sharing a side of mac and cheese and bottled water. We had twenty minutes until our "meal" was scheduled to arrive. Torin flicked on the television, but neither of us actually watched it. That wasn't really the plan.

"I don't think that stellar toothbrushing of mine should go to waste," he blurted during a commercial break of *Jeopardy*. I'd been tucked under the cover of the sheet while he rested on top, so when he turned to face me he'd inadvertently pulled the fabric underneath him.

"Argh," I growled as the sheets formed a tourniquet around me.

"I'm sorry!" Torin laughed and tossed off the covers to join me. It felt like the sleeping bag again, but more intentional, because in this moment, he knew I was there with him. "Is that better?" He slipped down next to me, tugging the duvet up to our ears. I wasn't really cold, but being under the comforter with him made me understand why it was named that: *comforter*. Because that was the exact sensation I experienced. Overwhelming comfort with the boy who I'd just discovered I more than likely loved.

"My mouth really does taste amazing right now, Darby." He pulled at the fabric draped over us. I slid toward him an inch, and our legs pressed closer together. Fabric on fabric, with even more cloaked over us. "You should taste it for yourself."

"Oh, yeah?" I teased, and he moved forward. Our arms tangled. Skin on skin. Not much, but enough to change the way my heart thrummed inside my chest.

"Yes. And really, to get the full sensation, you're gonna have to use your tongue. It seriously is all Doublemint-status fresh up in here." Torin waved a hand over his mouth and smiled so widely, I worried for a moment the newly formed scab on his face would burst.

"This is how you want our first kiss to happen?" I asked, hesitant because it didn't feel romantic or spontaneous the way first kisses should. Though in reality, I supposed it wasn't a first kiss at all. A third, but the first one that we'd both intentionally desired. And the first one that was okay for us to have together. For all intents and purposes, we were about to have our first kiss. I started to freak out.

"This is how I want everything about you. Like this. Making the mundane monumental." He scooted closer. "Seriously. Everything you touch turns to gold, Darby."

"Ah, there it is," I said, nodding, poking at him beneath the covers.

"What?"

"Your plagiarizing. It's been a while, but I see you're back at it."

Torin shrugged indifferently. "So what? I like quotes."

"I like your originality," I countered, because I did. I liked when Torin was just Torin; when I knew the things he said came from somewhere deep inside him, not from some surface level of past memorization.

"It is as though a thousand little garden gnomes chewed up mint-flavored crystals and then blew them into my mouth. In Antarctica." I burst into laughter so loud, I thought the neighbor on the other side of the adjacent wall might report me to the front desk. "That was a Torin original. You like?"

"I love," I giggled, instinctively covering my mouth with my hand.

Torin stretched over and pulled it back, coiling his hand around mine, his warm knuckles squeezing between my fingers. "I told you not to cover that up. Plus, it makes it a little hard to do this when you do."

His lips pressed to mine first, then our chests pressed together. Skin on skin again, but more intense than earlier because, it turned out, there were definitely specific patches of skin that held more sensitivity than others, and when those met, the body responded in a much different way. There were parts that made other parts feel certain things. When our arms touched, the hairs on them stood on end. But now, when his shoulder pushed against mine and the swell of my chest depressed against the muscles of his chest, I felt it in parts of my body that usually didn't feel anything. Which, I realized, was insane because I'd felt all of Lance's body on all of mine before, countless times. Skin on skin with no barriers between us. But there always had been a barrier, one made of emotion and not fabric. And that, it turned out, was a thicker barrier than anything else.

The commitment to our kiss lessened when Torin pulled back slightly to say, "Is this okay?" His eyes searched mine for confirmation, flickering over them. "Is it okay if I kiss you, Darby?"

"Yes," I said, nodding quickly. "It's more than okay."

And it was, because for all the things that felt so wrong lately, this felt so unbelievably right.

He moved in.

So did I.

He shifted closer, bunching the sheet beneath us, pressing the entire length of his body to mine. From our chests to our toes, everything lined up.

I waited for it—waited for him to lessen the gap between our mouths, because at that point, those were the only things not touching—but he paused.

"This is not a distraction," he said, locking eyes with me, referencing the flight. "This is me saying I love you, in this way. I've said it with my words, and there are hundreds of other ways I want to say it to you, but right now, this is how I'm telling you."

And he did. So clearly, Torin told me he loved me.

Slowly, but not hesitantly, he pressed in. I felt his breath against my lips and it was warm and, admittedly, very minty. When his bottom lip actually did make contact with mine, it was also slow, deliberate. Like he was savoring every part of this experience. Like he didn't want to rush it at all, but take it all in via one-second increments.

Then his upper lip touched mine. Both of our lips on the other, our mouths completely connected. I don't think I moved them at all, partly because I was stunned by the way something so small could make my entire body feel the way it did, but also partly because I was waiting for him—waiting on Torin's next move.

Again, he moved with caution.

With pressure that didn't really feel like pressure at all, he traced his lips over mine, guiding them in a way that made me mimic each movement. Some game of Simon Says where our lips were the players and everything he did caused me to instinctively do the same. He pulled my bottom lip into his mouth; I pulled his upper into mine. He coaxed my lips apart and slid his tongue in; I waited until he withdrew his and trailed my own into his mouth.

It amazed me, but he was completely right: His movements were his "I love you," and my reciprocation was my "I love you" back. And it wasn't all lust filled or frantic or even too entirely sexual. But it was an exchanging of our unspoken words with our bodies in this way, for this moment. Maybe later it would be in another way, but this was how we chose to speak to one another now. I loved this language.

Torin pulled away to gather air, and when he drew his head back, his chest pressed even closer to mine. The heartbeats ticking under his skin were fast and fluttering. For as controlled as our kiss was, Torin's heart rate was entirely uncontrolled, bordering on tachycardic.

"This is what you do to me, Darby." Scooping up my free hand, he placed the flat palm of it onto his chest. "That kiss may have been my 'I love you,' but this is my, 'Holy crap, if that was just a kiss, sex might kill me.'"

A laugh shot out of me so fast that it sounded like a snort, which must have made me utterly unattractive, but Torin's mouth on mine again proved otherwise.

"You are too damn cute. I can hardly stand it." He dropped a kiss onto my nose.

"I hope you can. I don't want you not standing me."

"But I like not standing." His eyes squinted along with his smile. "I prefer not standing, actually."

I lifted my hand to his face and ran the pad of a finger over his injured cheek. It was that in-between stage where the scab wasn't quite a scab, but it wasn't a gaping, open wound, either. I pressed at it lightly and said, "I'm so sorry, Torin."

"Don't be. It wasn't your fault. Lance had every right to punch me. I pretty much stole his girlfriend."

"But that's not why he punched you. He didn't even know that at the time."

"Right, but I was fighting for you. It doesn't matter what it was over exactly—just that it was over you. I'd be gutted for you if that's what it took to make sure you didn't slip back into your shell again, Darby." I lifted up to place a kiss on his damaged cheek. "Plus, this is going to leave an incredibly manly scar. In reality, I should probably even thank him for it."

Torin propped himself up with his elbow, his fingers woven through his blond hair. "Lie on your back."

I questioned him with a cocked eyebrow.

"Just do it."

Obediently, I rolled over onto my back.

Torin left the bed for a moment, and when he returned, he was holding something between his fingers. "Close your eyes," he instructed. Again, I did as he said, still playing along in the game of Torin Says.

But I wasn't at all expecting him to straddle me. That completely caught me off guard, in a way that a clap of thunder catches you off guard. My entire body went rigid and my breathing matched my new posture: It was all hyperventilate-y, the kind of breathing that needed the assistance of a paper bag to get things back under control. That, or you just needed Torin saying, "Calm down," because when he did, it was like he had command over my synapses and my respiratory system. It slowed my mind and my breathing to a somewhat consistent pace.

"Keep your eyes closed. Sometimes it's much easier to see

with your eyes closed. And I want you to see me—with all of your senses."

I held my eyelids together tightly because if I didn't use a significant amount of pressure, they would flutter open, and that would be embarrassing because they really were very fluttery at the moment.

I felt him first as his fingers swept my hair away from my collarbone. Then I felt the goose bumps, thousands of them, that took the place where the hair once rested. Next it was his breath that hovered over my skin as I assumed he was looking at me. But I couldn't tell, I could only guess, could only read the cues that he chose to make known.

Torin shimmied his weight on top of me a bit as he lifted up onto his knees. I felt both of his hands bracketed around my shoulders as they pressed into the mattress. His head drew closer to mine. His mouth was at my ear. He left just one kiss there and pulled back up.

There were several seconds of silence and my mind tried to fill it with hundreds of different possibilities as to what he was doing. But he wasn't really *doing* anything, probably just thinking, and that felt more active than any of his actual actions.

Breaking into the silence, Torin drew in a quiet breath.

"It called out in the distance,
the caution silent, yet brilliantly illuminated.
The pierce of blinding hope in the dark,
among the turbulent ebb and flow of unstill waters.
Her light was always on,
though not all saw it.
The storm cloud, the rain, the gale swept through.
But they could not diminish what they tried to obscure.
She was there.
Even in the darkness, her light broke through."

My eyes fell open, though I saw through clouded vision as the tears filtered in. "Who wrote that, Torin?" I looked up at him in awe. "It's beautiful."

"You."

I tried to gulp back my emotion, but it was too hard to do. "I did not write that."

"You are my muse, Darby. You had every bit as much responsibility in writing that as I did."

I shook my head, unable to comprehend any of it, because it was so much. It didn't make sense that he could see that in me in such a short time. I never saw that in me. "Seriously, where did you come from?"

"I could ask the same of you," he said with a smile, then picked up a pen that he'd placed on the sheets. He pulled off the cap with his teeth and kept it there as he hovered the tip of the pen just under my collarbone. "I don't think it matters where either of us came from," he said around the cap still pinned between his teeth. "I think it just matters where we're going. And I want to go wherever that is with you."

"Me, too," I said in a murmur that was almost inaudible. The pen began to glide over my skin and Torin's brows tightened while he pressed it in and out as he wrote. I tried to keep my chest from rising and falling too fast and impeding his ability to work, but there wasn't much use in even trying. All of my nerves—all of my senses—were focused around the pinprick of the tip of the pen on my flesh.

Torin pulled back and replaced the cap. *"My Siren. My Lighthouse. My Muse."* He traced his finger over each word as he spoke. "You tempted me, you called me, you inspired me," he added, sliding back to my side on the bed. I rolled to face him and slipped my arms around him. "Since I'm getting this manly scar, I figured you could use a little ink."

I pulled at his hair and drew his mouth to mine. The slower kissing from earlier was apparently just a warm-up lap, because this time we definitely picked up speed. He didn't hold back and didn't ask permission again, because I'd already granted that, and truth be told, if he honestly wanted it, I'd give him an all-access pass.

Torin's tongue parted my lips and stroked into my mouth, trailing along mine, a back and forth of rhythm and reciprocation. His finger ran over my collarbone, from shoulder to shoulder, pausing in the shallow slope under my neck. He dipped his head and kissed lightly there, then just above the fabric where my neckline fell.

I let my hands wander over his chest, to his stomach and hips, feeling each muscle under my fingertips, memorizing what his body was like against my skin. I closed my eyes and he was right: I could see so much more of him, could sense so much more, with them closed. I relied solely on touch to guide me and it made me think maybe that was why it was human instinct to close your eyes when you kissed. Maybe it was the brain giving the body permission to take over the thinking. If that was the case, I really liked the things my body thought about Torin's.

"I want you," I breathed. Apparently, Torin wasn't the only one with the missing censor.

He didn't really answer me with a legitimate word, but more of a raspy growl that I understood the meaning of as clearly as any word in the English dictionary. Torin sucked my lips into his mouth, twisted his hands in my hair, and eliminated any gap that might have remained between our bodies as he pressed his weight fully onto me. We were all hands and sweat and racing pulses that frantically fought against our desire, keeping it at bay with just enough control to make sure we didn't rush things. But I wanted to rush. I wanted to tear through those hesitations full force.

Torin stopped me.

"Ugh," he moaned against my lips, shaking his mouth free of mine. He tossed his head back and forth briskly. "We have to stop."

I stopped because, just like all those other times he'd commanded me, the helpless tone in his voice let me know this was the most important time to actually listen to him.

"I'm sorry, Darby, but we have to stop."

"Okay." My voice was hoarse.

He whipped his head side to side. "Do you have any idea how hard this is?"

I was really tempted to turn that last statement into a mildly inappropriate innuendo, but I bit my tongue, even though I wanted him to be the one biting it.

"Seriously, Darby. It's like being given the winning lottery ticket, but not being allowed to cash it in." He smirked to himself, his green eyes twinkling. "No . . . more like finding a pot of gold at the end of the rainbow, but discovering it's fool's gold."

"That's not nice!" I punched him in the gut and all the air held within him burst out in one forceful gush.

"What?" His puppy-dog eyes innocently questioned me, and those lips of his tipped up at the corners in a totally enticing way that was all kinds of unfair given that he'd just put the kibosh on our make-out session.

"Fool's gold?" I widened my own eyes in disbelief. "That's like saying I'm not the real deal, Torin. You're comparing me to some major disappointment." The volume of my voice spiked. "I'd like to think I wouldn't disappoint."

"No," he began, laughing lightly. "I'm sure you wouldn't disappoint at all. I, however, would be a *huge* disappointment if we took things any further tonight. Like those rides at Disneyland that you totally hype up in your mind, wait in line an hour for, and then what? It's over in, like, sixty seconds and you hardly realize it has even started before it's finished." He laughed again.

I was really starting to love the sound of that laugh. "I do not want to be your monumentally disappointing ride."

"Oh, come on," I said, but it sounded more like begging than teasing. Torin rolled onto his back and ripped his hands through his hair. I could see his chest rising and falling out of the corner of my eye, his breathing gradually steadying. "Some of those rides are completely worth it." I stared back up at the ceiling. "Splash Mountain? That ride has, like, three pretty awesome dips in it before you get to the big one at the end. It's like four rides in one. *Totally* worth it."

"Oh, my God!" Torin threw his hands into the air. "You expect me to go that many times? Was Lance some kind of superhuman sex machine?"

"That's not what I meant!" I shouted, utterly mortified at the totally inappropriate comparisons that were being made between Disneyland rides and sexual encounters. "I just meant that the ride is worth the wait!" My cheeks had never been this hot in my entire life. "I swear that's all I meant."

"Oh, dear God. I hope so, woman!" Torin's voice cracked.

"I swear!" I said again, but this time the laughter that fell behind the words pushed through and I became nothing but a hysterical mess of uncontrolled giggles. "Seriously . . . I don't expect that much . . . honestly," I managed to get out through unreasonably loud fits of laughter.

"What?! You don't expect that much?" Torin dropped his hands to cover his eyes, mock shame cloaking his face. He turned his head toward me and grinned playfully. "Oh, I promise you, Darby, you can expect the ride of your life."

I was going to spontaneously combust.

"This is too much." I couldn't stop laughing. It was all kinds of laughter mixed together: nervous, giddy, excited, terrified. All the different ways one was capable of laughing wrapped into one irrepressible giggling bundle.

"I know, right?" Torin snorted right along with me, matching my laughter note for note. "You need to stop comparing my sexual capabilities to amusement park rides."

I rotated over to curl my body into Torin's side. He tucked me into the space under his arm and slid the covers up over us. "But it's the happiest place on earth," I defended coyly.

"No." Torin smoothed my hair with his hand and placed a feather-light kiss on my brow. "*This* is the happiest place on earth."

I pinched back a snort. "You mean, the *cheesiest* place on earth."

"That was pretty cheesy, wasn't it?"

"Um, yes. I hate to admit it, but it really was."

Torin's frame straightened. "Speaking of, where is that mac and cheese of ours?"

"Oh my goodness, you're all over the place!" I could hardly keep up with the conversation. "You're crazy!"

Torin rubbed his bare stomach in circles with the palm of his hand. "I'm hungry, which is probably close to the same thing." He dropped another kiss on my forehead like it was a totally routine gesture. I really hoped it would become one. "And I honestly can't be held responsible for anything I say when I'm hungry."

"Is that so?" I tipped the corner of my mouth up to challenge him.

"Yes, because I could say things like how I've wanted to kiss you since the first time I saw you—when you sat next to me at orientation back at camp." He pressed his cheek against my hair and breathed deeply, almost like he was inhaling me. "And I might admit to things like actually sneaking a peek at you when you changed into your swimsuit in the river during our overnighter."

With the hand wrapped around me, he skated his fingers up and down my arm. "I might also admit to really wanting to have sex with you just now, but being totally freaked out because you would be my first." His fingers stopped. "I might say things like that. You know . . . because I'm hungry."

"I completely get that." I snuggled closer to his side. "'Cause I'm hungry, too."

"So we're speaking the same language, then?" He nodded, half with that confident exterior I was used to, and half with an unexpected insecurity that caught me slightly off guard.

"Yes," I confirmed. Because we were. For once, someone was speaking my language. Fluently.

And I really liked the sound of it.

Chapter 20

The smell of coffee wasn't what usually woke me up in the morning.

At four thirty a.m.

I tossed off my covers and fumbled in the dark toward the door separating our suite. We'd gone to our respective beds hours ago, which was probably a good thing, because Torin all but admitted to wanting to have sex, and my body all but would have let him.

I rapped a knuckle on the door.

Within seconds, a bleary-eyed Torin flung it open and locked my gaze. "Did I wake you?" He looked equally apologetic and excited, like maybe he was actually trying to rouse me from my slumber with his middle-of-the-night barista skills. "I tried to be quiet."

"I'm not sure what woke me," I replied. I wasn't—maybe it was the smell of the coffee, maybe it was the unfamiliar hotel setting, or maybe it was the realization that Lance and I were actually finished and some other girl may or may not have his child growing inside of her that startled me from my sleep. Out of those options, number three was most likely the winner.

"Want some? It's decaf."

I shook my head. "Then what's the point?"

Torin had a mug tucked into his hands, his fingers curled around the handle. He made his way to his makeshift bed on the couch and sat down, flicking his head in a nod for me to come join him.

"Don't most people drink coffee *for* the caffeine?" I lowered down to the edge of his bed.

"Probably."

It was too late—or early. I never really knew how to classify the middle of the night that fell in between yesterday and today. "I should go back to bed." I twisted my upper half toward the door, readying to go, realizing sleep was probably what we both really needed.

"How do you sleep?" Torin asked. "Because I don't. I don't sleep."

Folding my legs up into a crisscross, I wrapped my hands over my ankles and held them there. "I don't sleep, either. At least not well," I admitted. "At least not well on my own."

Which was probably the number-one reason why I'd stayed with Lance. Through the cheating. Through the lies. The thought of being alone—alone with my thoughts, my nightmares—was what kept me clinging to his side, both day and night. But thinking about it now, and looking at Torin, I felt that tight grip on Lance start to slip. I almost wanted to shake it completely free.

"I'm up every night," Torin continued without pause, maybe not even hearing my reply. I guessed he wasn't really looking for one. "I wake up every night. That jerking, falling sensation." He stared at the painting on the wall that I'd tried to crawl into earlier that afternoon. "I would love to, for once, wake up peacefully. Not with the image Randy left me."

"That was awful what he did to your family, Torin."

I wanted to punch Randy, which I realized was completely absurd, because hanging oneself from the rafters was significantly worse than being punched by a nineteen-year-old girl with absolutely no fighting abilities or actual muscle to speak of. But I really wanted to. I wanted to punch him. Not to hurt him necessarily, because it appeared as though Randy had more hurt than I could ever have comprehended—to the point of numbness. You'd have to be numb to do something like that. But I wanted to punch him to make myself feel better. And that was stupid. There I was, thinking about how much I wanted to deck a dead guy. I needed some caffeine.

"Do you think he regrets it?" Torin continued. It was starting to feel like he was having his own conversation, some internal struggle that I got to witness.

"Do I think Randy regrets killing himself?" I sunk my head against the wall since there was no headboard. The back ridge of the couch dug into the middle of my spine, so I shoved a pillow in the gap to make myself more comfortable. "I'm not sure he's even capable of thinking anything. I don't know if we think after death."

"That would be awful." Torin's face fell. "That would be awful to not be able to think anymore." He deposited his coffee cup onto the nightstand, which was really an end table. He shook his head and again said, "Awful."

"Yeah," I agreed. "It would be."

"But I think it would be even *more* awful to be able to think and to have regret, you know?" He spoke quietly, but not because he didn't want his words to be heard. The opposite, in fact. It was like he spoke so that I had to really work to hear. "I have one rule in my life: to live without regret." He lifted his head slightly, tilting his chin up in contemplation. "So how much would that suck if I ended up regretting my own death?"

"It would completely suck."

"But here's the thing." Torin was on a road to somewhere with these thoughts of his, and my simple interjections didn't feel like they belonged. But I still said them—still joined in—because it seemed like it was a road he shouldn't travel down alone. "I think there is always some amount of regret involved in death."

I didn't interrupt this time.

"You die in a car accident. *I should have stopped at that red light.* You get cancer. *I shouldn't have spent all of those years smoking.* Hell, you die in your sleep. *I shouldn't have gone to bed tonight.* There is regret in every aspect of life and, ultimately, it seems, in death." Torin pursed his lips tightly. His brow was taut over his eyes. "And that completely sucks because if my one rule is to live without regret and yet I still regret the way in which my life ended, what is the point?"

He abandoned his coffee and joined me to lean against the wall. With clumsy inaccuracy, his fingers fumbled into mine and he dropped his head onto my shoulder.

It was quiet for a minute and then I spoke. "Then I think the only way to follow that rule is to live each day like it was your last."

"Oh, and I'm the plagiarist?" Torin chuckled loudly. I could feel the way his body shook with laughter at my side, his voice vibrating against my skin in a way that created a wake of goose bumps across my arms. "That's complete cliché status right there."

"True. It might be overused, but what's more overused than death? I mean, it happens to *all* of us. God should come up with another way to end us."

His head nodded against my shoulder. "I'm all for going out Elijah-style, on a chariot of fire."

"I don't even know what you're talking about, but it sounds awesome. So much better than taking one last breath here and then who knows what happens next."

"I have a hope for what I think might happen next." Torin pressed his head closer against my shoulder, the weight of his body leaning heavily into mine. Our legs lined up hip to toe and my fingers twisted tighter in his. "I have hope," he said again. "And that, I think, is stronger than regret."

. . . .

"Get your shoes on." The vision of Torin's pint-size mother flashed across my brain. I could see where he got his drill sergeant–like skills. Luckily, he wasn't nearly as intimidating.

Flipping onto my back, I shielded my eyes from the wash of golden light that flooded through the hotel window as Torin ripped back the curtains in one dramatic swoop. I smacked my lips, totally embarrassed to open my mouth for fear that I might contaminate the air with my breath alone. "I think I need to get dressed before I can get to the whole shoe thing."

"Nope." He shook his head with a coyness that it was entirely too early for. "Clothing optional. But we will be doing some walking, so you'll probably want the shoes."

"Where are we going?" Our flight wasn't until the next morning, and while I knew I would be in D.C. with Torin, I'd originally thought those hours would be spent with Lance. But, I supposed, I had assumed I'd be spending even more than just a few hours with him; I'd counted on a lifetime.

"I would completely regret it if I willingly put you on a plane headed back to California, knowing we were only eight hours from your very favorite piece of architecture *in the whole world*, and you didn't get the chance to see it."

"We're going to Boston?" I practically bounced on the bed with a giddiness I rarely exuded. I couldn't believe that, one: he'd remembered, and two: he was willing to spend an entire day driving to take me there.

"Yes indeed." He nodded. "And I managed to get us a rental car, too. *And* change our flights so we fly out of Boston tonight, instead of D.C. tomorrow."

I wasn't sure how he'd arranged that, considering you had to be twenty-five in most states to legally rent a car, but I was still too excited about seeing Boston Light that the possibility of breaking the law in order to make that happen didn't seem all that important.

"Get your shoes on." Torin scooped my Chuck Taylors off the floor, tossing each one at me with a dramatic windup and pitch. My left shoe hit me square in the chest. "Sorry!" He laughed. "You gotta work on your reflexes."

"You gotta work on not throwing things at your girlfriend!" I shot back. Immediately, I realized what I'd just said, and for a moment, I wished my shoe had clocked me in the head instead and knocked some sense into me. I wasn't Torin's girlfriend. Why had I just said that?

"Did you just say 'my girlfriend'?" His eyes were huge, like a deer's that had two headlights careening toward it. I could almost see my reflection in those big green irises.

"I didn't mean it," I quickly backpedaled, and Torin pursed his lips in disappointment.

"You didn't? How come?"

"Because I'm not your girlfriend."

I wasn't. I wasn't really Lance's anymore, that much I knew, but I wasn't Torin's, either. I wasn't at all sure what this reality between us even was, or if it could be classified as a reality at all. The more I thought about it (and I'd spent quite a bit of that morning thinking about it), the more our story had the telltale makings of a rebound written all over it. He'd said before that his longest relationship had been six weeks. It seemed like our time might be running out.

Striding across the room, Torin came to my bedside and slipped the neckline of my top down. His finger traced the ink on my skin he'd left there the night before. A shiver followed along that same path as the tip of his fingernail skated across my skin like fire lit on a fuse. Everything in me started to tingle, a buzzing that registered deep in my core. Just that slow, seductive touch brought me to a place where I felt like I could explode. "So you're not my girlfriend, huh?" he questioned, eyes snapping up to mine. "Because here it says you're my siren, my lighthouse, and my muse."

The pen was still on the nightstand, but not for long. Torin yanked it from its position, threw the cap to the floor, and pulled the neck of my tank down dangerously low, the arc of my chest exposed. He scribbled something frantically and then tossed the pen to the ground just before tossing me back onto the mattress. His mouth plunged down to mine, and the reservation I'd had about opening it earlier was gone. Forget minty freshness; Torin didn't seem to care one bit, so neither did I. His tongue pulled in and out of my mouth hungrily, and his body dropped onto mine in a way that definitely told me I was every bit his girlfriend. Because I was pretty sure you didn't do stuff like this with just anyone. At least I hoped he didn't do stuff like this with just anyone.

"You are most definitely my girlfriend," Torin breathed, and pulled away slightly, biting my bottom lip between his teeth. "I didn't think I'd need to brand you to let you know that, but just so you don't forget, I wrote it with a Sharpie." He grinned widely. "But you should know—that whole 'permanent' thing is totally false advertising. This will be gone in a couple of days." He ran the pad of his thumb across the top of my chest. "And I have no plans to leave you anytime soon."

All the reasons why that statement—however sweet and sentimental—couldn't be true flooded my brain in a wild current of emotion. But I didn't say anything or let him know that hesitation.

At least not with my words. Unfortunately, my expression apparently said it all.

"I have no intention of being your rebound, Darby."

"You're not—"

"Let me finish, 'cause this is pretty good," he said, pressing a silencing finger to my lips. "I spent all morning coming up with this, so let me at least deliver it in epic monologue form before you burst my bubble, okay?"

"There is no bubble bursting in my plans," I said, palming his jaw, running my fingers along the stubble that was starting to grow there. I loved the way he looked down at me, the way his disheveled hair hung around his face like it did the first time I saw him at Quarry Summit.

"Wait until I'm done to tell me that, because I want to do the convincing—"

"I don't need convincing," I interrupted.

"Damn it, woman, let me have my moment!"

I bit my lips to keep back the surge of laughter that threatened to burst out, and nodded for him to go ahead.

"Darby," he began, his voice much more theatrical than necessary. "I have admitted my love for you." He waved a hand into the space of air between us like he was some Shakespearean actor. "And you have done the same." He sounded like one, too. "But I have no intention of being your rebound." Things sort of turned serious, both on his face and in his tone. "I don't want to be the guy who helped you get over Lance. I don't want to be the guy who made you forget Lance. I just want me to be me, and you to be you, and for us to be that way together. I want that to be enough." He dipped his head a bit and widened his eyes, staring at me through a lock of his sandy-blond hair. I didn't feel the need to cut it at all anymore, and I kind of adored the way it fell across his brow. "Because you and me becomes an *us*, and that's its own entity. I want our *us* to be enough."

"It's enough." I stared up at him openly.

"I'm not a rebound. I'm not replacing the part of the *us* that Lance took from you—the parts he's *been* taking from you."

I nodded slowly and said, "I know that. And in all fairness, I'm not the same *me*, either."

The smallest smile broke onto Torin's face and he dropped his lips softly to mine. "I know that, too." He pulled me up to sit with him and placed his hands on my knees. "Do you ever stop to think how no one else in the world is experiencing what you and I are right now *in this very moment*? Like, no one gets to feel this"—he swept his full lips across my cheek—"or this"—he ran his fingers through my hair and tucked it behind my ear. "No one gets to know what it's like to feel the way I do about you." Keeping his hand at the curve of my ear, he looked me right in the eye. "Hardly seems fair. I feel like I should write a book or something just so people can get a small glimpse into what I feel for you."

"I wouldn't want others reading about us. I want to keep you all to myself."

"You greedy little thing!" Torin flicked the tip of my nose with his finger.

"Why would I want anyone else to fall in love with you?" I asked outright.

"People don't fall in love with book characters, Darby." Torin shook his head at me like I was saying something completely ridiculous.

"Oh, please! They do all the time!" I blurted. "Edward Cullen? Four? Christian Grey?"

"Well," he said contemplatively as he thumbed his chin, "I'm not a vampire, nor a dystopian teen with a number for a name, and I think I'm actually the complete opposite of a billionaire playboy with weird fetishes. Nothing about me is fictional. I'm just a guy who works at a camp with my mom and dad, and I happened to fall in love with an incredible girl who came to visit."

"That's all you think you are?"

He shrugged his shoulders to his ears.

"Torin, if you were a book character, I *guarantee* you would have hordes of women swooning after you."

"Oh, hardly—"

"Let me finish, damn it, because this is epically good." I winked as I stole his earlier words. "You are this unexpected guy who can't help but be the savior. With your campers, with me—you have the ability to pull people out of themselves. That's an incredible gift, Torin. Because sometimes people can get buried pretty deep."

"Oh."

"Oh, what?"

He flashed a wicked smirk. "I thought you were going to say I am so incredibly sexy that women fall all over themselves at the mere thought of me."

"That, too." He was such a tease.

"Right." He smirked again. "That, too."

We spent a couple of minutes staring at each other, and I thought maybe I should say something more, but I didn't know what to say. I didn't even know what to feel. It was crazy to me that things had happened the way they did between us. How, within the course of a month, everything I thought to be true about my life had been turned on its head. But now, instead of feeling like everything was upside down, it—for once—felt like it all had fallen into place. How insane to think that I'd had it wrong all of those years, and all it took was a chance encounter with Torin to flip it around and make it right.

"Get your shoes on." He jumped up from the bed and headed toward the door. "We have a lighthouse to find."

Chapter 21

"How can it be so hard to locate a freaking lighthouse?" Torin punched his finger against the GPS screen on the dash. Roads and arrows wove together in a jumbled mess of street names and intersections. The robotic woman with the British accent muttered something about turning left, but Torin just shouted, "It's a *lighthouse*! Its job is to be seen!"

"It's okay, honestly." I pressed my hand onto his forearm. We'd been driving for ten hours, only stopping to eat at a diner where the grease in the atmosphere was a physical weight that you could feel on your skin, and to fill up on gas before continuing our venture. Torin had kept his cool until about hour nine, but the past sixty minutes had been filled with curse words and rants on the current political administration and their lack of investment in satellite technology. How it was really all the government's fault and how it probably had some underground conspiracy in place to keep young kids in love from locating historical landmarks. As far as Torin's thoughts went, he really was all over the map.

"It's seriously no big deal."

Torin's grip on the steering wheel tightened and his knuckles grew white with the force of his frustration. "But it *is* a big deal. This is a very big deal. I wanted to do this for you."

"I don't need to see a lighthouse for my life to be complete or anything."

"Maybe not," he said, turning down the radio like it was Taylor Swift's fault that we weren't on the right path. "But this was a dream of yours, and I have every intention of making this dream come true for you." The light ahead morphed from green to yellow to red unusually quickly, and Torin rammed his foot to the floorboard in an effort to keep the vehicle from blazing into the intersection. "Gah!" he screamed. "This totally sucks!"

"Make a legal U-turn," the GPS woman chimed into the angry air of the car.

"I'll show you a legal U-turn," he growled through his teeth, his lips tightening.

"Good one, Torin." I adjusted my sunglasses and flipped the visor to shield the glare reflecting from the car in front of us. It was a hot, sunny, clear day, one on which—I supposed—you would not even need the aid of a lighthouse had you been a sailor near the shore. We really didn't have to do this.

"It's the best I've got right now. All of my creative comebacks are on hold until I get to our destination. I have to focus all of my efforts on the task at hand. No multitasking."

"I don't need to see the lighthouse."

"But you love architecture!"

"I love you more, and quite honestly, I'm worried that you are going to have an irrational meltdown of grandiose proportions if we don't scrap this whole plan soon."

Torin flicked the turn signal and guided the car to the edge of the road, the tires settling into the ruts on the shoulder. He took a breath, pulling it in dramatically so that his chest puffed up, and then he slowly exhaled. "I think you're right," he resigned. "If we don't start heading toward the airport now, we'll never make our flight."

I nodded, a little relieved that our wild-goose chase was over. Yes, I'd wanted to see Boston Light, but when it came down to it, just the fact that Torin tried to do all of this for me was enough. The lighthouse was just the path, not the destination.

"Before we do that, though, there is something I have to do." He pressed a finger to the GPS pad and our British guide began reciting, "*The route guidance will begin . . .*"

"Route guidance my ass!" Torin megaphoned his mouth and shouted into the touch screen. "You couldn't punch your way out of a wet paper bag!" He started on the idioms full force, and I bent over in laughter so hard my seatbelt locked up on me. Once he was done with his tirade of comebacks, he turned to look at me, rotating his body in his seat. But I couldn't see him. All the tears filling my eyes made it incredibly hard to even make out his shape. Everything hurt from laughing: my face, my stomach, my head.

"Sorry you had to witness that."

"It's fine," I giggled, covering my mouth as another laugh escaped. "I told you I was ready for an irrational meltdown of grandiose proportions."

"Well," he said, looking over his shoulder and coasting back onto the highway, "I'm glad I didn't disappoint." He changed lanes and picked up speed until we were right there along with the other traffic that sailed down the interstate. "You're not at all disappointed that we didn't make it to the lighthouse?"

"Not even a little bit."

Torin turned to smile at me, and he held his gaze longer than was probably safe to do while operating heavy machinery, but I didn't mind. I loved the way his eyes were so vulnerable and so telling, how he must have felt safe with me to expose his emotions so freely. I hoped that I was able to do the same for him.

"How come you're an architectural design major?" he said, swinging his head back to stare out the front windshield. "That's a pretty specific field."

"I like buildings." I bit on the jagged edge of my thumbnail and said, "I like that there are these structures that get to hold so much life within them. And that people get to create them." My own eyes remained fixed on the stretch of highway out my passenger's side window, the whirling landscape blended together like the brushstrokes on a painting. "I like the idea that I can create something, and that someone gets to fill it up with their own memories and experiences. Like, I can make the outside shell, and they can breathe the life into it." I began feeling too lost in thought, and insecurity swept through when I realized I was actually verbalizing all that I was thinking. "It's weird, I know."

"It's not weird." He looked at me again. The vehicles blurred past our periphery at seventy miles per hour, but it was just us. In this rental car, in this moment, it was just us. "It's beautiful."

I dropped my eyes down to my lap and twisted my fingers. "I don't know."

"Well, I do, and I think it's beautiful. And the irony is the most beautiful part, Darby."

I lifted my face up to him. "What irony?"

"That you were this empty shell." He didn't look at me when he spoke, and I was grateful for it, because my cheeks were hot and red, coated with my emotion. "You were this empty shell that needed life breathed into it." He switched lanes and caught my gaze on the way. "I'm honored I got to be the one to do that."

I gaped. "Oh my word. Seriously, *who are you*, Torin?"

"Is that going to be your go-to every time I say something that blows your socks off?"

I giggle-snorted again, realizing that was the type of laugh that Torin elicited from me.

"Because if it is, I'm going to have to get used to hearing you ask me that, since I plan to blow your socks off quite frequently." He glanced down at my feet. "You might as well just wear flip-flops from now on."

The signs on the freeway indicated our turnoff for the air-port, and Torin guided the car in the direction of the closest exit.

Part of me worried that things would change once we got back to camp. I had no idea what the next couple of weeks would hold, but I was certain they would be different from our past twenty-four hours together. They couldn't be the same—not with the strict limitations on boys' and girls' cabins, and with our responsibilities to our campers. I wouldn't see much of him, and I wondered what that would do to our newly created *us*. It was obvious what the distance did to Lance and me; I hoped that wouldn't be the case when it came to Torin.

"What do you say we get a one-way ticket outta here?" I blurted without reservation.

"Are you quoting a movie? Or are you serious?"

"I'm serious, Torin," I said quickly, before I had the chance to come to my senses. "What if we just pick some random place and go there? Start a life. Start over. I know it sounds crazy"—*because it was*—"but I think we should do it."

His smiled. "You're right, it is crazy. But I've told you, I kinda dig crazy."

"So let's do it!" I straightened up in my seat and pressed a hand to the dashboard to brace myself under my illogical excite-ment. "Let's do this, Torin. Let's create our own adventure and just go wherever. Just start over."

"Are you asking me to run away with you?"

I supposed I kind of was. "Yes," I admitted playfully. "Torin, will you run away with me?"

"I would, Darby," Torin began, but I couldn't help but feel the letdown in his tone. "I would run away with you . . . if I was sure it was because you wanted to run away *with* me, and not *from* something." A thick pause. "But I'm not sure, so that's why I hesitate."

"I'm not running from anything. I'm running *to* something, and I want you to run with me."

I could see the airport parking lot up ahead and the car rental return sign telling us where to go. Our vehicle curved along the indicated path.

"See, I don't think we need to run anywhere. I'm happy walking. Hell, I'm happy sitting. I'm happy just being with you, Darby. Just like this. Driving ten hours together and ending up absolutely nowhere. I don't mind being nowhere with you, Darby, because you make even my nowhere feel like somewhere." He tossed a glance in my direction and quirked up the corner of his mouth. "Go ahead, take your socks off."

"You really are too much, you know that?"

"I actually think I'm just enough."

. . . .

The plane taxied on the runway for several minutes before the seatbelt sign shut off and a chorus of metallic clicks filled the cabin. Torin reached a hand across my lap to unhook my belt.

"Was I successful in keeping you distracted?" I smirked, my lips still buzzing from our mildly inappropriate airplane make-out session.

"More than successful." Torin pressed his mouth to mine once more. His lips felt warm and pliable like always. "And I think we distracted a few others, too." He gestured two rows up at an elderly man who stared unabashedly at us, scorn held in his eyes. "I think we gave that guy a heart attack."

"I think you gave *me* a heart attack," I admitted, still feeling the aftereffects of his kiss surging throughout me like the warmth of that first sip of alcohol. The subtle hint of impending intoxication. "Your kissing skills are totally heart attack worthy. You nearly killed me."

But as it would turn out, I'd used that statement too early on in our day.

And about the wrong person.

. . . .

"Darby." Torin shook me awake, my back pressing in and out of the lumpy mattress. The bent springs creaked with each jolting movement. "Darby, wake up."

I knew better than to bolt upright this time. The faint scar near my hairline was a clear reminder to rise gradually from my slumber. But Torin obviously didn't want me to wake up slowly. No, his firm grip on my shoulders totally indicated otherwise. He was wrestling me out of sleep like a ravenous lion batting at its prey.

"The campers!" I shouted, disoriented and dazed. We'd gotten into Sacramento after midnight and then headed back up to the Trinity Alps immediately after. I'd slept the entire car ride, and all but zombie-walked to the cabin, only to have found it completely empty. "Where are my girls?"

"On their overnighters," Torin clarified. The latest set of campers were out with their parents for the weekend, and I'd known that, but the fog took a while to lift from my eyes and my brain. "Darby, last night . . ."

"Was amazing." That much I remembered. "Who would have thought making out at thirty thousand feet could be such a rush? I can think of a few other things I'd like to do at that elevation—"

"There was a car crash, Darby." Torin's eyes were bloodshot; spiderwebs of red wove in and out of the whites surrounding his irises. He had to be so tired. It was a miracle we'd made it back to camp without him falling asleep at the wheel. Something was clearly looking out for us.

"Oh my God." I paused. "Are we dead?" I knew it was stupid to think—even stupider to say—but maybe this was death. Maybe the afterlife was just another extension of this life. Maybe that's all it was. Or maybe I was deliriously sleepy.

"No, Darby. We're not dead," he said softly, the way a mother gently breaks bad news to her child. His one hand was at my cheek, and he held it there in a way that made me nervous, because the look that draped across his face matched the desperate feeling that pulsed from his fingertips onto my skin. His other hand clutched my cell phone, the one I'd accidently left in his Jeep last night. "But Lance is."

. . . .

My stomach twisted violently, and my eyes swirled round and round, following the whirlpool of water that pulled back down into the base of the toilet. Before it had even finished flushing, I filled it with vomit again.

"It's okay," Torin whispered against my clammy forehead, his hand holding my hair in a makeshift ponytail. "Shhh . . . it's okay, Darby."

We did this for a while, Torin shushing and me puking. It might have been a few minutes; it might have been a few hours. It was hard to tell because it felt like a dream, and time wasn't something you could register in a dream. I wanted it to be a dream. I prayed for it to be one. But it wasn't. It was a very real, very tangible nightmare.

"What the hell was wrong with him?" I shouted, gripping

Torin's chest as we sat curled up on the chipped tile bathroom floor. "Why did he come after me?"

"Because you were running from him." It felt like a slap in the face. I would have preferred that, actually—Torin physically punching me with his fist rather than backhanding me with his words.

"I wasn't running *from* anything, Torin!" I buried my face into the fabric of his flannel shirt and it stuck to the wet slope of my cheek. The fibers scraped my skin like the scratching prickles of a cactus.

"But you were. *We* were. It wasn't right for us to leave without talking things out with him once more." Torin shoved the heel of his hand to his nose and wiped it quickly. "It was like I was kidnapping you or something. Like I had to get you out of there and away from him before you had any second thoughts."

"That's not what you were doing, Torin." I looked up at him. His head tilted back against the stall wall, his neck stretching completely, his face directed toward the ceiling coated with splotches of mold and dirt-filled cracks. "We both know that's not what you were doing."

"Maybe not consciously, but my subconscious is apparently an insecure prick that feels threatened quite easily." Torin brought his lips to my forehead and dropped a hesitant kiss onto it, like maybe it was something he shouldn't do. He kept his mouth there as he said, "Because in all honesty, Lance wasn't that much of a threat, having cheated and possibly gotten another girl pregnant and all."

It felt weird to be talking about him like he was still alive, but I supposed it felt even weirder to acknowledge he was dead. So far, I hadn't been able to do that. Maybe my body had, judging by the way it retched and convulsed, emptying my insides of any sustenance it might have held. But I had a much harder time acknowledging it with my mind.

Lance is dead, I spoke in my head. But just forcing myself to think it didn't make it feel real. Just like the way believing the phrase *"It's not your fault"* never felt real to me, either. It hadn't felt real these past six years, and it definitely wasn't real now. I wasn't sure what was actually real anymore at all.

"He'd probably been drinking because of our fight."

Torin's arms pulled tighter around me, a vice grip that refused to let go.

"You can't say things like that, Darby. You can't blame yourself for something you didn't have control over."

"Then what is the point, Torin?" My volume raised and my ears flooded with the angry pounding of my heart. "What is the point in any of it? Because ultimately, we don't have control over anything at all!" I pulled from his hold and rose to my feet, turning my back to him and bracing my hands on either side of the cracked porcelain sink. The tormented reflection that stared back at me from the mirror should have caught me off guard, but it didn't.

This was what I deserved to look like; this was how I deserved to feel. "He got in that car because I left. There is no other reason that he should have been heading to the airport last night. He would have stayed in D.C." I dragged my fingers down my face and clenched my eyes shut. "Me." I pushed a finger into my chest. "*I'm* the reason he got drunk, got in the car, and died. I'm responsible for it, Torin."

"Maybe, maybe not." His voice quivered with a shaky unsteadiness. "There is no way we can know what he was thinking."

I flipped around to face him, pressing my backside against the ledge of the sink. He looked so vulnerable, so childlike, with his knees tucked to his chest, his eye sockets pressed into the caps of them. Torin rocked back and forth in a disturbing rhythm that was probably meant to soothe, but it didn't appear to be working. The way his shoulders rose and fell betrayed any attempt he made at covering up his emotion.

"Torin . . ." I muttered his name, but he continued to rock without acknowledgment. "Torin."

"I can't bear the responsibility implied in that statement, Darby." He didn't look at me. He didn't even lift his eyes from his knees. He spoke into the floor. "I can't." He shook his head, but since he was still balled up, his whole body shook like one of those Weebles from back when we were kids. *What was it? "Weebles wobble, but they don't fall down."* Torin never seemed to fall down. He swayed back and forth and caught himself at the last moment before angling to the other side every time.

But my statement—that was enough to knock him completely over. He rammed his head against the solid frame of the stall.

"Saying things like that?" With uncharacteristic frustration, Torin's eyes impaled mine. "Blaming yourself for the choices *Lance* made? God, Darby. Do you realize what that means if that's what you honestly believe?" I didn't. He continued. "If you really think that way, that our argument with Lance last night resulted in his death . . . *do you know what that means?*" There was a fury that pulsed in that bathroom, and it scared me. Not that Torin scared me; I wasn't afraid of him. But he was scared, and something I'd said brought that fear out in him.

"I don't know what that means." My hands were so drenched with sweat that they started to slip off the counter. "I don't know, Torin."

"It means that we're all ultimately responsible for one another." He cracked his head against the paint-chipped wall again, intentionally. Intentionally ramming into the blunt surface, like he was trying to hurt himself. Or maybe replace one hurt for another, something I'd mastered long ago. "And that is more responsibility than any one of us is strong enough to bear."

Chapter 22

Two weeks later

"This still smells like him."

I knew that. In reality, it probably smelled more like me, because I'd had it pressed to my nose for the past week. Pressed to my cheek as I slept at night. Pressed to my skin as I walked around campus, retracing the daily path we'd taken to O-Chem last fall. But maybe there wasn't much difference. We'd shared so much else. Maybe we smelled the same. In some odd way, I almost hoped we did.

Lance's mom held the sweatshirt to her face, smothering herself with it like she could somehow still feel him inside it. Like Lance's arms filled the armholes and wrapped around her in a cotton-coated embrace.

"I don't ever want to lose that." She closed her eyes and swayed back and forth, the red hoodie draped across her chest. "When I would get him after his nap," she said, her eyes still drawn shut, "his curly hair would be so sweaty. He'd bounce up and down in his crib with his arms stretched up to me." She lifted hers to the sky as she replayed the memory. "I would scoop him up and just hold him in my arms." She rocked again, side to side. "I would keep him there and just nuzzle my nose against him—breathing him." She took a deep, prolonged breath. "But I can't breathe him anymore." The sobbing started. "I . . . can't . . . breathe."

Lance's dad wrapped his hand around Sarah's heaving shoulders, rotating her body away from me, like seeing her cry would trigger my own waterworks and he somehow wanted to shield me from it. But you couldn't shield someone from death. We started experiencing the effects of it the moment we were born. Life, as I'd come to find out, began its process of ending with our first newborn cry. And then we continued to cry over the deaths of others who affected our lives. Death was sad. It involved a lot of crying. I figured the only death that you couldn't cry over was your own. I longed for that day when there would be no more crying.

Lance's dad was muttering something into Sarah's ear. She nodded. They left.

Three minutes went by.

He came back.

I was still in the same position, still sitting on the empty floor of my apartment, staring at the P7036 on the walls.

"Darby." Lance's dad shut the door into its frame, leaving his hand there for a moment on the oak that encased it. I didn't know what he did with Sarah, but I assumed she was waiting in the car. He slipped down to my level and crossed his legs underneath him.

"Paul."

He let out one of those breaths that would lift the hair from his face, had his hair been long enough to lift. Instead he had a closely shorn cut that masked the fact that his hairline receded nearly all the way to the back of his skull. "You don't have to pretend that he was a saint just because he's gone."

I kept my eyes to the wall.

"You don't even have to pretend that you still love him. I know what he did, Darby. Lance was my son, and as much as I loved him—worshipped the ground he walked on, practically—I know he had his faults, and how those faults greatly affected you."

Even though I didn't want to, I turned to look at him. "But I *do* still love him," I whispered, my chest tightening as I spoke the heartbreaking words.

"I know all about Clara and how she thought she was pregnant." Turned out she wasn't. What an awful twist of fate that was, to find out that the girl partially responsible for our breakup had no claims to him, either.

So there it was. Lance had died completely alone. That broke my heart even more than anything Lance had ever done to me, the thought of him alone in his final moments here on earth.

It was Paul's turn to memorize the color of my apartment now as his gaze switched from me to the beige expanse opposite us. "That's why we told him to fly you out for the weekend. To be honest with you. Come clean."

You would think we were both looking at the Mona Lisa based on our intense scrutiny of the blank wall before us.

"You blame yourself." His body tilted and his shoulder pressed mine. "You think he drank because of your fight. And that he got behind the wheel because he was coming to see you. Because you left."

It wasn't necessary for me to nod, so I didn't. I just stared.

"You were not responsible. Lance chose to drink. He chose to get in that car."

"Okay." It was all I had. I wanted to say more, to truly believe him, but guilt and grief had taken ahold of me so strongly that they even stole my words.

Grief, I'd learned, didn't just occur when something was taken away, like when my sister died. It didn't end there. It continued to take as if it owned you and fed off your being for survival. Like a leech, it siphoned from you—things like your hope and hunger and your chance at living a normal life—it took all of those things into its bloodthirsty possession until you were only a shell. Then it was up to you to fill it back up.

I'd spent way too long trying to figure out what I was supposed to be filling that shell with, and losing Lance felt like another parasite attaching itself to my existence. It hurt beyond belief.

"Please, Darby." Paul slipped his hand into mine. It was weird because it felt like Lance's, just rougher, older. Slightly more calloused. "If you need someone to blame, blame me. I told him to go after you after the gala. I didn't know he'd been drinking. Or at least not that much." There was a distinct tremble in his voice. "Let me take that from you."

It didn't help hearing that. Maybe it should have, but it didn't. I was already being crushed under the weight of "the impossible responsibility" that Torin spoke of. So what? Paul told Lance to follow me. Maybe he was responsible for that piece. But I was responsible for my own pieces.

It felt like my pieces were bigger.

Paul's fingers were loose in mine. I didn't like holding them, but I didn't want to shake them free, either. So we sat there for a few moments, our fingers in this weird stage of almost holding.

"You can trace responsibility back to every action Lance ever took, and every interaction he ever had. We don't live in a vacuum. What I do affects you, what you do affects someone else, and so on and so on," Paul said, looking at me. "This is where people get the notion that God is to blame for things like this, if you trace it all back far enough."

"I think he must be." My foot was asleep. Pins and needles.

"Of course he is." Paul squeezed my hand tightly within his knotted fingers. "Let *him* be responsible, Darby." The squeezing got tighter as he tried to convince me. He had his courtroom lawyer skills playing out in full effect and I tried so hard to believe every word, I really did. "Let him take the blame. He can handle it."

"That just feels like a way of deflecting responsibility." I had to stretch my leg in front of me because my foot was all prickly and began to twitch, and it was sort of embarrassing when it jumped up and down. "To blame something that may or may not exist, just so I don't have to take ownership. That feels like the easy, cowardly way out. I can't be a coward about this. I can't do that to Lance."

"It's not cowardly to lean on something greater than you."

"I don't know how to do that, Paul. I really don't." My foot pulsed again and I shook it out with one shallow kick thrust into the air. "Do I place the blame on this entity that can't even defend itself, just so I—what? So I don't have to feel so guilty about my role in it? That's not fair to Lance. I won't do that to him."

Paul sighed, lighter this time. "Honestly, Darby, you're already blaming some*one* that can't defend *herself*," he said. "Because it's not like you're going to come to your own defense. You've sentenced yourself to this irrational punishment, just like you did with Anna."

"This isn't about Anna." If I had a penny for every time I'd uttered that phrase . . .

I pulled my hand from his, but he'd already sort of let go, so it just left me feeling alone and abandoned. Even though I didn't like holding his hand, I wanted to curl up in his lap like a little girl did with her daddy. Paul was family to me and I needed that reassuring, everything-will-be-okay hug.

"This is about Anna." Paul's red-rimmed eyes locked with mine. "This is about Lance. This is about any person that ever crosses your path, Darby." His eyes were the same color as his son's. I wondered why I had never noticed that and I started to cry at the realization that I'd never be able to compare them side by side. "And this is about your life and how you're going to choose to live it." I waited for him to blink, but he didn't. "Because you can think that you played a part in their deaths, or you can think you played a part in their lives." Pressing his palms to the floor, he pushed up to stand, then he walked toward the door, about to open it, but not before he turned his head in my direction and said, "In my opinion, I think you need to focus more on the living, and less on the dying."

My phone vibrated on the carpet. I couldn't look at it. I couldn't even pry open an eye to sneak a glance at the screen. I pressed a lazy finger onto the off button and curled back onto my side.

A few hours passed. The only way I could really tell it was a few hours was from the increased pain of the crick in my neck. After sleeping in the middle of the empty family room of my old apartment (which Gustov was kind enough to let me squat in while he looked for a new tenant) for the past three nights—or days, all of it, really—my bones felt like they were going to break. And after sleeping several hours straight, they felt like they were about to become unhinged. So that's how I knew I'd been asleep for a while, because not only did my head and my heart hurt immensely, but my bones ached to the core.

The front door flew open.

"God, this color sucks." I rolled onto my back, my joints all popping with the slow movement, like a twisted-up section of bubble wrap. "Seriously, Darbs. I *hate* this color."

Sonja dropped a bag of Cheetos onto the floor and they landed inches from my head.

"But it matches," I said, swallowing. When was the last time I'd brushed my teeth? My mouth felt like cotton.

"Matches what?" She ripped open the chip bag and tossed an unnaturally orange puff into her mouth. "There is absolutely nothing in here to match."

"My mood."

Sonja threw another chip in. "Darby. That is *so sad*." I could hear her teeth crunching around her words. "This color is awful, and if this is how you feel, then I'm truly sorry. This has to be the worst color in the history of colors. It's not really even a color."

I propped up onto my elbows, my bones locking into place. I prayed they wouldn't snap beneath the pressure as I stretched my neck out toward her. "It is a color. Just, like you said, an awful one. White is not a color. Or maybe black isn't. I don't really know. But beige is. And this one is P7036."

"Let's repaint." She held out the bag to me and I dipped my hand in. I hadn't eaten in—I actually didn't know when I last ate—but for some reason that I couldn't explain, Cheetos were exactly what I craved. "Come on. Get in the Jeep. We're headed to the hardware store."

Though I hadn't left the town house in days, it didn't sound like a bad plan, so I forced myself into a sitting position, readying to stand, not entirely sure the bones in my legs were actually going to do their expected job and support me.

While I was figuring out how to best stand without snapping in two, there came a knock on the door. Sonja flicked a glance in my direction, as if to ask, "Are you expecting someone?" and I shrugged, as if to say, "No." She crossed the room and tossed open the front door.

"Is Darby here?" He didn't have to say it, because we'd actually made eye contact before the words even had a chance to fall out of his mouth. There they were: two wide, green eyes that leveled me with just one glance.

"And you are?" Sonja gave him a sidelong look, and then tossed one toward me.

"Torin. Darby's friend."

"Can you paint?" Both of her hands were hooked on her hips. She was practically tapping her toe. "How good are you at painting?"

Torin's dimples—how I'd missed those dimples—pulled into his cheeks. "I'm an excellent painter." He almost sounded like Dustin Hoffman, *Rain Man*–style.

"Good!" She grabbed him by the wrist and flung around toward the empty room, waving a hand at the wall. "Because today, we paint."

We both sat in the back of my Jeep. Sonja drove. She liked being in control, and I liked letting her. That was how our friendship went, and there was comfort in that predictable consistency.

There was also comfort in the silent way Torin's fingers twisted with mine.

We hadn't talked since Lance, and we still weren't actually talking with words, but we didn't need them.

I'd left Quarry Summit that day—that same day that I heard about the crash. I didn't look back. I just ran. I ran *away* from it all, that much I was willing to admit. Because in reality, there was no way I could keep up with my summer duties as a counselor to troubled youth. I was every bit as troubled as their worst-case-scenario camper. It would be the blind leading the blind, and any way you sliced it, you always ended up lost.

Torin had tried calling, but I didn't have it in me to answer. I worried that somehow the grief I'd felt for Lance would hurt him, and I couldn't do that. The whole unexpected scenario was so unbelievable, so fresh and raw, and Torin didn't need to be dragged into the middle of it. Somehow he'd gotten mixed up with me that summer, and I'd bet everything I had that he wished I'd never set foot at Quarry Summit.

But his presence in my Jeep and his hand tangled with mine hinted otherwise.

The first week after, I was with Lance's family mostly. Going through his things. Watching old videos. Talking about him like he was some incredible person who was too young to die. Which probably he was—especially the "too young" part. That was what everyone always said about Anna: that she was *too young* to die. I was beginning to believe that was just what people said because it sounded good. Was there really an acceptable cutoff age when it suddenly became *okay* to die? Like, at forty-two, was that an appropriate time for death? When did death no longer become tragic? When was it finally allowed?

It struck me that it never was.

This thing that would eventually happen to *every single one* of us was never accepted by *any* of us. I wondered if there were any other things that humanity experienced universally yet had an impossible time coming to terms with. I didn't think there was. Death was it. Death was the socially unacceptable experience that we would all, at some point in time, experience.

All I knew was that if I were to die right then, I didn't think I'd feel too young for it. If anything, it would make me want to ask the cruel hands of time, "What took you so long?" Maybe that's what happened when the people you knew and loved died before you. Maybe that's why everyone always said the words "too young to die." Because, in reality, they believed—or at least hoped—*they* were too young to die also. No one ever felt old enough to stop living.

I vowed at that moment to never utter that phrase again.

Sonja angled the Jeep into a parking spot near the sliding-door entrance of the store, and we funneled out in one line of three, like we were on some mission and were joined at the hip. I was grateful that Torin had scooped my hand back up after getting out of the car, and our arms swung loosely between us as we walked.

"Mark, where is your paint section?" Sonja took charge and asked the first guy she could find in a red apron with his name embroidered across it in unraveling white thread.

"Aisle 23."

We all nodded a thank-you and then headed that direction.

"Can I help you?" a boy who was probably close to our age asked from behind a metal counter. He pounded on the lid of a paint can with a rubber mallet and wiped his hand across his brow, streaking it an aqua hue.

"Yes," Torin spoke up. "We need paint."

The guy gave us a look that should have made us feel stupid, but it didn't, because we were on a mission, and this was more than just paint.

"Do you have a swatch?" He pulled another can from some contraption that rocked and vibrated like a washing machine, spinning the containers around furiously.

"No." Torin glanced in my direction. "What color are you thinking?"

I thought for a moment. "Black."

"No way." Sonja thrust out a pouty bottom lip and furrowed her brow. "Absolutely not. We're doing an actual *color.*"

The guy behind the counter wasn't listening to us anymore, but that was okay because it wasn't like we were anywhere near ready to place an actual order.

"I think black is a color. I think it's actually all of the colors mixed together," I suggested, feeling like I'd heard that somewhere once.

"That is very right-brain thinker of you, Darby." Torin squeezed my fingers, but I just gave him a confused look. "To an artist, black is all the colors. To a physicist, it's the absence of color." Again, the blank look of confusion cloaked my face, not knowing where he was going with this. "In terms of light, black is not a color. No light equals darkness, which equals black." I wondered how Torin had learned such things up on that mountaintop of his. "White is the blending of all the colors together. Like light from the sun. All colors on the spectrum composed together equal bright white." He paused, waiting for us to catch up, but my brain was working hard to process and lagged behind. The look on Sonja's face proved hers was working at an even slower rate. It was obvious Torin really wanted to be understood, so he continued, "But from an artist's perspective, you can't combine colors together to make white, so white is the absence of color."

"How does this help us decide on paint at all?" Sonja wasn't going to get it, but I was close.

"We have a choice to make." Torin cocked his head and thumbed his chin. He looked absolutely adorable, and I nearly felt guilty for thinking it because being with him really did bring me joy—a joy I wasn't sure I was supposed to deserve just yet. "Today, are we going to be scientists, or are we going to be artists?"

Sonja shrugged, not caring. But I did. I cared.

"Logic and reason, or emotion and feeling?" Concrete and structure, or trees and flowers?

I dropped his hand and walked toward the vast wall of paint-chip samples. They were organized into a rainbow of colors, all blending from one shade to the next like their own work of art. I didn't want to pull one out to look at it, for fear that I'd disturb this beautiful cohesion of so many different hues all existing in one space, all playing their small but significant part.

I felt Torin's body come up behind me before his chest touched my shoulder blade. "Lots to choose from," he murmured. Sonja was a few feet away comparing paint rollers, holding them up and mock painting in the air.

"I know, right?" I fingered the corner of one strip, but left it in its holder on the wall. "I don't want to take any of them out. They look so perfect like this."

"I doubt anyone would notice," Torin said, and that statement pulled all the wind out of my sails.

"That stinks, Torin." I shut my eyes and swallowed hard, breathing in. "That completely stinks that you could remove one of these very integral pieces to the puzzle and no one would notice."

"This a metaphor, right?" He wrapped his arms around my waist from behind. "We're not actually concerned about paint, are we?"

"We *are* concerned about paint. Someone needs to be concerned about this wall and someone needs to be responsible for keeping it like this. It's beautiful!" I tossed my hands toward the thousands of paint chips in front of us.

"Stunning, really."

"I know, right?" I nodded quickly, encouraging his agreement. "They need to devise a new system so people don't have to remove these cards in order to choose their paint."

"We should write a note and put it in their suggestion box." He was right there with me and my crazy. It might have just been humoring, but it felt like love.

"We *need* to. We can't just have people haphazardly removing such important players in this artistry of color. It's an injustice."

"A *complete* injustice."

Sonja waltzed up to us and reached her hand into the display that was our hardware store masterpiece.

"What are you doing?" I gasped, swatting her hand away.

"Ouch!" She grimaced and shot me the look that she often reserved for her boyfriend when he'd done something to royally piss her off. "I'm picking out a color since all you two seem to be doing is staring."

"We're not staring, we're appreciating," Torin said.

"Appreciating what?" Her hands were on her hips again.

"We're appreciating the very important role that each one of these little paint chips is playing in creating this gorgeous myriad of color and substance." I looked at Torin and he smiled down at me. I loved the wavelength we were riding together.

Sonja didn't have that same smile when she said, "Have you been drinking? Because it sounds like you've been drinking."

"No, we haven't been drinking."

"All right," she resigned. "If I'm not allowed to take it out, then let's write it down. Here—" She paused, scanning the rows of samples before landing on one. "This one." She thrust a finger onto an off-white sample that was only slightly less depressing than the one already coating our walls. "Gimme that pen."

Torin handed her the pen that rested on a five-gallon can of paint near his feet. Sonja scribbled the code onto the palm of her hand. "I'll tell him to mix it up. Enjoy your masterpiece, weirdos."

"We will," I replied, slinking my arms over Torin's, which were still held around my waist. "I know it's stupid and I know it makes me crazy, but it really is beautiful. Even if it's not actual art. Even if it's just a display some minimum-wage-earning sixteen-year-old put together."

"It's not stupid, you're not crazy, and it *is* beautiful." His mouth drew closer to my ear, and the way he breathed against it was chilling, in a good way. "You're beautiful," he said quietly, but I heard him clearly, even over the intercom speakers that announced a cleanup on aisle 4. "And you may not realize it, but you are a beautiful, bright piece in my world's masterpiece." The chills intensified. "You are this one." His finger fell on a stark-white chip. "To me, you are all of the colors combined. You are light, Darby, like that beloved lighthouse of yours."

"I feel really, really dark."

"I know." He didn't say anything for a few moments; he just let me feel the way I did without reprimanding me, or telling me it wasn't my fault, or that I wasn't responsible for it, or whatever it was that people had always been saying to me and continued to say to me.

"My fear is that my world will never be a beautiful master-piece with Anna and Lance gone."

"Right" was all he said, giving me the silence and the space I needed to continue.

"My fear is that somehow it was my job to keep their paint chips in place and now they're missing and it's all messed up." I inhaled through my nose, out through my mouth. "My fear is that I've messed it all up."

"Do you want to know what I think?" That phrase always struck me as odd because most people coupled it with a tone that came across as condescending and belittling. But the way Torin said it, he was actually asking my permission. Asking if it was okay for him to share his thoughts and feelings on my thoughts and feelings.

I nodded. It was.

"The way I see it, that sixteen-year-old hardware store worker of yours—he's got a pretty important role. Sometimes he discontinues certain colors, and sometimes he creates new ones." I could hear Sonja at the counter behind us arguing with the paint guy about how many gallons we would need, and I left her to that task. Torin continued, "And sometimes he moves them around into an abstract design that might not make sense to us, but he sees the whole picture and it's his job, not ours, to interpret it."

"I wish I could see things that way." I really did; I wished I could believe in something more, the way Torin did.

"Maybe someday you will," he said. I felt his heart against my back, that soothing pulse that steadied my own.

"It's exhausting talking in metaphors. Like, this has been the most taxing hardware store trip ever."

"Agreed." He smiled, dimples and all. "But sometimes it's easier to say what you feel when it's masked under something else."

All of the quoting finally made sense.

I flipped around to face him and ripped off my own proverbial mask.

"I'm in love with you, Torin," I said. "And I feel like I don't have a whole lot to offer because I was on the path to finding myself, and now Lance is dead, and I have to create who I am without him in my life, even though he *was* sorta out of my life, since we broke up and all. But now he's completely gone, with no chance of coming back, and I don't know what that means for me and for us." The sentences ran on. "And I left. I just left you there. Lance died and I freaked out and I left and didn't answer your calls because I felt guilty since I was not only mourning Lance's death, but had just started mourning my failed relationship with him. Which didn't even seem fair since I'd already started falling for you. So I was so trapped in my grief, and I didn't want you to think that me mourning Lance and his life and his death and *my* life with him and *my* death with him meant that I had stopped loving you. Because I hadn't. I haven't." Torin's eye softened with understanding, which was exactly what I needed. Always what I needed. "So I love you, and I don't want to mask that under anything else. I want you to know that I still love you, no metaphors."

"I love you too, Darby." He brought his lips down to mine and suddenly we were kissing in aisle 23, amid the paint-chip samples and blue tape and the tarps and the brushes. We were kissing. Like inappropriate, you-really-should-get-a-room kissing. And I loved every second of it because we weren't masking anything. We weren't hiding our feelings or holding anything back. We were full-on making out in a hardware store in front of this exhausting metaphor of paint chips.

His hand was on my cheek; my fingers were twisted in his hair. His chest leaned into mine; I pushed back with equal pressure. It was a lot of heavy breathing, racing pulses, and lips and tongue and sighing and wanting. And it lasted for several minutes, to the point where, even though we weren't doing the whole masking thing, we sort of had to in order to keep things decent and somewhat appropriate. While I wanted Torin to know that I loved him, I didn't need every patron in the store getting a complete visual of just how much.

He pulled back first, taking my bottom lip between his as he slowly broke our kiss.

"I don't know what I have to offer you right now, but whatever is there, it's all yours," I said, looking at him, trusting him with my heart, my grief, and my crazy.

"We love the things we love for what they are." I knew the words weren't his own, but this time he wasn't using them to shield his feelings at all, because I didn't think he could have said any other combination of words to create a thought or sentence that rang truer than those in that exact moment. "I love you, Darby, for what you are. Not what you will become once you're out of this valley." He dipped down and pressed his lips to mine in a sudden way that made the floor completely fall out from under me. "Not what you hoped Anna would become. Not what you allowed Lance to make of you. I love *you* for you."

"Look at my feet."

Torin shrugged his head back into his neck, completely perplexed. "What?" But then he did as I said and a smile stretched across his face, ear to ear, as he glanced at my sandals. "Blew your socks off."

"You warned me you would," I said, covering my mouth to hide the laughter.

"You forgot to recite your 'Who are you?' line," he said, pulling my hand from my lips.

"I didn't forget," I answered quickly. "I know exactly who you are, Torin." Pushing up on my toes, I sealed my lips to his in one more prolonged kiss. "You're the one who's helping me figure out exactly who I am."

Chapter 23

"I don't notice a difference, really." Torin dropped his brush into the open can of paint. "Is it bad that I don't notice a difference?"

"If we were still talking in metaphors, then yes, it's catastrophically bad, because then you're saying there's nothing special about paint chip P4560." I sat down in the very middle of the room and tucked my feet underneath me. "But since we're done with that and this is just paint, I sorta agree."

Sonja had left a couple of hours ago because her boyfriend was back in town for the weekend, so Torin and I were alone in the empty town house.

"Let's get pizza." Torin pulled his phone out from his back pocket. His jeans rested low enough that the toned edge of his hip peeked out above it. "You hungry?"

"I am."

He scrolled on his phone with his index finger and asked, "What's around here? I honestly don't even know where we are."

It was a funny statement coming from the guy who knew every square inch of Northern California's wilderness.

"Papa Pizza's is decent. They deliver," I said. "And, Torin?" His eyes flickered up to mine. "How did you know how to find me? I sorta left without giving you any clue."

He bit his bottom lip and squinted as he thumbed through the list of pizza joints. "Your application."

"Oh." I guessed that made sense. It didn't really matter how he'd found me, though. I was just glad that he had.

"Pepperoni okay?"

I agreed with a nod and he called in our order.

As he conversed with the worker on the other line, I couldn't help but stare at him. His hair curled around his ear and his dimples pressed in and out of his cheeks, sometimes more prominently with certain syllables and words than others. I tried to pinpoint which ones brought them out, deciding those would become permanent words in my own vocabulary with the hopes that maybe they would rub off on him and he'd start using them more frequently, too. I really loved when those dimples made an appearance.

He'd been so focused on ordering our late-night dinner that he didn't notice me gawking at him until our eyes caught after he'd hung up the phone and dipped it back into his pocket.

"You see something you like?" he asked, his eyebrows shooting up in a "I totally know you were just checking me out" kind of way.

"Definitely," I admitted, returning the same encouraging grin.

But Torin didn't need any encouragement.

In an instant he was down at my level, his face inches from mine, his eyes locked with an intensity that made everything else disappear. And not just our surroundings. Everything in my brain disappeared, too. Every emotion that existed outside of this realm that was just the two of us completely vanished. It was only us. No grief. No anxiety. Just us.

Like he was on the prowl, he walked his hands across the ground and pressed his chest solidly to mine. I fell onto my elbows, then onto my back completely as the tantalizing weight of his body guided me slowly onto the carpet.

This wasn't at all how I pictured our first time together—on the floor in the middle of my empty shell of an apartment with an unnecessary coat of paint drying on the walls. I'd pictured it happening, obviously, but not there. And not just weeks after losing Lance in the way that I'd lost him. In the way that we'd *all* lost him.

I wondered when the time would come to move on, and how that could even be determined. People moved on in their own ways and at their own speed, I supposed. Part of me—most of me, actually—began moving on over a year ago when Lance started that process on his own with another girl. What he'd given to her took from what we had, and no matter how hard we'd tried to get it back, it was hers, not mine anymore. The heart he'd once professed to me was parceled out, and even in death, it belonged to other girls, too. He'd given himself to them and he wasn't all mine. Maybe he never actually had been. The finality of it all broke my heart beyond repair.

I knew it wasn't his responsibility, but I needed Torin to help put it back together.

We kissed for a long time. I was sure our pizza-delivery guy would rap on the door at any moment, but each time things started to really pick up, something in Torin's posture shifted. There was a tangible hesitation that made me feel like maybe I was doing something wrong. I was pretty certain, after all the times I'd been with Lance, that I knew what guys liked, what got them going, but Torin's visible pauses made me feel like I had it all confused. The humiliating grip of insecurity took hold.

"Torin?" I asked after a kiss that nearly made me pass out. I marshaled my breathing before I continued. "Do you want to . . . um . . ."

He pushed his mouth to mine and swallowed my words. His tongue ran across my bottom lip and his hands roved over my body with frantic, fueled movement. There was no question that we were on our way to doing this. Our hips, our mouths, our bodies, everything begged for more and moved synchronously in a way that felt more intimate than anything I'd ever done. I wanted him. That was not the question at all. And I was ready to give all of myself to him. Completely.

The problem was, it didn't seem like he wanted to take it.

"Darby." My name came out in the form of a throaty groan. I gripped his shoulders with my hands, my nails digging into his back, just above his shoulder blades. "This is amazing."

And it was. Even with all the layers of clothing between us, it felt incredible. I really wanted to feel just how incredible it could be.

"Do you think we should . . . ?" I tried again, because even though I'd kind of hinted at it, I wasn't entirely sure he'd gotten that hint, since we were still just limiting things to making out.

With his hands bracketed around me, he straightened his arms and propped himself up. The hair that hung around his face and the flush that painted his cheeks made him look so incredible that I was beyond tempted to rip his clothes off right there.

"Do I think we should have sex?"

Hearing him actually say it made my body temperature elevate to thermometer-breaking status.

"Um." I gulped between breaths that I absolutely could not control. "Yeah."

He dropped down onto me again, pinning me beneath him with his legs twisted in mine. The kissing became too much at that point. His lips were hot against my skin as they trailed from my earlobe down to the curve of my neck, stalling right around my collarbone. "I." Another kiss on my throat. "Want." His lips brushed back to my ear and his ragged breath echoed into it, shooting chills down the entire length of my body. "To." His fingers raked through my hair, nearly making it stand on end. "So." His other hand pressed flatly against my stomach, lifting the hem of my shirt to push his palm to my bare skin, making my stomach quiver with anticipation. *"Bad."*

"There's a *but*." I had to acknowledge it before he did just to save a little face.

"No, there's no *but*." His words totally shocked me and seemed to snap me out of some daydream. "I completely want to."

"Are you serious, Torin?" It had never taken so much effort to swallow in my entire life, but somehow I managed it. "Like . . . you want to . . . ?"

"It's honestly not a matter of wanting." The kissing had stopped momentarily, mostly so we could actually get the words out, but the movement of hands and bodies didn't let up. "Because I've wanted to do unmentionable things with you from the moment I saw you. That's not the issue."

"But, Torin . . ." I couldn't believe we were *actually* talking about *actually* doing this. "You haven't . . . I mean . . . you said you were a virgin."

"I am." His body pushed down onto mine even harder and our legs coiled together, our chests heaved against each other, and our mouths hovered to no more than a sliver of space apart. "But it's not because I have something against sex." He really shouldn't have, but he licked his lips—unintentionally, I was pretty certain—and it almost made me lose it. I imagined that tongue licking across my own, and that was just about more than I could handle. "I'm pretty sure I have nothing against sex. Sex is good."

"Sex is amazing."

"I'm going to choose to believe that is just a blanket statement and you're not pulling from prior experience, even though I know that's not the case." He smiled when he spoke and a slight laugh followed his words. "Because I don't like thinking about you and Lance."

And just like that, the brakes were completely pulled.

"I don't like thinking about Lance," he continued, this time sitting up, drawing away from me, "but I can't stop thinking about Lance."

Neither could I. Only in momentary waves was I able to block him out of my mind. There wasn't much that could distract me from the fact that he was gone and that the way we'd left things was absolutely awful. Lance was at the forefront of my mind, no matter how hard I tried to shake him free. He was there, always there.

"And since I can't stop thinking about him, I think maybe we shouldn't do this," Torin said, his voice thick with emotion and his eyes welling with that same sorrow. "Because I don't want to be thinking about Lance when we, you know, *do* this."

Of course I agreed with that. I had to. I didn't want to be thinking about Lance, either. I just wasn't sure when that time would come that I *wouldn't* be thinking about him. I wished for some magical hour to occur, when the grieving process would come to a close. But the more of life I experienced, the more I came to realize there was no end point to grief, just different stages of it. And those stages were long, drawn-out, ceaseless chunks of time.

"Okay." I didn't feel rejected. If anything, it was a relief because Torin seemed to have more clarity in the moment than I did.

"I hope it is. . . . Okay with you, I mean."

"Of course it is, Torin."

A cautious smile spread across his face and he added, "Plus—you might make fun of me for this—there are a few other quotes I'd like to say to you before we actually do it."

"Oh, yeah?" My interest piqued. "And what would those be?"

Even though it was nearly black, the floodlight we'd used as we painted the wall cast curved shadows across the room, creating its own painting of light and dark. Torin's profile was illuminated and I could see his Adam's apple pull up and down in his throat as the ball at the back of his jaw pulsed. Nerves rose to the surface and took the form of a slight twitch of his lip and the tightening of his mouth. "As long as we both shall live."

I didn't say anything. I couldn't say anything.

"Does it freak you out to hear that?" Torin asked quickly, a rush of words. "Because it freaks me out to say that."

"It doesn't freak me out," I said, though it did just a little. Okay, maybe more than a little. "I just wasn't expecting that."

"Expecting me to quote from wedding vows? I guess I haven't done that yet, have I?" He smiled apprehensively. "I realize it's totally unconventional, but I really like those words. How it's just two people, committed until death. When we are together, I want it *as long as we both shall live*, Darby."

When he said that, my heart physically hurt inside my chest for Lance and the brutal fact that he didn't have that with anyone in his final moments. He'd died alone. Without me. Without Clara. And he'd died in pieces, having parceled himself out to so many different people, no one to fully claim him as their own.

Maybe he had the hope of me as he got in that car—and I prayed that hope was enough. Because in this quiet that pulsed between Torin and me, I realized how sad it would be to die without that hope of a future. To die with regret. I clung to the thought that he did have hope, and that what Torin had once said was true: that hope was stronger than regret. I needed that to be the case for Lance. I needed that to be the case for all of us.

"Can you say something?" Torin's fingers lifted my chin. I'd been staring at the carpet—I hadn't realized it—and I'm sure I looked like I was off in some faraway place. "Is it okay for me to tell you things like that?"

"Of course it's okay, Torin. It's what I want, actually."

"So we'll wait. I mean, for now, we'll wait."

"We'll wait," I agreed.

"This is not me saying I don't want this, Darby." He still cupped my jaw in his palms. "Because I want to do this. Just maybe a little differently from the way you've done things in the past."

"Different is good," I agreed. Honestly, different was probably what I needed. And since I didn't do a very good job of knowing what I needed—having up and left Quarry Summit, having repainted a wall in a house that I no longer even inhabited—I thought Torin was a good person to help me make those decisions. I needed someone to guide me.

"When I'm with you, I want to be able to give all of myself to you, and I want to have all of you." He reiterated, "I think a piece of you is still with him. And that's okay, it should be." We were sitting now, and Torin pulled me onto his lap, my legs wrapping around him, squeezing his body closer to mine. "But it wouldn't be fair to either of us to do this until all of our pieces were put back together. When our pieces fall into place, then we'll be ready for each other, whatever that looks like."

"It might be a long time before that happens."

With a reassuring smile that was heavy with love and understanding, Torin said, "I'll wait for you, Darby." His fingers trailed slowly up and down my bare arms and I looked deep into his eyes, seeing my own reflection illuminated in his wide-open expression.

That's when I began to cry.

"Hey," he whispered, lifting my chin up. "It's okay."

"I know." I nodded, sniffing back my tears and pushing the heels of my hands to my eyes. "I just feel crushed."

"Of course you do. You have every reason to, Darby." There

wasn't anything he could really do to comfort me, but he tried as he wrapped his arms around me and cradled my head onto his shoulder. "I know that Lance and I didn't have the greatest encounter, but it honestly does break my heart that he's gone, because no one deserves to die when they're nineteen." Smoothing my hair with his palm, he continued, "Or thirteen. Or seventeen." I knew he was referencing Anna and Randy. "In a perfect world, we'd all grow old on our porch swings with our glasses of lemonade, watching our grandchildren run through the yard."

The vision brought a smile to my face even though the tears continued to stream.

"In a perfect world, we'd all die in our sleep, wrapped in our loved one's arms." I wasn't sure if he did it on purpose, but the tightness of his embrace grew stronger around me. "Car crashes and abductions and suicides—that's not how it's meant to be, Darby. It's awful and tragic and unfair in so many ways. And it's so unfair that you've had two people you've loved so strongly ripped from your life so early," Torin said. "It's unfair, but it's not unrealistic."

I blanched. "It's not?"

"It's all of our fates. We'll all die eventually, as much as we'd like to pretend we can avoid it. There will be others. Lance and Anna are not it, but you have to keep loving and you have to keep living. It's the only thing we can do."

"I hope I can," I muttered into his hair.

"I'll wait for you until you can, Darby," he assured, his lips pressed to my forehead. "I think I've actually been waiting for you all along."

. . . .

We ate our pizza and fell asleep in the middle of the room, just like I had for the past however many days it had been. At about two thirty in the morning, I thought I heard scratching, like a cat clawing on the door, but I didn't own any cats and this wasn't even my actual residence anymore. I awoke slowly, gradually, and the fuzziness of sleep stayed with me even as I opened my eyes.

Torin was at the wall, a pencil in his hand, the floodlight centered in a circle of light around whatever it was that he was etching onto the smooth surface in front of him.

"Torin?" I pushed my hand into my eye sockets, rubbing them in an attempt to find some focus. "What are you doing?"

"Come look at this, Darby." He waved a hand over his shoulder, all the while continuing his scribbling on the drywall. "I want you to see something."

I rose from the floor and joined him at his side.

"What is this?"

There were columns of names etched in graphite, all across the wall. At least fifty names, maybe more. It resembled those walls of remembrance that list the dead at cemeteries.

Turned out, that's exactly what it was.

"These are all of the people who I know that have died."

"Wow." I gulped. "That's an awful lot."

"Well, yeah, I suppose it is. But they weren't all people I was close with. Just people I knew or met who are no longer living." He scrawled another name onto the wall. "And I'm sure there are hundreds more I'm not counting. Like, a grocer at a store who I might have met once. Or someone I sat next to at a red light. Or the garbageman or mailman. That hiker who died a few years back just a couple miles from Summit . . . what was his name? Brent, I think. No . . . that doesn't sound right." He paused. "Bryant!"

"What's this all about, Torin?" I scanned the memorial in front of me and my eyes locked in on *Lance McIverson* like it was written in blood rather than lead.

"Before you left—before you took off—you said we are all responsible for one another." He must have remembered another name, because he added one to the list. "And I told you that was a responsibility I couldn't bear. Which is true. I couldn't be responsible for keeping all of these people alive. And these are just the people who I *knew* that have died—the ones I'd had some sort of relationship with." His explaining didn't really feel like explaining, because the words he spoke didn't clarify anything about this cryptic display. "Tony Gonzales," he said, running his pencil over the wall. "Forgot him. Anyway," he continued, "this is my list."

"It's a long list. I'm so sorry, Torin."

"Right. It is."

"I don't think my list is that long."

"I think you're wrong," he said in a no-nonsense kind of way. "Your list is probably exactly the same length as mine. Maybe even longer since, as you say, you grew up in civilization. More paths to cross. More interactions. More opportunities to change the course of someone's life."

I combed my fingers through my hair, the nervous energy taking form in my anxious hands. "That really doesn't make any sense, Torin."

"It doesn't? You sure about that?"

"I don't get this metaphor. The paint one of mine, that kinda made sense. But this? This doesn't make sense to me."

"Good." He snapped the pencil between his hands, shards of wood splintering onto the floor. "Because I want you to see just how crazy a statement like that is." Dropping both palms onto my shoulders, he all but shook me as he said, "The thing is, Darby, we never know how an interaction with someone will change the direction of their life, but inevitably, it will change it."

"If you are doing this to make me feel less guilty about Lance, I appreciate it, but I don't know that it will change things. I'm still part of the reason for his death."

"I'm doing this to show you how I think we're meant to live.

I don't think life should be full of what ifs. *What if* we hadn't left a day early out of Boston? *What if* you'd left the light on for Anna? *What if* you hadn't picked up the phone that night he called? You're giving the what ifs too much power."

"I don't know how not to."

"You focus on the things you know—the opposite of the what ifs," he said.

"What is the opposite of *if*, Torin?"

"Truth." It didn't take him any time to answer, like the response had been waiting and balanced right there on the tip of his tongue. "And the truth of it is, we all play a part in all of this. We've all been assigned our roles. I think we're responsible for the living part, not for the dying part. You can't look at each interaction as a possible turning point toward death. You have to look at each interaction as something that adds to life."

"How do you think like that?" I shook my head at him, completely awed. "Like, how does your brain even work that way?"

"Don't know. Honestly, sometimes it hurts," he admitted, rubbing his scalp with his fingers. "But I knew I had to think this for you because you wouldn't allow yourself to believe it if you came up with it on your own."

"That's probably true." For knowing me only a short while, he knew me so well. Probably more than I'd ever let anyone know me before. I wondered if that meant that I was giving all of myself to him, at least as much as I had to give. I hoped that's what it meant.

"I'm going to paint over this now." He motioned back toward the wall while turning at the waist. "I just really wanted you to try to see things from another perspective. Don't live in the what ifs, Darby."

"I'm trying not to."

"I know. Me, too."

And with a roll of the brush, the names were gone.

Chapter 24

One week later

I desperately did not want to be that girl again. That girl who stumbles into depression and doesn't really ever come out of it, just wallows through it, sometimes with greater, more stable strides, sometimes with visible faltering. I would not wade through depression like I lived there in its murky waters. I would cross through it. I would come out on the other side.

I had to.

I had to focus more on the living, less on the dying. That was good advice.

Lance's physical body was no longer here, and neither was Anna's, nor Randy's, nor the fifty-odd other names hidden under the most recent layer of paint in the town house. But their memories were still alive, and how they impacted this world was still present in the form of recollections and footprints and conversations and stories.

Interactions. When it came down to it, that was all life really was. Sets of interactions: Me interacting with you. You interacting with me. You interacting with someone else. That someone else interacting with the someone else next to them. We were all just a bunch of someone elses strung together in a network of interactions. Like that whole Six Degrees of Kevin Bacon thing, only much, much bigger. More like Six Billion Degrees of Someone Elses. That's what we were, and we tangled into one giant, messy web.

The truth of it was, we *were* all responsible for one another, just not like I'd thought. Maybe not so much in the dying (though inevitably we did hold some responsibility there, even if we didn't want to believe it, because life ultimately pointed toward death), but in the living. The way I lived affected the way you lived, and the way someone else lived affected others because that's what we did: we interacted and we lived our lives and we rubbed off on others and hoped that the mark we left was a positive one.

That was why I couldn't allow myself to drown in the depression of grief. Because I would continue leaving my mark—even if I tried not to—and I wanted it to be more than I'd left these past six years. I had to work at leaving a better mark.

"I still think about her every day."

"I know." Mom took another sip from her martini glass, swishing the cool contents in her mouth, her eyes held shut.

It was ten o'clock in the morning.

"Does that help?" I waved a hand toward her glass and could see the reflection of *Sesame Street* playing for my youngest sister on the television in the adjoining room. Big Bird's long neck looked even longer than I'd remembered, and his oversize beak appeared more pointy and sharp, like a razor blade. I felt drunk just looking at him, and I'd only had a glass of orange juice. "Drinking . . . does it help?"

Mom let out a soundless huff of a laugh. "No, Darby. Nothing helps."

"Why do you do it, then?"

She tipped the empty glass to her lips and sighed so loudly I worried she'd momentarily run out of air. "Because it allows me to hide, Darby." It was an honest statement, and I wondered if whatever she'd been drinking gave her the ability to speak it so freely. "It hides me from the things in my life I don't want to face."

Sitting across the kitchen table from my mom, watching her drain her liquid courage, it dawned on me that maybe that's what we all did. We hid behind famous people's words and the buzz of alcohol and even another person's memories because we were afraid of what would happen if we didn't provide some type of shield against the hurt that would inevitably come our way again. So we crouched in our corners and drew up our defenses and cowered from the things that scared us. Losing Anna scared me, so I didn't allow myself to lose her. I held on to her with all I had.

And holding on to Anna when it seemed like everyone else was letting her slip away was the only way I could protect myself from the hurt of that reality. The reality that life moved on. That people died and, yes, it was sad, but people also lived. And moving on, and even forgetting to an extent, was part of that living.

I thought, finally, that I really wanted to start living. And I thought, maybe, that letting go of Lance might be the right, and only, thing to help me do that.

"I'm so sorry, Darby." Mom twirled the stem of her glass back and forth between her fingers, studying the drop of clear liquid that pooled at the lip of the rim. It matched the ones that balanced at the edges of her eyes. "About Lance, about your sister. God. It's all so awful. It's like the universe randomly drew your name and you've been dealt these horrible cards."

"It doesn't feel random." I knew when I spoke it that I was beginning to sound an awful lot like Torin, but I was okay with that. I was okay with believing—however guardedly—that maybe it wasn't random. And it didn't make me feel depressed or anything, it just made me feel like maybe there was a picture. A bigger blueprint. There was comfort in thinking that, and more than comfort, there was reason. A reason why some people experienced so much tragedy, while others skated through life without ever really living in the valley. I'd been in the valley for longer than I liked. I was ready to reach the summit.

"I met a guy."

I expected a "Seriously? Already?" but instead Mom just said, "What's his name?"

"Torin."

"Goofy name." She laughed, and I realized how much I missed the sound of her laugh because she didn't allow herself to do that much anymore.

"So is 'Darby.'"

She smiled, another thing I missed. "What's he like?"

It really had only been a month since Lance died, but my mom didn't make me feel horrible for talking about Torin. I didn't think I'd ever be able to show her how grateful I was for her not judging me for that.

"He's quirky. He quotes movies and philosophers and books." I'd never really described Torin to anyone, but the characteristics came out effortlessly. "His brother died when he was twelve."

Mom nodded knowingly, like that statement spoke volumes. I supposed it did. "He sounds good for you, Darby."

"He gets me, and right now, I think I need someone in my life who gets me." I paused. "But I still miss Lance." I had to add that. I was pretty certain I'd always be adding that.

Standing up from her seat at the table, Mom came up behind me and wrapped her arms over my shoulders. "You will always miss Lance, sweetie. He was a huge part of your life. Like family."

"We didn't end things well." I really didn't like admitting that out loud. It was easier to pretend I was the grieving girlfriend who had lost her knight in shining armor. That's what others believed and that's what I wanted them to believe. Just because he wasn't perfect didn't make it necessary to tarnish his image that way. Allowing people to think that he was nothing but a stand-up guy felt like one final gift I could give him. Maybe I couldn't have saved his life, but I could at least save his image. Deep down, I knew he'd have done the same for me, and I think my own image needed just as much saving. "We didn't end things well. We both made a lot of mistakes. Honestly, we probably should have broken up years ago, just so we could have ended things better, you know?"

Mom squeezed me tighter, then drew in a sharp breath. "Did you know that Anna and I had a huge fight that day?"

I shook my head, surprised by the turn in our conversation and her tone.

"She had been asking all day for me to take her to get something she needed for an assignment that she'd waited until last minute to start." Mom's grip loosened and she stood back a few feet. I rotated in my chair to face her, feeling like I was looking at my partner in crime. Like she was confessing to part of the responsibility I bore on my own for all those years. "I was so angry that she'd procrastinated, and Joey had a game, and Sarah had ballet, and then there was dinner and baths and bedtime for the little ones. I yelled at her and told her she wasn't the only child in this family." The tears that refused to fall earlier skimmed down her cheek. "The last words I said to her were, 'You need to understand that the world doesn't revolve around you.'" Mom closed her eyes and paused before saying, "That was the last thing I said. What mother says something like that?"

"Every mother on the planet." Which was true. I think it was in some script that they'd all been given, with comebacks and one-liners that would stand the test of time. "Seriously, Mom. I think every single mother has said that."

Mom sighed. "It doesn't make it right."

"No, but it makes it okay. I think there's a difference." I reached out to take her hand in mine. It was so much more frail than I'd remembered. The knobby bones of her knuckles dug deep into my fingers and her once manicured nails were jagged and rough. "Maybe it's not right to say or think things like that, but it's okay to do things that aren't right sometimes. We're human."

"Yes, we are." Mom shook my hand free and grabbed me and kissed me on the crown of my head. "Being human is hard."

"That's an understatement."

"I feel so awful for Paul and Sarah." I'm sure she did. She knew exactly what it was like to lose a child. "And Lance. Poor Lance."

"I think out of all of us, he's got it the easiest. He doesn't have the hard work of being human anymore."

She smoothed down my hair with a palm and tugged me close to her chest. "Being human is hard, but I do think it beats the alternative."

I shrugged and let her hold me there for a bit, leaning into her, knowing she needed this just as much as I did. "That honestly depends on what you think the alternative is."

. . . .

It was all tucked neatly into two shoe boxes on the top shelf of my closet. That was it. It all fit in there: a half-dozen dried corsages, two albums of photographs, a couple of letters (he wasn't a big letter writer), a small stuffed animal we'd won at a carnival junior year, and a handful of newspaper clippings featuring images of Lance and his parents in black-and-white print.

What I had left of Lance fit into two boxes. What was physically left of him fit into a box buried six feet underground. Had he been cremated, that box would have been even smaller. And what of those people whose bodies weren't even intact when they died? Like, if you died in some explosion, there wouldn't even be anything left of you to have a box. That thought, however horrifically morbid, really made me sad. Everyone deserved at least a box.

I stared at the two containers on my shelf, grateful for what was hidden in them. I did love Lance, and in a way, I knew I always would. And I didn't think I'd ever really get over him, so maybe he'd always own a piece of me. Maybe I'd never be completely whole.

Every recent memory I had involved him in some form. Some memories were good, others were bad, and a lot were just mediocre, which was how our relationship had evolved—the downward slope toward breaking up. But the memories were a part of me and a part of him, so I held on to them. It felt like having those memories in my grip was the only way to make things good again. In my mind, I could remember when things were good with Lance. I would choose to do that, because I hoped that when I died, others would choose to remember the good in me, too.

I slung my duffel bag over my shoulder, glancing around the room, taking a final inventory. It really hadn't been my room for quite some time. My younger sister Natalie had taken it over while I was at college, but whenever I came back home, it was where I slept. There were still a few things in the room that were mine, but most of what was left of me blended in with Natalie's posters, her books stacked high against the far wall, and her cosmetics strewn across the dresser. It was funny how what was once solely mine morphed into someone else's. I couldn't tell where the blur between Natalie and me started, but it was there and the room was a weird amalgamation of that.

I bounded down the stairs, the weight of the bag bouncing against my side as I approached the landing. Chris, my oldest brother, passed me on the way up, shifting his shoulder slightly to slide by, nodding his shaved head in my direction without looking up from his phone. That was his good-bye to me, I figured, and I wondered if it had ever occurred to him that maybe it could be our last.

Of course it hadn't occurred to him, which was good, because he was normal. He didn't think of life in lasts. He probably just thought of life in the present, and that was the way it should be.

No one else was home, so no other "almost" good-byes took place on my way out the door. I tossed my bag into the back of the Jeep and fit the key into the ignition. I'd made a run to the store earlier, and my stash of junk food littered the passenger side. I was ready for this.

He wasn't expecting me for another three weeks, so the entire drive I felt that giddy, nervous sensation that wasn't only mental, but physical, too.

I knew I loved Torin.

I couldn't describe it in a way that others would get, like with those common phrases "It was love at first sight" or "We were meant to be." I didn't think I really believed either of those things. They felt too simple for the emotions evoked when I thought about him. Words, even though there was an endless number of them at my disposal, couldn't be arranged to form my feelings. At least, I couldn't do that on my own, with my limited vocabulary. I knew I'd have to borrow someone else's for this one.

I began the drive in the morning, and by early afternoon I was rounding the turn into Quarry Summit, the SUV kicking up copious amounts of dust from the dirt road, the once formidable evergreens rising up on either side of me, framing me in like a welcoming hug.

He was up ahead in the distance, and my body instantly reacted to the sight of him as he inched closer into view. He was shirtless and shoveling some loose gravel at the edge of the parking lot. The sun wrapped around his body, defining his toned and muscular form. He brushed the sweat from his brow at the same moment he caught sight of my Jeep. Like nothing else existed, he dropped the shovel from his grip—almost throwing it—and raced toward me as I killed the engine. His hand was at the handle to the door before I could push it open and his mouth was on mine before I could even say hi.

He tasted like sweat and salt, but I dove right in, my lips curling with his, my back arching as he bowed over me.

"What are you doing here?" he gasped with an excitement in his eyes that made every hour of my lonely, carb-fueled car ride worth it.

"I had to tell you something."

"And it couldn't wait three more weeks?" His lips met mine once more, this time teasing them apart so his tongue could slide in. My legs went all Jell-O and my heart started a hundred-meter dash. I pulled away, light-headed and dizzy.

"I have one rule in my life," I said, pushing my back against the driver's side door. Torin's hands slid into the back pockets of my jeans. "To live without regret." I lifted a hand to his chest and pressed my palm onto his heart. "I haven't done a good job with that so far. I figured I should start now."

He shook his head a little, his hair tossing side to side. "What do you regret?"

"Honestly, in life, a lot of things. But with you, not many." It was strange, but with Torin, I seemed to do and say what I felt without keeping much in. Regret came when you held something back. With Torin, there was no holding back.

"That's good. No regrets."

"That's beyond good. And that's why I didn't want to wait the three weeks to see you again. I would regret that."

"I'm glad you didn't wait." He shot me a smile and pulled me into a hug that was almost a headlock. As he breathed into my hair he asked, "So what is this potentially regret-inducing thing you have to tell me that can't wait?"

I very nearly cleared my throat. "We're born alone, we live alone, we die alone. Only through our love and friendship can we create the illusion for the moment that we're not alone." My shoulders lifted in an insecure shrug and I added, "That's from Orson Welles."

"Yeah." Torin nodded, but seemed a little unaffected.

"You make me feel less alone in this illusion we've created," I clarified as Torin squinted down at me. In this moment, with the sun highlighting it in slight golden waves, his hair was definitely blond. I wondered how red mine looked in this same lighting.

Torin smiled at me, pausing before he spoke. "But we aren't born alone, I don't think. We're born out of love between two people, and even in the instances when that ideal isn't the case, we're still born *from* someone." He started with the reason and logic, which I found pretty darn attractive. I loved the way his brain worked; how he could pull so much meaning from a grouping of words strung together. "And living alone? I don't think there's much truth in that." He shook his head and his hair skated along his jaw. "The dying thing? Maybe. . . . That might be the only instance we're ever alone, but even on our deathbed, we have life's memories to keep us company."

He paused.

"I think the illusion isn't in pretending we aren't alone, the illusion is in pretending it's ever possible *to* be alone."

"I really thought I had something with that." I sighed.

"I think you did," he assured. "Absolutely. I just interpreted it a little differently than you did."

Torin interpreted more than just words differently than I did. He had his own way of understanding life unlike any other interpretation I'd ever read or heard. It made me want to learn his language. It made me want to continue learning from him in any form he wanted to teach me.

"I think that quote was a good one, Darby, I do. But there's going to be one that speaks to you at the core of who you are. You'll find your quotable quote yet, trust me."

My bag was still in the SUV, so Torin opened up the back and pulled my bag up onto his shoulder. I wasn't quite sure where I'd even be sleeping, since camp was done and the cabins were locked up for the season. I hadn't prepared much, other than that one quote, and even that fell a little flat.

"I'm actually glad you came up early."

"*Actually* glad? I was hoping for 'exceedingly glad.'"

"I'm actually exceedingly glad that you're here, because there is something I want to show you." He stretched his hand out for my keys and I dropped them into his palm. "I thought I'd have about three more weeks, so I'm a little behind." He slid into the driver's seat of my Jeep, motioning for me to join him in the cab, tossing my bag back in. "I've got something I want you to see."

Chapter 25

It was strange to drive in a vehicle through the forest when we'd spent so much time in the expanse of wilderness on foot before. For about ten minutes we coasted across carved-out dirt roads, ever increasing in elevation until Torin abruptly shut off the engine right where the Jeep sat, like there was some imaginary stop sign I couldn't see. "We have to walk the rest of the way."

I nodded and unbuckled my belt.

He waited for me to join him and then twisted his fingers into mine, a gesture that didn't go unnoticed. Before, I had always trailed him. Now, we were side by side.

Last time I was in these woods, I didn't know that the process of falling in love with Torin was already underway. I wondered what was underway right now that I wasn't aware of, because life apparently occurred in hindsight. It was only when you looked back on things that you could see clearly.

Had Anna not died, I probably wouldn't have ever gotten together with Lance. And had Lance and I not been together all those years, I wouldn't have come to this camp in the first place.

Life, in itself, was inertia.

Even when you left everything alone, it continued to move forward, continuing on its journey. There was a momentum to life, and the only thing that could stop it was death. It didn't feel as rewarding as I thought it would to finally figure all of that out. It just felt real. Living finally felt real, because even when you stood still, everything else kept moving, with or without you. I had to face that reality, and even if I couldn't, it wouldn't really have an effect on how the mechanics of life worked. It would just keep going: that was the hard truth of it all.

"This is it," Torin announced as we crested the hill. The air was thinner where we were, the forest more sparse. "Over here."

When he stopped, I glanced around him, craning my neck, expecting to see just what it was that he wanted me to see, but there was nothing. Only an open expanse of dirt with a few boulders rising out of it.

"I feel like I'm missing something." I looked around again.

"Technically, there's nothing here."

Good. I was glad that my interpretation of this wasn't as skewed as my apparent interpretations of other things.

"But there's the potential of something, and that's what I want to show you." Torin kind of bounced on the heels of his feet as he spoke, a giddiness that couldn't be contained within the confines of his body. "So this is the summit." His hand outstretched to the left in an encompassing wave. "On the property we have here, this is the highest point."

Just past his hand I could see the sloping mountains that slanted toward the valley and the tops of the trees that, earlier,

I'd viewed only from their trunks. The trees felt smaller from the summit, and it was incredible how their looming grandiosity was diminished so much from that perspective.

"You can't see the forest for the trees," I muttered, my eyes sweeping across the miles of evergreens that blanketed the hills like a green, crocheted afghan.

"Holy heck, Darby! You just did it!"

"Did what?"

"Your quote!" Torin half shouted, his pale eyes lighting up with intensity. His hands gripped my biceps and shook me excitedly. "And a damn good one at that."

"It's so true." I continued staring at the valley, my eyes unblinking. "This perspective is like . . . it's un*real*. Like there's this big, beautiful forest that you can't even see until you're actually out of it."

"*C'est la vie*," he murmured, his fingers looser on my skin, sliding up and down the length of my arms in an affectionate, swirly motion.

"Such is life," I repeated.

And it was. Life was the big, beautiful thing that I wasn't sure I'd ever appreciated for the actual beauty it held. Not until I saw it from another perspective. Somehow, Torin had been able to do that, but I was still working on getting there. The paint chips, the trees. I was close, but I hadn't reached my summit point of view.

"Anyway." He snapped me back around to face away from him. "I have something for you." Torin briefly let go of me and walked toward a small, rust-coated shed that I'd overlooked in my whole forest-realization moment. The door had a padlock with a key still in it, and he twisted the key to pop the lock off of the metal handle. The door creaked on its hinges as he held it open, and for a second he disappeared inside. When he came out, he was holding a roll of blueprint paper.

"This is for you," he said, handing me the paper. "This—and this." He motioned toward the dirt underneath us with a stomp of his boot-clad foot. "I want you to make the shell. And I want us to fill it up."

"What?"

"It's all yours. Like, seriously, do whatever you want with it. Design a house or a cabin or a tepee if you feel so inclined." His smile spread wide across his face and I lifted my finger to trace his full bottom lip like it was instinct. "But it's all for you," he spoke against my skin. "Well, for us, hopefully . . . but only when you're ready."

I replaced my finger with my lips as I stood up on my toes to meet his mouth with mine. Torin ran his fingers through my hair, tucking the strands around my ear before cupping my jaw in his palms. The way he looked down at me, like I was the only thing that existed in this world, left my stomach feeling warm and heavy.

"I know things aren't in our favor, Darby. Had you and Lance only broken up, that would have been a ton to deal with." His hands stayed in place on my chin. "But he cheated and you fought and then he freaking died, and I'm not naive enough to think that we won't have our struggles because of that." I couldn't break my gaze with his eyes. Everything about him drew me in. "But I want to struggle *through* it with you. I think the noble thing for me to do would be to step back and let you have your space, but I don't want to give you space." He paused, ever so briefly, before saying, "I want to be *in* that space with you. And I want to share this space with you, too." Turning around 360 degrees, he met my eyes after the full-circle rotation. God, he was gorgeous. I didn't know how I missed it in the beginning, but he'd turned into this gorgeous boy, on the inside and out. "Your own summit, Darby. Your own corner of the world," he said. "I want to share this mountaintop with you."

Again, there weren't a lot of my own words readily available and I stunk at reciting others', so I just held him there and thought of how amazing it was that this guy had just given me my own mountain to build dreams upon.

You couldn't plan for anything in life. It happened to you. But holding the blank blueprints in my hands felt like a promise: a promise of a new start, a new hope. I could make something there and we could fill it up with *us*. In all of my life, I didn't think I'd been given a greater gift than the grid-lined paper that rustled between my fingertips.

"I love you, Torin."

"I love you, Darby." He didn't say 'I love you, too,' like it was a response to my saying it, but he spoke it as a declaration, as if it stood all on its own. "I know I have this tendency to get attached to things easily, but even if that weren't the case, I'd have fallen for you just as quickly." He pulled me closer to him, his hips pressing against mine, his chest still bare and suntanned, the filmy layer of dirt and sweat that coated him creating a rugged aura that was hopelessly irresistible. "Maybe it's our experiences, maybe it's our similarities. Whatever it is, I recognized something in you. It was like my heart recognized yours."

I completely got that. Our beats becoming one, morphing into the same metronomic pattern.

"So there's this . . . get this—" he teased, his eyes opening more, "a *quote*—I heard that says we're given two hands to hold, two legs to walk, two eyes to see, two ears to listen. But why only one heart?"

I shook my head to encourage him to continue toward the punch line.

"Because the other was given to someone else. *For us to find.*" Torin smiled a soft, thoughtful smile, and the hip pressing became more intense and our foreheads touched as we moved closer. "I found my heart in you, Darby." I swear we were so close I could feel the flutter from his eyelashes whooshing against my skin. "I know I told Lance I was the one who took the time to look for you, that I'd found you. But maybe I was just looking for myself all along and I found myself mirrored in you. Does that even make any sense?"

"Does it make sense that you'd find yourself in finding me?" I pushed up a bit so our noses aligned. "I think that's exactly what love is, Torin. I think that's what happens when a *you* and a *me* become an *us*. In finding what you love, you find more of yourself."

"I think you might have just written your own quote with that one, Darby." Foreheads, noses, and hips all touched. "Just you wait and see. You could go down in history for that."

"If discovering what love is through loving you is what I'm remembered for, then I think that's a pretty good legacy."

"It's definitely what I will remember." Foreheads, noses, hips, and now chests.

"Then that's enough."

To be remembered—even if by only one person in this world of seven billion—for how much I loved was infinitely more than I could ever have hoped for.

"Um . . ."

"Um what?" Hands. Now our hands touched, too, as Torin wove our fingers together and brought them up by our shoulders. I felt a little like a marionette as he waved them back and forth slowly, my arms and hands directed by his movements.

"Um-I-want-to-make-out-with-you."

"Um-I-think-that-is-an-incredible-idea."

Just like with the eyelash fluttering, I could practically feel his smile as he beamed a wide, toothy grin. "Um-it's-sorta-dirty-here."

"Um-I-kinda-like-dirty."

I smiled and wondered if he could almost feel it, too.

"Um-you-really-shouldn't-say-things-like-that."

So I didn't. But that was because Torin released his grip from my fingers and instead slid his hands down to the backs of my thighs and in one effortless lift, hiked me up onto him. I curled my legs around his waist and he planted his hands on the pockets of my jeans. My elbows were on his shoulders and my hands were in his hair, pulling his head closer to me, needing him to press up against me with his whole body.

Torin looked up at me with eager eyes that instantly flooded me with what felt like helium, because I was completely weightless, about to take off.

"You," he breathed against my skin.

"Me what?" I smirked down at him, biting the corner of my mouth playfully. I decided to flutter my eyelashes a little, too, just to see what it would do.

"That's all. Just you." He pulled his bottom lip into his mouth, too, nearly mimicking me.

"You kinda sound like a caveman."

He dipped his hands into my back pockets, grabbing my backside and pulling me even closer. I tightened my legs around him and crossed my ankles to bracket myself there.

"I'm kinda thinking like a caveman. The fact that I have my hands on your ass right now makes it a little hard to form complete thoughts, let alone sentences."

"And what if my lips were on yours? What would that do?" I brought my forehead down to his and looked at him from under my eyelashes. I probably batted them a few times more than necessary.

"I'm not sure what is more prehistoric than a Neanderthal, but I'd be that."

"We wouldn't want that." I shook my head slowly.

Torin almost chomped through that bottom lip. "No," he said, his lip still pinned, making him a bit of a ventriloquist, which I actually found remarkably impressive. "No, we wouldn't."

"Well . . ." I tugged his golden hair. "Maybe we would."

"Yeah," he agreed quickly. "Maybe."

"C'mere." I yanked his mouth to mine with my hands coiled in his hair. There was just a slice of space between us. His breath rushed out of him and I pulled it in like I needed it to survive.

"Mmm-kay," he muttered against my skin, then took my bottom lip between his teeth. I jumped noticeably in his arms, startled, and he used his biceps to squeeze me closer, our chests pressed so hard against each other that I couldn't make any sense of whose erratic pulse belonged to whom. It was all just drums and cymbals and rhythm.

Torin pulled back an inch as he smiled gently, his dimples deepening, his green eyes hooded. Releasing my lip from his teeth, he let his lips take hold of it, sucking it into his mouth so slowly it made me physically ache. My stomach clenched as his mouth pressed to mine, pulling and tugging my lips in a painstakingly deliberate rhythm. I ran my tongue across the fullness of his bottom lip and parted my lips to let his tongue slide into my mouth. He was really good at this, like too good, considering I knew he wanted to take things slow for the time being.

Still holding me wrapped around him, he walked forward several feet. I felt the sudden roughness from the bark of a tree against my back as he pushed me up against its surface. His hands slid out from under me and he used his weight to press me against the trunk, his chest heavy on mine. One palm was at my jaw, the other trailing down the angle of my neck to my collarbone. "Sleep with me," he murmured against my skin. Waves of emotion pulsed through my body, taking on a physical form in goose bumps rushing across my exposed arms, legs, and neck.

I managed to get out a dizzied, "Huh?"

"Tonight, under the stars. In the sleeping bag, for old times' sake." He spoke quietly in between light kisses and nips at my bottom lip. "Because at any moment you're going to realize the permanence of what happened with Lance, and I'm worried you'll run again." Holding his head directly in front of mine, our eyes aligned and locked. "Before you run, I want to share tonight with you." His brow furrowed and his jaw tightened. "Just the two of us, up here, under our very own canopy of stars."

"And all you want to do is sleep?" I teased. I dropped my mouth to his again at the same time a low groan slipped through his lips and I swallowed it up.

"No, I obviously want to do more." His tongue darted into my mouth and ran along all the sides of it. Mine danced with his, trailing the same path in his mouth instead. Our lips were hard against the other's, opening and closing on cue, stealing all control of my breathing because everything right then was centered on our lips. Even breathing at a steady pace took a backseat to kissing Torin. "I'll always want to do more, but I'm waiting for you, Darby. So for tonight, I just want to stay with you, asleep in my arms, the way everyone dreams of it all ending." His steady gazed penetrated me. "If this is it for us, that's the only way I'd want us to end."

"I'm not going to run." He didn't give me much opportunity to get the words out, but I managed to speak them. "I don't plan on running from you."

Torin brushed the pad of his thumb against my bottom lip and looked me directly in my eyes, like he was studying me. "You already know my philosophy on making plans."

"Then I'll give you my promise, because that's more than a plan."

"You don't need to promise me anything, Darby. Just tonight. That's all I need." Slowly, he slid my body down the length of the tree, the friction of our bodies as I slithered toward the ground almost too intense to bear.

"I'd stay here forever with you if you asked me."

Torin sighed. "If I honestly believed forever was an actual possibility, I'd ask for yours."

"You wouldn't have to ask. I'd have already given it to you."

"Then can I have your *for now*?" His eyebrow arched with the question. "Since that's all we're guaranteed?"

I shook my head. "Forever might not exist, but my *for now* isn't enough," I said. Because it wasn't. We'd had a summer together and that felt like just the beginning. There was no way I could let him go now; this wasn't enough.

I'd learned something about love and loss and knew the inevitable heartache that accompanied it. If I had any say at all, any remote ounce of control, I'd never willingly lose love again.

"You can have my everything, Torin. Everything I possibly have to offer," I continued. "As long as you and I are on this earth, I want to be yours," I vowed, pressing my cheek against his chest, loving the sweat and the dirt that all combined to make Torin who he was, this unexpected boy who brought me to the summit. "I promise you that."

"That's a promise I'll gladly accept." His lips swept against mine with featherlike pressure. "Because whether you know it or not, you've been my everything this whole time."

Chapter 26

"There are so many of them."

"I know, right?"

"Is it possible that there are more here than in other places?" I craned my head back closer to the crook of his elbow, tugging the nylon edge of the sleeping bag higher. "Because I've never seen so many all at once before."

"When you're this high up—without all the lights, without the trees—it's all you can see." His fingers combed through my hair and he played with the frayed ends with his fingertips. "And it's incredible to think that we're only seeing a small portion of it all. Like it goes on forever."

"Feels infinite."

"That's because it sorta is. I mean, when it comes down to it, we're looking at time," he said. "Like, all of those stars are blazes from explosions years and years ago. Or at least I think that's what it all is. I'm no astronomer."

"No," I agreed. "Sounds right. We're looking into the past. I think that's what it is." I sighed and curled against the solid line of his body. We'd retrieved a sleeping bag from the shed, but Torin didn't have any other clothes to wear, so he was tucked into the sack wearing just his jeans, his upper half bare. I ran my fingers over his torso, over the curves of his stomach, and could feel his muscles tighten under my touch. "I wish we could be looking into the future instead," I murmured, continuing to trace along his heated skin.

"No you don't." Torin didn't offer more than that and changed the subject by saying, "So there's this star called WR 104."

"I thought stars had names like Sagittarius and Aquarius."

"Those are astrological signs," he interjected.

"Which, I believe, are derived from stars, Torin."

"Yeah, you're right," he conceded, chuckling. He trapped my wandering hand in his and brought it up to his chest, resting it on top of his heart. "Anyway, WR 104. That star apparently is like total Death Star status. I guess there's a big likelihood of these gamma rays hitting Earth once it goes all supernova, which could be tomorrow, or five thousand years from now." Our legs had been wrapped together in the sleeping bag, almost pretzeled, and he drew me closer with his knee hooked around mine. I settled into the heat he provided. "Anyway, we wouldn't even know what hit us when it actually did. It would all be over. Just like that." He snapped his fingers. Dust to dust.

"Kinda scary to be staring down the gamma ray barrel of a star."

"Sometimes it's easier to live life under the false pretense that we're invincible, isn't it?" A light breeze kicked up in the dirt and Torin tugged the top of the bag up under our ears, sheltering us from the crisp air that skirted around us. "Like nothing can stop us. Not like we have a proverbial gun to our heads the way we all kinda do, huh?"

"I'm starting to believe it's the only way to actually live at all." I was starting to believe a lot of things about life. Some more concretely than others.

"But how do you do that?" His heart echoed steadily against my ear and I pressed closer against his chest to swallow up the sound. "Like, reconciling the invincibility feeling and the mortality factor—they're two opposites on the same coin," he asked thoughtfully, like he always did. I'd never met anyone like Torin who thought so deeply about life. "What, do you just flip each day? Today I live like there's no tomorrow. Today I live like I have endless tomorrows."

"I honestly feel like I'm teetering on the edge of that coin. Like it's spinning and spinning and wobbling, but sorta balancing at the same time."

"I get that," he said, and I felt his head nod against the top of mine, his chin pressed to my temple. "And maybe they're not actually opposites at all. Maybe we *are* both mortal and immortal. Looking up at that midnight sky, it kinda changes the whole picture. Maybe we're mortal here, that might be true. But maybe we're invincible there." He didn't say what "there" was, but we were both looking up at that same sparkling abyss, its vast expanse of infinity shining on us in thousands of bright, white, has-been stars. "Maybe—hopefully—this isn't it for us, you know?"

I wanted to agree by saying "Yes, I know." But I didn't know. As Torin said, I hoped, and for now that felt close enough to knowing. Sometimes hope was all we had.

"I'm fine balancing on that edge," he continued. His chest rose and fell consistently. "Balancing on the edge of that possibility. I wouldn't regret living like that, I don't think. I wouldn't regret living for today and hoping for tomorrow."

"I like that rule." I wrapped my arms around him tighter—even though the one slunk underneath him was tingling with numbness—because, finally, nothing else about me felt numb. I'd experienced so much death that I'd forgotten to experience life, and that was the greatest tragedy of all. Torin brought me back to life. I wasn't sure he'd ever be able to know the extent to which he saved me, but I was determined to spend the rest of whatever time I was given letting him know.

"So I remember you saying your parents started this camp to try to use Randy's death for good."

Torin angled toward me, smoothing my hair so he could look more clearly into my eyes. "Yeah?"

"Do you think that's our job? To look for the good in the bad?" I'd never lived my life like that, but instead had just refused to believe the bad had even happened. Refusing to come to terms with death by ignoring the permanence of its power had been my default for as long as I could remember.

"I think there is always a silver lining. I don't necessarily know if it's our job to find it, but I do know it makes life a hell of a lot better if we do go in search of it." It was incredible to think that something so simple had eluded me for so long, and that Torin could speak it so freely. "Like those stars," he continued, waving a hand toward the blackened blanket above us. "It kinda sucks that only after they burn out do they finally get to shine that brightly, but I guess that's the good in the bad for them. Their silver lining."

My gaze tried to take it all in, the limitless sky and its millions of sparkles of burned-out energy. I knew there was bad in the world, but in this moment, all I could see was the good. The beautiful creation of light and constellations and shooting bursts that crossed over the galaxy—that was all I could see. And it was honestly the most captivating, breathtaking scene that my eyes had ever, and probably would ever, taken in.

"I want to do all of that, Torin." I closed my eyes for a brief moment, and the black that shielded my vision made me crave the twinkling illumination instantly. "I want to live for today, hope for tomorrow, and try to look for the good in everything in between." I opened my eyes again. "I think that's the only way I can truly live this life without regret."

"I like that, Darby. The rules of regret," he said softly with an understanding that made me feel not only wholly understood, but significant beyond anything I'd ever experienced.

"I think I can follow those."

In fact, I knew I could. For once, I was completely confident in that answer. I could live. I could have hope. And I wouldn't allow myself to dwell on the bad, but would give myself the freedom to seek out the good. I would allow myself to do that, and Torin would be the one to guide me. He'd guided me so many times before, and that was just around the tree-dotted trails back at camp. His guidance through life, though much more important on every possible level, felt so much easier to surrender to. And surrendering to the idea of hope felt just as natural. I could do this—I could live this life without regret. "Let's follow those rules together," I said, pulling him so close I could hardly tell where I ended and he began.

Curling me into his side and holding me with the most gentle but secure embrace he possibly could, he kissed my forehead, suspended his lips just above my brow, and said, "I think we just might regret it if we don't."

ABOUT THE AUTHOR

Megan Squires is a writer and photographer and she loves to photograph based on what she writes and write based on what she photographs.

She's fueled by Diet Coke and an overactive imagination and can't do without the San Francisco Giants, her mini iPad with the Kindle app, and a daily dose of snuggles with her one-hundred-pound golden retriever.

And she loves *love*. Like seriously adores those butterflies you get when you think about that first kiss or reminisce about holding hands with someone you'd been crushing on for years. Even if it was cringe-worthy and terrible, there's just nothing quite like connecting with another human being on that nervous, hesitant level. Relationships are complex and wonderful and scary, and Megan gets a rush each time she has a chance to write about them and all of their layers. This is why young adult literature is her genre of choice.

A graduate from the University of California, Davis, with an international relations degree, Megan currently resides in Sacramento with her husband and two children. She documents her dreams with both her keyboard and camera and has enough characters in her head to keep her busy for years.

You can visit Megan online at www.megansquiresauthor.com.